Readers love *Obsidian Sun*
by JON KEYS

"The world building was great and I loved that the author had inventive creatures and plants that inhabited it. There was a lot of time put into making the world stand out."
  —Prism Book Alliance

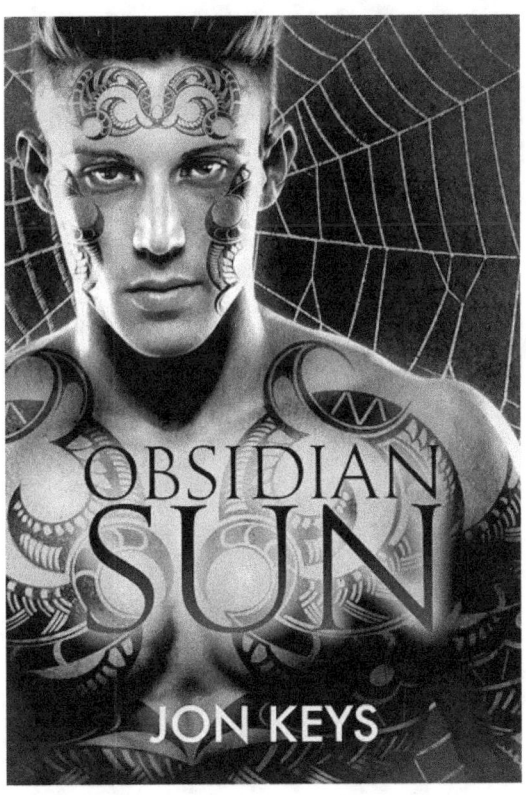

"Wholly unique, *Obsidian Sun* takes readers on a road of vengeance and discovery."
  —Joyfully Reviewed

"The fantasy is solid, and the romantic elements are a delightful bonus. Whatever you enjoy, I think you'll enjoy *Obsidian Sun*."
  —Queer Sci Fi

"…I would not hesitate to recommend *Obsidian Sun*."
                              —Joyfully Jay

By JON KEYS

Heart of the Pines
Home Grown

OBSIDIAN SERIES
Obsidian Sun
Obsidian Moons

Published by DREAMSPINNER PRESS
www.dreamspinnerpress.com

OBSIDIAN
MOONS

JON KEYS

Published by
DREAMSPINNER PRESS

5032 Capital Circle SW, Suite 2, PMB# 279, Tallahassee, FL 32305-7886 USA
www.dreamspinnerpress.com

Obsidian Moons
© 2016 Jon Keys.

Cover Art
© 2016 Paul Richmond.
http://www.paulrichmondstudio.com
Cover content is for illustrative purposes only and any person depicted on the cover is a model.

ISBN: 978-1-63477-717-9
Digital ISBN: 978-1-63477-718-6
Library of Congress Control Number: 2016910622
Published September 2016
v. 1.0

Printed in the United States of America
∞
This paper meets the requirements of
ANSI/NISO Z39.48-1992 (Permanence of Paper).

GLOSSARY

Talac Terms

Akhir—Offensive magic from a Spellspinner against an attacker. It strips all emotion from the person and kills them. The backlash against the spinner is fatal, with the exception of a few individuals through history.

Arrowweavers—Talac who specialize in creating the tribal longbows and arrows.

Blessed ones—The deities of the Talac.

Bloodfruit—Deep red berries found on the grasslands. They're considered a treat.

Bloodweaving—Ritual revenge. The pair declaring a bloodweaving must petition the gods for their blessing. The ones declaring the bloodweaving are bound to it until they fulfill the quest, or die trying.

Cloudflyers—Colorful flying insects that move in large swarms.

Corcra—The emotions of intimacy. It presents itself in the spinning as shades of purple.

Council of Five—Another term for the five clans that make up the Talac.

Crawlers—Tiny biting pests that can infest the bedding, and velvet, of the Talac if the proper spells are not performed.

Daggerhorns—Grazing animals from the Talac homelands. Medium-sized and brown in coloration, the animals are known for their long horns that are tipped with poison.

Deathspinner—Large spiders similar in size to two adult fists. They live in enormous colonies and create landscapes of webbing to trap their prey. Their silk can be harvested and is a critical element in Talac magic.

Featherleaf trees—A low-growing tree commonly found along permanent waterways in the Talac savanna. They are a deciduous tree with bipennate leaves.

Fingerwidth—The time it takes for the sun to move the width of a single finger.

First Spinner—One of the pair of avatars comprising the Blessed Ones of the Talac.

First Twining—The combination of First Spinner and First Weaver.

First Weaver—One of the pair of avatars comprising the Blessed Ones of the Talac.

Great Weaving—The Talac afterlife, where a person's life fibers go before being woven into a new life.

Guardian bush—Head-high bushes thickly covered by toxic barbed thorns. The toxin paralyzes the chest muscles and stops the victim's breathing.

Herdweavers—Young Talac of both sexes who watch over the herds of kuri. They are armed with slings as their primary weapon against predators.

Hollowfruit—A melon native to the savanna with a hollow center filled with seeds.

Hunter grass—A coarse perennial grass used by the Kuri to make baskets.

Iceweaver—The deity of winter and the season of telling oral traditions. Also used as the common term for the cold season.

Ironwood tree—A medium-sized tree with palm-sized leaves and a dense cell structure in its wood. The tree also absorbs silica from the soil and deposits it in the tissue.

Kit—The term used for Talac children who haven't reached puberty.

Ko—The riding animals of the Meke clan. They domesticated the animals from the wild [and highly protective] snowgrazers.

Kuri—The grazing herd animals raised by the Kuri clan of the Talac people. Kuri is also the name of the clan who specializes in rearing the animals.

Longtooth—Predatory mammals that hunt in packs. They are tan in color with long tails used as counterbalance as they run. They have retractable claws and long incisor teeth that extend far past their bottom jaw.

Matama—Emotions given off by people. These are gathered by Spellspinners and combined with deathspinner silk for the spell weavings created by the Spellweavers.

Meke—The Meke are the northernmost Talac clan. Their territory includes the Iceweaver's mountains. They breed large, longhaired animals that they use as pack animals, as well as a source of fiber and meat.

Mezi—Same-sex pairing. The terms are specific to the pairing, not the person. So a person who is bisexual could be either mezi or nisa, depending on the gender of their pairing. There is no stigma or significance for either among the Talac.

Needle bush—A perennial plant that grows to waist high on an adult Talac. Its leaves are covered with a coating of tiny needles. If you brush against them, it causes a burning sensation. While not fatal, they are painful.

Nisa—Opposite-sex pairing. The terms are specific to the pairing, not the person. So a person who is bisexual could be either mezi or nisa, depending on the gender of their pairing. There is no stigma or significance for either among the Talac.

Pairing-bond—An almost telepathic connection between twined mates. In some cases they can share the harvested emotions via their connection.

Pero—One of the clans making up the Talac council. They are known for creating woven cloaks and finery that incorporate feathers from many different birds. They were a small clan, and the Varas raids have largely decimated them. The few remaining members were rescued by Anan and Terja and are now with the Kuri.

Rattleback—A medium-sized mammal that has their offspring four at a time. The name comes from the finger-thick spikes that cover the animal's back and make noise when they hit each other.

Rugza—The harvested threads of anger or violence. Usually not harvested other than in times of dire need.

Snowgrazer—A large mammal that typically moves in herds. They are native to the more northern mountains and extremely aggressive. Herds move into the plains during the winter moons to escape the worst of the harsh weather. The Meke clan has domesticated a smaller version, called ko, for riding and their fiber.

Spellspinners—Talac who are born without the hallmark velvet of the other Talac. They are trained from birth to spin the fibers of emotions that are made by other people. But they can only spin the fibers; they cannot create weavings of magic.

Spellweavers—Talac who have the special sight needed to create spells from fibers spun by the spellspinners. Spellweavers discover they have the ability at puberty and are trained. They also are the type of Talac who are almost completely covered with plush hair finer than velvet. At puberty they also get their adult velvet, which is a rich pattern of spirals and marks unique to each spellweaver.

Spinner/weaver—The term spinner or weaver, when combined with other skills or materials, such as hideweaver or bowspinner, indicates a high level of mastery and the ability to manipulate the materials with small amounts of personal magic.

Springtail—A small mammal common throughout the region. They have a distinctive upright carriage and muscular hind legs that can allow them to jump many times their own height. They are a common quarry for young Talac who are learning to hunt.

Staffweaver—Talac who are trained to fight with a bladed staff. The tradition has been lost to the Kuri clan for several generations.

Strands—Mild profanity.

Sunbird—Smaller, bright yellow birds that move in flocks of several hundred.

Talac—A group of seminomadic people who form a number of clans based on a weaving specialization. Most Talac are born with velvet: short hair in detailed, swirling patterns that covers their body. A minority of the Talac are born with no velvet, which marks them as a spellspinner. The other half of the Talac magic is formed by spellweavers, who are identified when they reach puberty.

Twined Ones—The reference to First Weaver and First Spinner as a collective.

Twining (societal)—The rituals typically performed by a couple to formally announce their bond to each other. It also creates a physical connection between the couple. The strength of the connection varies from pairing to pairing.

Twining (weaving)—A weaving technique where two or more flexible elements cross over each other as they cross the warp threads, or spokes in basketry.

Unraveling—Ritual for sending the dead to the afterlife.

Visionspinner (or visionweaver)— The ability some Talac have to see into the future through visions that come to them during their sleep. The terms are interchangeable but describe a gift applicable to a single person.

Warp—The elements of a weaving that are generally under tension and provide the structure for the weaving.

Warriorglass—Another term the Talac use for obsidian.

Weft—The thread that traverses the warp threads in order to create cloth.

Varas Terms

Blackrock—A porous volcanic rock commonly used to carve effigies of the Varas's gods.

Burning Twins—Primary gods of the Varas. Also called the Red Twins or Red Gods.

Century—A full unit of Varas soldiers that numbers one hundred people.

Forever Words—The written sacred teachings of the Red Twins.

High Regent—Highest rank of the Varas ruling class. Somewhat of a figurehead as most of the power in the Varas culture rests with the slavers who can provide Talac slaves.

House of the Sun—The highest caste of the Varas. The High Regent is always from this caste.

Red Gods—Primary gods of the Varas. Also called the Burning Twins or Red Twins.

Red Twins—Primary gods of the Varas. Also called the Burning Twins or Red Gods.

River Serpent—Large aquatic animal. Adults are longer than two people are tall. The Varas believe it is the Red God personified and sacrifice people to it by throwing them in the river.

Sun-drenched Talac—A Talac whose velvet is a golden blond rather than the typical brown. It's a rare occurrence and highly valued by the Varas.

Varas—A people with extensive permanent towns flanking the Great River. Many of the Varas are addicted to sex with the Talac who have velvet. As a result they have an extensive slave culture to meet the demand for sex slaves and houses of pleasure.

Ubica Terms

Amia—Ritual suicide if a Triad kills someone other than the target of their assassination agreement.

Great Anvil—The Anvil portion of the Ubica deities making up the Holy Triad.

Great Forge—The Forge portion of the Ubica deities making up the Holy Triad.

Great Hammer—The Hammer portion of the Ubica deities making up the Holy Triad.

Honor duel—The only type of fighting allowed between two Ubica. Highly regimented with many rituals designed to prevent loss of life. But often the death of one or both combatants does occur.

Iron People—The term the Ubica use quite often for themselves.

Nikata—Shared intimacy between members of a Triad. It is the ultimate level of intimacy and usually represents a life bonding.

Red-legs—The slang term the Ubica use for the Varas soldiers. It is due to the red pants they wear.

Rockdivers—Small rodents that live in the rock piles formed by avalanches.

Spiritknife—A steel knife made by a Ubica smith that has illness matama embedded as part of the process of creating the alloy.

Triad of Ancients—The combination of Ancient Forge, Hammer, and Anvil, the three lead deities of the Ubica religion.

CHAPTER ONE

THE FINAL strands of Llyca's unraveling drifted past the tops of the massive featherleaf trees the Talac sheltered beneath. They'd had far too many last rites so far as Terja was concerned. Every day they moved closer to their homeland and farther from the Varas who had held them captive, but for the ones who were dying, it was not enough. Llyca joined the Great Weaving shortly after they had stopped for the night at one of the islands of trees scattered across the eastern hills. The sun touching the western horizon served as a reminder of their goal: the unending sea of grass, and the massive earth lodges that made up their winter village. The region's blazing hot summers and brutally cold winters made it an inhospitable land, but it was home to the Kuri clan of the Talac people. His home. But Terja worried none of the Kuri they'd rescued would survive the trip.

Known for their fine weavings, the clan and their herds were so intertwined that they shared a name. For as long as any of the Talac Elders could recall, the weavings of kuri fiber were the hallmark of the Kuri clan. A clan almost wiped from the savannas by the Varas and Xain, the traitorous Talac who aided them. The band of slavers attacked the Talac because of their value as pleasure slaves. The velvet covering the spellweavers was a sexual addiction to many of the Varas, including the High Regent. The people who survived and were trekking to the Kuri winter village had suffered many days of abuse and neglect after their capture, and subsequent rescue, by Terja and Anan, with some guidance from the gods. Now they had lost another, and he knew Anan took each death as a personal failure. As Llyca's last fiber disappeared from sight, Terja felt the same sense of defeat he did each time they sent someone to the Great Weaving.

"She shouldn't have died. What am I doing wrong?" Anan asked.

Terja studied his twining for a moment before shaking his head. "Anan, she was free. She died a free woman. You gave her that."

He shook his head. "No. I'm past the guilt of trying to save everyone. But we shouldn't have so many injuries that aren't improving.

1

We certainly shouldn't still be losing people to wound fever. Our kilt panels were filled with the matama you spun from us. And even though some colors have been used and the thread faded to dust, my healing weavings should be working."

Terja thought for a moment. "What about the trap Xain set inside Joven? The twisted healing warped him until he tried to kill you. That bit of treachery almost cost your life, and Xain was the one who crippled many of the captives."

Anan's lips narrowed to a thin line. "That isn't something I'd forget. I checked for traps in the wounds, but found none. I don't think he had the time. But the cuts Xain made on the Talac who were captive won't heal."

Terja slowed his pace for a moment then stopped. "They possessed Ubica locks…."

Anan spun on his mate. "The assassin people? You think Xain had one of their spiritknives?"

"The former captives are slowly dying. Their wounds will not heal. The Elders said the Ubica smiths could embed their blades with forces, something similar to matama."

Anan let out a dismissive snort. "That's just a story for Iceweaver's season."

Terja shook his head and considered his twining for several moments. "The Varas believe we spellspinners are the healers. They pursue us in the hope of finding a skilled healer while in truth we velvetless spellspinners could do little more than the Varas could do themselves. I have a few skills given to me from the First Twining."

Anan considered him for several moments before speaking. "It can't hurt to weave a healing targeting a spiritknife. All I've been looking for is twisted matama. I know little of the assassins' weapons and how they function."

A heartbeat later, Terja shrugged. "I don't remember much either. The spellspinner Elders were strangely silent on the assassin people. It is said they always work in threes, and each member has a specific role as dictated by their gods. One of the Elders called them Ironweavers. Their talent in the smithy is as extensive as ours at the looms. But they are not hired for their talent to create, but their ability to destroy. They

2

are masters of their weapons." He struggled to remember more, but then looked to Anan with a frown. "That's all. They didn't tell me anything else. Perhaps to be certain I was not the object of a Ubica contract."

"I'm sure the two of us can stop three Ubica, regardless of their reputation. We wiped out a Varas slaver company and rescued the Talac they had taken."

The conversation concerned Terja. "Hopefully we'll never find out. Come, let's see if Xain wielded a spiritknife."

Terja and Anan made their way to the main camp and found Joven and Soneri waiting for them. Terja considered the two men for a moment while Anan explained their new idea. Both of them would be willing to do anything to keep from being recaptured. Between the value of Soneri's sunbird-colored velvet and the living trap they had made of Joven, they would rather die than be returned. Terja stepped closer so he could hear their ideas.

Joven motioned to the people spread around the camp. "You're doing all you can. They just aren't healing. Soneri and I have tried too. Even Morea cast a weaving."

Anan studied him for a moment. "Is her weaving progressing?"

Soneri held up his hands in a helpless gesture. "I can sense the vision inside her. Her weavings are perfect. But they have little strength. She's becoming discouraged."

Anan nodded, and Terja could tell this was one more burden he placed on himself. Terja sent him a wash of comfort through their twining connection. Anan flashed him a smile that Terja savored for a moment before refocusing on the others.

"We've been talking about it too. The Varas had locks made by the—"

Soneri immediately saw the connection. "You think Xain had a spiritknife?"

"Maybe," Terja said.

Soneri looked pensive for a heartbeat before turning to Terja and Anan. "You might be right. He had other surprises no one would expect from a Varas slave."

Terja swept the people surrounding them with his gaze. "Who is in the greatest need?"

Joven used his chin to point. "That one. The Talac from the Pero clan. He's getting worse in spite of all we do."

3

They walked toward the man. The object of their attention had been lying as if he were asleep until it became obvious he was the focus of the small group. Matama poured from the weakening member of the feather-weaving clan, with fear dominating all other emotions. To Terja's senses he reeked of stale sweat and sickness.

His face became drawn and the fear seemed to grow. By the time Anan was close enough to touch him, the young man shook. Anan paused and smiled at him. "Try to relax, Reni. There is nothing to be afraid of. We think we know why you aren't healing, but I need to examine you. I promise there will be no pain."

The fear receded from the man's face, at least to a degree. "Since I'm the closest to death… I would be the one to welcome any new healing."

This time Anan touched the man and Terja could feel the wave of comfort flowing from his twining. A few heartbeats later, Reni relaxed enough for Anan to work. Terja knew the healing would be tedious. Terja sat close, ready to help. He could sense the movement of the matama between them as parts of the spell panels from their kilts faded away, but could only sit quietly and will Anan success. Terja dropped out of his drowsy state when Anan opened his eyes. He glanced around for a moment as Terja watched him through the growing night.

"I think I found the problem, but it's nothing Xain created. This is different. Not a weaving, but like it in some ways."

"You can explain the details later. Can you cure it?" Terja asked.

Anan considered for a moment and nodded. "I think so. Thank the Twined Ones it isn't the spell Xain set in Joven. We would not have been able to spare him."

Joven paled slightly and then nodded at the patient. "But for him?"

"I don't have to remove every tendril of the magic. His body can heal; it just needs some help."

"You think you can cure me?" Reni asked.

Terja glanced at the patient who resembled an injured child more than a battle-hardened man. He could see tears trailing across the patterns in the velvet covering Reni's face. He reached down and touched his cheek lightly. "It looks hopeful. Do you want us to continue?"

"Yes! Please."

"All right, but I will lay a sleeping weaving over you. This shouldn't be painful, but when you work with unfamiliar forces…." Anan looked apologetic.

"Do it. Otherwise you'll be doing my unraveling, and I'm not ready to join the Great Weaving."

Anan began without any further discussion, and Terja felt the pull for extra matama along their connection. He slipped into spellsight as Anan began his weaving. The matama he pulled from their kilts formed familiar patterns, and Reni slumped into unconsciousness. His pain had been more than Anan realized. His entire body fought the agony until he fell under Anan's sleep weaving.

From there, Anan's work was largely invisible to Terja. The effort was obvious, though, as the sweat began to show on the velvet covering his body. Terja couldn't help but feel the attraction when Anan's musky aroma washed over him. He fought desperately to keep his arousal from traveling to Anan. Deepest night wrapped around them by the time Anan tucked the last thread of his healing weaving into place. He rocked onto his heels and studied the young man for a moment.

"I got a lot of it. Not everything, but most. He should begin to heal. His body was trying to fight off the invaders, but it was outmatched."

"You are sure it was not Xain?"

Anan shook his head. "No. What I see wasn't woven by a Talac, certainly no one of Kuri training. It was bits of darkness slowly spreading everywhere."

"Could it have been a spiritknife?"

Anan gave a tired shrug. "I'm not sure. I've never seen the damage it leaves. But if it is, I've beaten it back."

Terja tensed slightly. "Won't it spread again?"

"No, not now."

"Why?"

"Because I trained his own weavings to fight back." Anan's face broke into a smile. "Maybe I should've armed them with slings like you use."

Terja couldn't help but grin at the idea. "Quite a fierce little army he'd have."

"You've killed longtooth with yours. I'm sure his could fight off the darkness he has."

"Regardless of how it happens. He will not lose this battle." He studied the sleeping man for a moment and then glanced at Anan. "He looks more comfortable."

"He should. The weave I used was one of my more potent, and most difficult. If what I fought resulted from a spiritknife, I hope one is never used on me."

The youngster snorted and rolled to his side. Terja smiled, grabbed Anan by the sleeve, and pulled him away from the obviously sleeping figure. A young Kuri woman hovered close by, and he felt certain Reni would be well cared for. Terja searched for a moment before finding her in the shadows. He motioned her closer. "He should heal now, but he needs rest and food. Wake us if something happens."

He pulled Anan toward their tent. "Come. Let him sleep. The nights are getting colder and I don't have your thick covering of velvet. Besides, I am exhausted so I'm certain you need sleep."

A few steps beyond the low fire where final bits of the evening meal were being eaten, Anan stopped and pulled Terja against his chest. With his arms wrapped tight, Anan planted tender kisses along Terja's smooth jaw as Terja traced through the complex patterns in Anan's velvet. His heart raced when Anan pressed his lips close and whispered, "Your bare skin excites me like few other things."

Terja moaned softly and ran his spread hands over Anan's thick chest as he nibbled at Anan's neck, rewarded by a throaty growl.

"I can see why the Varas become addicted to spellweavers. I could spend a lifetime enjoying your velvet," Terja said.

He gasped, focusing on his twining as he bit down on the inside of Anan's neck. His thoughts fogged over with lust as he ground against Anan.

"Hey! Anan! Come here. We need to show you something." Joven's voice sliced through the pleasurable haze Terja had created. Hesitantly, he separated from Anan, his fingertips lingering, and turned to discover what was so critical it demanded their immediate attention.

They moved to the cluster of people at one side of the fire who stared at an animal someone had brought down during a hunting trip. At first Terja couldn't see the fascination with what seemed to be an ordinary springtail, but then he started to note the differences. Its coat was easily double the length of the springtail Terja had hunted since he was a kit. Its ears were so small they almost disappeared in the fur. But the most notable things were the fangs.

Springtail didn't have fangs. They were plant eaters. But this one had fangs easily as long as the first joint of Terja's finger. A small green drop oozed from the tip of one. Terja reached to touch it, and Anan grabbed his wrist.

"Don't. I'm not even sure we should eat it. The meat might be tainted."

"Let Soneri check it. He could always tell when the food the Varas fed us was bad," Joven said.

Terja turned to the big Talac. "Soneri? Is this true?"

"Yes. My family is, was, very skilled at that weave. It's part of how we managed to survive outside of a clan."

Terja nodded toward the still animal. "And this?"

Soneri squatted beside the carcass and wove a spell. While they waited, the firelight reflected off Soneri's golden velvet. Terja couldn't keep from recalling the ravenous hunger the Varas had for him simply because of the color of his velvet. Terja was startled into the present when Soneri began to speak.

"It's safe to eat. But discard the head. The poison sacs are along the jaws." He turned to Anan. "I'd burn the head to ash. That would be the only way to not taint the lands."

"What is it? Any idea?" Terja asked.

Soneri shrugged. "No. But we are on the border of the Meke clan. Our Elders said the Meke could make changes in an animal. Perhaps our northern cousins have done something to their springtail."

"I don't know why you would change a simple springtail into a poisonous animal. But until I get a better answer, I will follow your instructions." Terja glanced at the others who had gathered close. "We're going to stay here for a few more days. Anan found a way to help the injured, and we can use the time to hunt."

THE LOW fire sent up tendrils of smoke that curled around the drying rack Anan had built to help preserve the meat from what game the hunters found. After several days of hunting their reserve of food had become less concerning, but Anan wanted to increase their stores as much as possible.

Anan sliced the daggerhorn carcass before him as thinly as possible and hung it over the thin rods making up the drying rack. Several others duplicated his efforts, but keeping the group fed was a concern for them all. One he wasn't certain how to conquer.

"These bits of meat will not be enough to get us to the Kuri's winter pastures," Terja said.

Anan frowned at Terja. This discussion was becoming more and more annoying. He couldn't seem to get Terja to see his concerns. "We can't stay here. I've told you. It's too close to where we fought the Varas, and we aren't far into Talac territory. If Xain survived, he might be able to convince the Varas to come after us."

"How would he do that? We wiped out an entire slaver company. What could possibly convince them to send more soldiers after us?"

Anan was about to answer when Soneri and Joven walked back into camp. He was relieved to see the golden man had taken a small daggerhorn and Joven's game bag wasn't empty either. They moved to the same set of drying racks Anan had laid strips of meat across. After nodding at Anan and Terja, they started to skin and prepare their take.

The men worked silently, readying the meat while Terja slowly fed the small fire creating the smoke needed. From his expression, it was obvious he was not happy. Joven glanced between the two of them and frowned.

"What's wrong?"

Without glancing upward, Terja answered. "Anan thinks we have to travel to the Kuri's winter camp. I think his weaving has unraveled. Why would we want to begin the journey to the village when Iceweaver's season has begun? We've already moved much farther north than the Varas brought the slaves, and we are moving into the lands of the Meke. Even the ice mountain clan doesn't travel in this season."

"Xain. He would chase us to the ends of the world. We can't stay here," Soneri said.

Anan and Terja both looked at the young man. Anan knew Soneri understood the danger. But the expression on Terja's face said he was not happy with Anan's allies.

Terja bit off a reply. "Xain's just another Talac slave to the Varas. Why would they listen to him, and more importantly, why would they help him?"

Soneri swept his hand over the golden velvet covering every exposed bit of his body and then nodded toward Terja. "The two of us. The Varas slavers made it clear a Talac pleasure slave with golden velvet was worth any price to present to the High Regent. And you are the other. Your velvetless skin labels you as a spellspinner as clearly as I am marked by the color of my velvet. Either would be enough for them to support Xain. For both of us? I don't know if there is a limit to the amount of help they would provide."

Terja tried to appear dismissive. But Anan could feel his doubt through the connection between them. "What's the worst they could do?"

Anan waited. He hoped Soneri could convince Terja how great their danger would be if they stayed close to the Varas border.

Soneri's gaze bored into Terja. "What could they do? Find someone to lead them who is not addicted to sex with spellweavers? Discover the beast riders from across the waters? Use trained soldiers instead of mercenaries and murderers? Perhaps the pleasure houses would release Rock soldiers in exchange for us. Or, they had Ubica locks. What if they hired a Triad of assassins from the worshipers of the Great Smith? That's a few of the things they could do."

Terja's mouth opened and closed a few times before he managed to form words. "No. That's impossible. We aren't that valuable."

Soneri somehow flared his golden velvet, with its intricate silver patterns, and made himself even more physically appealing. Anan licked his lips at the sight. He wasn't tempted from Terja, but it was a mating flair that would have its effect on any unattached Talac and he couldn't begin to know what it would do to a Varas addicted to intimacy with the weavers.

Anan untangled himself from the spell Soneri cast on them. The gold-velveted Talac turned to Terja to continue. "And you might be more valuable to them than I am. They have never captured a spellspinner. Always before the spinners wove akhir and destroyed themselves along with a fingercount of attackers. They also think you velvetless spinners are the Talac healers. They have many reasons to want you."

Soneri moved closer to Terja. "Yes, Terja. We are that valuable. Given all that could happen, do you still want to stay here through the winter and hope I'm wrong?"

Anan watched as Terja met the eyes of each person and saw the same acceptance.

"That's just the way it is, Terja," Morea said.

Terja stopped and stared at the young woman. "Even you feel the same?"

"Yes. Even me. We need to go or they will catch us."

He turned and Anan felt his claustrophobic desperation. "Why don't you send Soneri and me away? If we are the only reason to hunt this group, we'll leave and lead them far away before they snip our warp threads."

Soneri began to chuckle, tinted slightly with hysteria. "You forget so soon, little spinner. I made a similar request when you rescued us from the slavers, and I'm fairly certain your voice was among the loudest that I not be left behind."

Terja tensed in a stance Anan had seen many times. He was going to argue. But then he deflated. "I'm not going to waste more time when I have a feeling I'd just be strapped to a drag and brought anyway."

Anan smiled broadly and nodded. "It was a nice large drag, but it was already chosen."

CHAPTER TWO

XAIN'S CHIN drooped against his chest as the iron cuffs ripped open the flesh of his wrists. Suspension from the monolithic altar to the Red Twins of the Varas was not how he foresaw his return to the Grand Hall of the Varas's High Regent. The hiss of the inquisitor's whip was his only warning before the braided leather and iron blades ripped across his shoulders. His gasps echoed off the white stone lining the hall as pain washed over him. Blood dripped thickly on the altar's fitted slabs beneath him. His muscles failed to hold him one after another until his entire weight hung from the rings.

I will live through this. I didn't survive the Varas pleasure houses to die on the Grand Hall's altar. He refused to accept a role as simply the latest Talac sacrificed to the Varas's Bloody Twins. He would have his revenge against his fellow Talac too. But the emotionless visage of the High Regent told him nothing about when his thread would be cut. The man lay on the dais, stroking the skin of his latest favorite among his slaves while he watched with dispassion.

On either side, and behind him, the Ubica Triad towered over the Varas in the room, meeting Xain's own stature. The dark-skinned smiths were infamous for their assassin Triads. Standing motionless in their robes and pants of black, with dark boots reaching to their knees. The only variation between the three was in the complex patterns of their sashes and in the unique hairstyle worn by one of them. No one could guess their goals. Their faces were as impassive as the dark stone columns he was suspended from. He hoped it was to aid him in recapturing the escaped Talac and punishing the spellweaver and spellspinner who freed them. But for all the expression on the Ubica's dark brown faces, they might as well have been carved from blackrock.

The silence drew out with only the sound of Xain's labored breath filling the room. A welcome breeze entered the arched windows that overlooked the bloodred waters of the Great River. The massive doors opened to allow

11

admittance to a trim figure that he studied through the fog of pain. The red-uniformed officer came to a crisp stop and executed a perfect bow.

"You called for me, High Regent."

The regent rose to his feet and snapped a quick nod at Xain. "This vermin is the only survivor of an ill-fated excursion by a distant cousin. They allowed the Talac animals to free the slaves and the Varas lost a company of harvesters." His eyes narrowed to tiny slits as he studied Xain. "This one tells me they also have a gold-pelted Talac. The first one in several lifetimes."

He shifted his gaze to the officer. "Captain Kosemi, I want those slaves back. I want each Talac returned even if all I receive is their filigreed pelts. The golden one particularly."

The captain knelt on one knee and dropped her head in acknowledgment. "Yes, High Regent. It will be done."

"Choose a century of soldiers to aid you." He motioned to the Ubica. "They will accompany you also."

The captain looked displeased at the last bit of information, but kept her expression to the smallest of frowns. Once the information had time to settle in, he continued after a twitch toward Xain's limp form. "You will also take that with you. He seems to know of a way to circumvent the Talac magic." A dark look passed across his face as he studied Xain. "Or he is the cause of the death of Geir and all his men. If the latter is the case—kill him."

Kosemi bowed again, having regained her composure. "So it will be done."

The High Regent made a slight motion toward the Triad. Instantly three knives flew through the air and sliced the leather binding Xain to the columns like they had rotted in the red waters of the Great River. He landed hard, but managed to keep his silence as the feeling painfully returned to his hands and feet. The Ubica removed the iron from his wrists and ankles as he writhed slowly, each movement sending new waves of pain through him. Fighting the agony, he pulled himself into a semblance of a slave's bow, his forehead against the blessedly cool stone.

As he waited, he heard a soft movement followed by the closing of a substantial door.

"Get up," a gravelly voice directed Xain.

He tilted his head to see the crimson pants of an officer of the Red Twins' army a few feet from him. He waited a moment longer to ensure there were no other commands before pressing himself into a seated position. He wasn't certain how this officer would receive him. She wasn't one he was familiar with. He glanced upward. A tight grip fastened on his jaw and yanked his head to her. Their eyes locked and her cold stare left no doubt as to her opinion of him.

"Talac, I would gut you here and now if it were up to me. I've never seen this mystical healing magic you claim. But I did see my father lose himself in his addiction to Talac pleasure slaves. He came to kill to feed his addiction, and was given to the River Serpent."

Xain dipped his head lower while keeping an eye on the soldier. "Of course, Captain. I will help however I can. I have no love for my fellow Talac."

A feral smile formed on her face. "I'm aware of your traitorous history with your people. Your loyalty to the Varas must be proven to me. You will be watched carefully until we return with the escaped slaves."

To Xain's surprise, she spun to the Ubica who stood silently to the side. "I also have little use for you three. It has long been a mystery to me why each High Regent purchases a Triad as their personal guards."

The largest of the assassins spoke, his voice a whisper, one that reminded Xain of a steel sword slipping from a boiled-leather sheath. "The Ubica are purchased because we stay bought. But keep this clear, red-legs, we are not slaves and there are limits to what is allowed by the Master Smiths."

Careful to school his expression, he chuckled to himself at the Ubica's use of the slang term for the members of the High Regent's army. A term he was certain the Ubica knew was hated by the wearers. Xain refused to point out the woven sash worn by each of the Triad contained the same crimson.

The captain stood for a moment, fingering the braid of the whip tucked into her belt. When her touch shifted to the short sword at her hip, the Ubica tensed. A common rumor said the Ubica carried many fingercounts of weapons, both hidden and openly displayed. The moment passed with neither Kosemi nor the large Ubica man blinking.

Xain detected a shift in the captain's body, and she retreated a step. He could almost smell the fear coming from her. The other two of the

Triad somehow flanked her. She glared individually at each of the four of them, and the look of contempt never shifted.

"Remember. I command this century, and they are absolutely loyal to me. Cost me one of their lives and I will not save enough pieces of you for the offering to the River Serpent." She paused for a heartbeat more, and then spun and escaped the room.

Silence enveloped the four of them for several moments. Xain drew up the courage to meet their gaze. Their glares locked and Xain's emotions swirled until a faint smile formed on the Ubica's face.

"This should be a trip worthy of the best dark-time stories. A Triad working with a Talac traitor and a century of Varas to recapture a group of escaped slaves. How could this be?" the large Ubica said.

Xain slowly rose to his feet, his jaw clenched against the renewing pain. He looked into the eyes of the thick-armed assassin. "I am not sure how they succeeded. But two things I do know. First, one of them is a spellspinner. The second should be of interest to you." He paused for a moment. "They opened the Ubica locks we used."

One dark eyebrow lifted on the man's face. "I see...."

He motioned to the other two with a barely noticeable flick of his hand. They swept from the room with more power and grace than any of the House of the Sun could manage, including the High Regent himself. Before Xain could blink, he was alone for the first time since he'd left the savanna.

CHAPTER THREE

GURVAN AND Daya entered the dark lodging provided for the Ubica Triad by the High Regent. Oka lagged behind them, and tonight Gurvan found no issue with allowing the newest member of their Triad a moment alone with his thoughts. The dark stone walls consumed what little light came through the thinly scraped hides stretched over the windows. A slight glow of red emanated from the few coals remaining in the center fire pit, and the faint scent of drying herbs lingered in the air. Preserving the silence, Gurvan lit lamps spread throughout the room, and while he did, Daya checked the tells they put in place to let them know if there had been intruders. After they'd inspected every spell, Gurvan allowed himself to relax. "They searched the room, as we expected. But they found nothing more than a fingercount of ordinary blades."

Daya shook his head slowly. "They hammered an agreement with the Master Smiths. We are ironsworn to uphold the contract they made. The Varas know the quality of our contract, and our locks. Our locksmiths are renowned for creating works of art in gray metal that can't be picked. They could not have opened any of the locked objects. But they jeopardize our contract by searching the lodging they provided us."

Daya paced the small open space, agitated far past his typical calm demeanor. "They must be aware we would know if they try to open our locks. Why would they feel the need to search our lodging? Is their world so filled with subterfuge that they see it in every possible source? I do not understand what else they thought they would find. It seems they question our integrity."

"Perhaps they don't understand the work of our smiths. They claim Ubica locks were opened by the Talac, after a moon deprived of food other than what they feed freshly captured slaves. The Varas took great delight in reducing the payment because of the failure."

Daya shook his head. "Were the locks truly ours? I've never heard of anyone tricking one of our locks open."

Gurvan said, "According to Xain, two Talac destroyed an entire slaver company and freed the captives. We must forge this mission carefully."

"We lost Satu during our last contract, and Oka does not seem to have the alloy to form a life triad with us."

"What is an Anvil and Hammer without a Forge? Our coupling must echo that of the Ancients," Gurvan said.

"You have a Forge. I am the Forge in this heating. But you don't trust my temper?"

Gurvan and Daya turned to find Oka standing in the doorway, his arms folded across his chest and his stance rigid. Inwardly, Gurvan groaned. This would weaken the already brittle welds. Their connection had been tenuous and might shatter under new stress. He glanced at Daya before meeting Oka's glare.

"You are correct. We have a Forge. And you are also right. It's untested by Daya and myself. I'm sure you feel the same, being the only survivor of your Triad."

"I've acknowledged their deaths were my fault. But the ones who bought the forging used us. It was a death trap no one should have survived. But apparently the Great Smith wanted me to suffer the loss of my Triad."

This time Gurvan did let out an audible sigh and lifted his hands into the air. "We've all suffered loss. We must make these new welds stronger than before. I do not think the weavers will be the helpless quarry the Varas believes them to be. I think some Varas already know this, or they wouldn't be concerned."

"Does each High Regent hire a Triad as personal guards?" Oka asked.

Gurvan stared for a moment as he adjusted to the sudden change in topic. Finally he nodded. "I'm not certain what brought on this question. The Triad of Master Smiths approved our contract. But to answer your query, yes, there is a tradition of Triads with the Varas ruler. Why do you ask?"

"Because we're on the wrong side of the Great Smith's teachings."

"It is not our place to question the Triad of Master Smiths. They are the holders of all knowledge. Also, you well know each forging has many folds, some of which are only known to me."

Oka rolled his eyes. "I know the leader of our Triad is the Anvil. I am not an apprentice new to the bellows. But, as Forge, I have the duty to question when I feel it is needed."

Daya stepped between them. "Enough." He focused on Gurvan for a few heartbeats and then said, "Honesty is always needed. To have a true forging requires the work of all members of the Triad." Shifting his gaze to Oka, he continued. "And Gurvan is our Anvil. You must respect his decision as final once it's been passed down."

Both men nodded, and Gurvan wrapped himself in his own thoughts as he undressed to his inner clothing. He unsheathed his sword and began the nightly ritual of sharpening.

"See now, this is why my war hammer is superior. It doesn't need a nightly sharpening. Each new notch and scratch adds to its effectiveness," Daya said.

"No, you're both wrong. I carry the legendary century of blades, and each one is lethal," said Oka.

Gurvan felt the spirit of a smile develop on his lips at the friendly banter. It was the first time since leaving Ubica lands that they had been comfortable enough to tease each other. But he did wonder. The century of blades was an old saying Satu quoted to them frequently, but he'd never actually shown them the blades.

"Oka?"

The young man looked toward the Anvil of their Triad, some of his tension returning. "Yes?"

"A century of knives? Where do you put them all?"

Oka's smile bloomed back, larger than any Gurvan had seen on the young man before. "I have the legendary number. But you might question calling them knives."

He reached inside his robes and brought out a short stick covered with bright tufts of feathers. Oka grasped it by its ends and tugged. It grew in length until it stretched from his fingertips to his elbow. He held it out to Gurvan with a smile. "Here are at least a double fingercount of knives."

Oka moved beside him as Gurvan studied it. "A blowgun? That's part of your century?"

"Each part of the Triad has their secrets. The blowgun is part of the Forge's."

Daya reached to pull a dart from its resting place. Oka stopped his hand. "They are coated with daggerhorn poison. Enough to easily kill a man."

17

Gurvan carefully handed the weapon back to Oka and watched as it disappeared into his robe. After a moment he shook his head and smiled. "How many little secrets do you have hidden away?"

Oka seemed to consider his reply but reached in his robe and pulled out a narrow tube, wider than the blowgun, but still small.

"These hold throwing needles, which are also poisonous." His smile grew even larger as he reached up to the tight bun he always styled his hair into. He held out what Gurvan now realized were throwing spikes.

"So, you can see. I probably have more than the requirement of legend."

"Smith protect us. I had no idea how many little nasty tricks the Forge hid," Gurvan said.

Oka tucked everything into its place before meeting the gaze of the other two. His smile had diminished, but not disappeared.

"Perhaps sometime you can share the teachings of the Anvil and Hammer."

Gurvan studied the smaller man for several heartbeats. "A fully forged Triad shares all."

As THE lamps were extinguished and the room darkened, Oka curled up facing the wall and tried to sleep. He listened to the night sounds around him, but they brought no comfort. They served only to emphasize the foreign setting. He'd surprised himself by sharing a secret of the Forge sect. It wasn't forbidden, but as Gurvan pointed out, it wasn't common unless the Triad was forged. For Oka, it seemed the right thing to do.

He felt the wounds of loss reopen as he thought about Ata and Lanvi. His Triad had been on their final contract and planned to forge the mating bond afterward. But things went terribly wrong. Oka missed an impossibly easy knife throw, and the target's personal guards had burst through the door with crossbows loaded. The chaos had been short and lethal. His Triad had practically thrown him out the window to save him.

"Questioning their choice is not helping, Oka. They wanted you to live or they wouldn't have protected you so you could escape," said Gurvan when the silence stretched longer.

"And I let them. I fled faster than a rockdiver." Oka cringed at the memory of scurrying away in fear. Retracing the event brought the same feeling of hollowness and pain it always did.

"The time will come when you must forgive yourself, or when you go to the Master Smith for reforging you will be found faulty."

IIe searched for a response when a knock came from the thick wooden door. Gurvan motioned Oka to light a lamp.

He quickly struck the back of a blade against a piece of firestone he kept. The spark hit the lamp's wick and a flame formed quickly. Gurvan moved beside him, and Oka handed him the flame. Oka saw he had a blade palmed as he moved to open the door.

Holding the light low, Gurvan cracked open the entrance. During the heartbeat that followed, Oka readied himself for a throw. He could only guess Daya was arming himself too. Only a fool disturbed a Triad under contract. But these Varas didn't seem to understand the nuances of working with the Ubica.

"Let me in, fools!" hissed the voice from the other side of the door.

Gurvan's eyes narrowed, causing Oka to tense, but then he opened the door wide enough to allow the nocturnal visitor admittance. The shadows moved but more lamps were not lit. Oka wondered why, but knew Gurvan would have his reason.

Oka's vision adjusted to the flickering light and he recognized the furry Talac. Why would he come here? *I can see Gurvan's hand twitch with the need to feed his iron with this one's blood. The Talac should state his business quickly.*

"Why are you disturbing our sleep, slave?" Gurvan asked.

Oka was a little surprised Gurvan spoke so abruptly. Ubica tradition dictated a more hospitable approach, but he was the Anvil of their Triad. He waited to see what the Talac's response to the offense would be. He was surprised to see the tall man fold into a bow of subservience.

"My apologies for disturbing you, Anvil. But I hoped for a moment of the Triad's time."

Gurvan's only response was a low grunt.

The slave slipped into the room, his movement echoing those of a hunting longtooth. This was no helpless slave. Gurvan held the lamp higher and the two locked eyes.

This time with a short, less formal bow, the slave began. "My name is Xain. This mission is important to me. I know your contract is with the High Regent, but we will be working together and you will need my help, or you will be unable to complete your agreement."

The muscles in Gurvan's jaw tensed at Xain's words. Oka could imagine only the forging with the Master Smiths kept the Talac alive. Then he noticed something else about the visitor. The Talac was wearing a spiritknife at his waist. *How did he get the short sword? Only certain Triad Anvils carry that weapon.* It was an incredible blade in the right hands. But even for someone of the Iron People, it was not to be treated lightly. Gurvan hadn't been awarded a blade because their Triad wasn't life forged. How the Talac had gotten one was beyond Oka.

"We will finish our mission, furry one. There is nothing you can tell us that we do not already know," Gurvan said.

"You know the Talac magic? You know, the two you are assigned to kill have more skills than any Talac I've ever seen. I think they are blessed of the Twined Ones. I believe the spellspinner somehow survived akhir. No one since the clans were joined has survived akhir."

Oka caught the twitch traveling along the dark skin on Gurvan's face. A wash of surprise came over Oka. *Gurvan doesn't know. Or he hadn't known. Interesting.*

"What of it? And what do you ask of us? I'm sure even you are aware we will not go against the forging we have already created with the High Regent."

The Talac's expression changed even further. This was not a man Oka wanted at his back. "I want those two. The spellspinner and his mate. They destroyed my plans. Now I am living only at the grace of the High Regent. Do you have any idea what that means?"

Oka shook his head in a negative, but Gurvan nodded, and his expression seemed to soften. After a moment of silence, he spoke to Xain. "We cannot help you directly. But our goals are similar. I understand you are marked, but our current forging is with him."

Xain glared at Gurvan until the tension became palpable in the room. "You want to be my ally, Ubica. I am not a person you want to be pitted against. I am not the helpless slave you think I am." Xain rested his hand against the spiritknife's hilt.

Oka stepped from the shadows at the same instant Daya moved to Gurvan's other side. Oka could see the eyes of the other two were echoes of their roles. Gurvan's became the coal black of the anvil and Daya's the shining silver of a working hammer. He knew from past experience his own eyes were the deep red and yellow from the forge.

Oka was pleased the combined energies of his Triad drove the Talac back until he was pinned against the door. Oka's fire built as he watched the man who was rapidly becoming his prey. The feeding hunger sensed the fear from Xain until Oka twitched his arm and held three throwing spikes in his palm. *Three, the sacred number, it's a sign from the Great Smith.* Oka tensed to launch the lethal missiles, but a heavy hand closed on his shoulder.

The fire he was about to unleash drained from him. He tensed as his desire faded faster than a drop of water against red hot metal. *I will have words with Gurvan later. But I will play my role for now.*

Gurvan spoke and this time it had the true ring of the Anvil. The almost crystalline chime in his voice traveled through Oka, soothing some of his fire. He glanced at Daya and got a small nod. Daya agreed with Gurvan. Tonight his fire would not be fed.

"Leave now and we will forget this ever happened. Don't interfere with our forging again. Know that whatever you feared from the pair of weavers would be nothing compared to the wrath of a Triad of the Iron People," Gurvan said.

The conflict in the room built until Oka thought he felt the waves traveling through him. Xain reached behind him, slipping across the face of the heavy wooden door until he reached the latch. Oka enjoyed the moments of fumbling as the Talac tried to open the lock. With the bolt's click, the door pivoted open, and Xain slipped through.

Oka glared at the door as he calmed his racing heart. Once he thought he could speak to Gurvan with the respect due his station, he turned to catch his gaze. "Why would you—"

Gurvan silenced him with a flick of his hand. "You were unleashing the hunger of the Forge. I know the outlander carries a spiritblade, which will make our forging more difficult. I couldn't allow you to send him to the Ancients for reforging. We have many obstacles ahead of us. There is no need to make it more difficult."

The heat inside Oka built for a moment, and then he allowed Gurvan and Daya to calm him. Without looking at either of them, he returned the throwing spikes to their sheaths and moved to the corner and his sleeping mat.

"Oka, come. Sleep with us," Daya said.

Oka stared at the two men for several moments. *Do I want to become close to these two? They are different from Ata and Lanvi. Ata would never have quenched my fire. He enjoyed seeing me use it. But Ata is dead, and I have a second chance with Gurvan and Daya.*

"Come. You can give us some of the heat you are filled with. These Smith-cursed northlands are cold," Gurvan said with a throaty tone to his words.

Oka chuckled at the idea of Gurvan being affected by the cool temperature. It served its purpose too.

"All right. But don't complain to me in the morning about feeling as if you'd slept with a live ember."

CHAPTER FOUR

ANAN WATCHED Morea as she sat with her back to the encampment, seeming to study the endless sea of tawny grass ahead of them. Light from the emerging sun cast part of her in deep shadow that echoed the expression on her face. When a sudden gust of wind sent a ripple of movement over her short hair, she sat unmoving. Anan waited a moment longer, then lowered himself beside her. They sat quietly as the time stretched out.

"Joven told me," Anan said at last. "You might as well talk to me about these visions of yours."

"Joven died once. His weaving is more than a little tattered in places," Morea said.

Anan dropped his gaze to the ground and smiled. "Yes, well he didn't quite die. The matama Terja and I wove wasn't as strong as the stories would have you believe. But he said you are seeing into the future."

Morea replied without changing her position. "And you believe visionspinners are less useful than three-moon-old rancid daggerhorn meat."

Anan lifted his head until he met Morea's gaze. "No, Morea. But I do not believe you can see how the threads of the future are woven."

"Then any argument that might change our plans for the future will be ignored." Morea said.

Frustration tinged with anger slipped into Anan. Morea was proving herself invaluable in treating the more severe wounds. But this nonsense of visionspinners... he couldn't let it go any further.

"Morea, I think you have found something to believe in, and after being taken by the Varas slavers and living through the moons' cycle under their abuse, I'm glad you can put faith in anything. I believe in a sharp knife and a sure hand on the bow."

Morea tilted her head slightly and drew her lips into a thin line. "So the words of the Firsts telling you to take the survivors to the Kuri winter village mean nothing more to you than a cast-off husk from a deathspinner colony?"

"That was completely different. Terja and I called a bloodweaving to avenge the Kuri clan. It's not the same as seeing spirits at night and trying to give their strange dances a meaning when there is none."

"So you've given my visions to the same realm as the ghost stories we tell kits. After you freed us, when we were preparing to begin this trip, that was just ghost dreams too? First Twining didn't give you information to help get us back alive?"

Anan's face grew hot as the young woman outmaneuvered him in their discussion. This wasn't the way he envisioned the conversation going. A moment passed and then he exhaled slowly. "We're not moving the camp because you saw red beasts with teeth the length of my arm attacking us and killing everyone. No animal is that large. If they were, what would we do against them?" He paused for a moment before continuing. "Besides, it was already decided we would not stay. But tonight has the feel of more rain. It would be foolish to move through that weather."

She looked so dejected Anan wondered for a moment if he had made the right choice. But as he glanced around them, he couldn't see anything threatening to a group of Talac this large. Even a pack of longtooth would find attacking them difficult. He stood and squeezed her shoulder lightly. *I feel there is more to be said, but I don't know what. My parents said silence was sometimes the best reply.* He decided this time he would take their advice. After an instant of hesitation, he turned and walked to the cluster of tents. He studied the darkening clouds coming from the north and felt Iceweaver's breath in the fitful wind.

"You know, you aren't always right."

Anan cringed at Terja's words. But he refused to doubt his choices. "I have to get all these people to the winter village. Fleeing from every bad dream will not get us there faster."

He moved to help a trio who were having difficulty with their tent lashings. He barked out a few instructions, and moments later the tent was tightly stretched. Anan couldn't help but be pleased at the simple success. He turned when Terja stepped beside him.

"See. Some things are that easy," Anan said.

"You know, I don't believe you."

Anan turned, avoiding Terja's gaze. "It's fixed. That tent won't fold under tonight's storm."

"I am not talking about the tent."

Anan stopped, the weight of this entire mission pressed on his shoulders. "I can't appear weak. How would it look if I were making decisions based on a visionspinner? Some aren't even sure they believe in a spellspinner. Do you think you can change their mind about their beliefs?"

Terja scanned the small valley where they had sheltered. The waning moon's darkness made it easy for Anan to see the approaching storm's fury. They would be glad for the protecting shelter before the night ended. Jagged white bolts of lightning raced across the dark southern sky as he considered the future.

"This isn't her first vision. She's had others."

Anan met Terja's gaze. "Why haven't I heard anything about it before?"

Terja made a gesture of helplessness. "None of them were of anything significant. This is the first one that challenges the group's safety."

"And before...."

"All her visions have been proven to be true."

MOREA WOKE with a twisting pain in her gut. She sank her teeth into her lip to keep from calling out. Waiting, she hoped the agony would pass, but it built until it felt as if she were wrapped in a needle bush. A bolt of lightning struck a huge ironwood tree nearby and wove a pattern through its bark more intricate than what appeared on any Talac velvet, before exploding in every direction. Two more followed quickly behind, increasing the weaving's complexity.

She gasped for air as the intricate pattern inside her continued to grow. Fire jumped from tree to tree, taking on depth and reality. The shape it created was achingly familiar. Fangs materialized as the web moved around the ironwood, liquid covering their length. It was followed by a snarl that vibrated through Morea's being... and jarred her awake.

"Soneri! Joven!"

The men materialized at her side within a heartbeat. She glanced at first one and then the other until she gained her wits. Joven grasped her wrist and squeezed, giving Morea the composure to speak.

"Something's coming. It's huge and deadly. We need to leave."

Soneri gripped her shoulder, but the terror of her vision built until she thought her heart would escape her chest.

"Are you having dreams again? We just can't—" he began.

Morea jumped to her feet, her voice shrill with panic. "No! It was not a dream. I am becoming a visionspinner. We must leave."

A long breath escaped from Joven's lips. She spun to him as her anger and desperation grew. "We have to run. I'm telling you. None of us may survive if we don't do something immediately."

Joven motioned for her to lower her voice, but it had the opposite effect.

"No! I will not be quiet. We need to move. We need to leave. All of us."

"And where would you suggest we move the entire camp?"

Morea spun to find Anan glaring at her with crossed arms. Behind him was Terja, and the expression on his face was not sympathetic. She kept her resolve and returned the scowl. The moons' positions along the northern horizon at least made it possible for Morea to make out the disbelief carved onto their faces. She turned her developing anger on Anan.

"You have to move the camp. Something huge and dangerous is coming. It might kill all of us."

Anan locked eyes with Morea "What, exactly? The Varas aren't following us. There are far too many for a pack of longtooth to attack. What would be so big and dangerous?"

"I don't know, but it's going to be bad if we don't move. We must leave now!"

Anan shook his head and sighed. "No one will move in the middle of the night based on the word of one girl."

"But they would move on your command. Can you risk being wrong?"

"She has you there, Anan."

Everyone's eyes shifted to Terja, and Anan looked as if he were ready to strangle his twining. Morea took the offered ally and rounded on Anan. "See! Terja agrees. I know it would be a desperate chance, but I swear to you if we don't move, there may be no Kuri left."

In the dim light of the moons, she could see the tightening of Anan's jaw muscles. His eyes seemed to bore into her and study her very core.

"Strands, Morea! If you're wrong, you will never wake me with your visions again. Agreed?"

She shivered and nodded. A moment later Morea realized he couldn't see her in the impending storm's thick darkness as the clouds wrapped around the moons. "Yes, I agree. But I'm not wrong." A chill ran through her and she couldn't keep the quiver from her voice as she continued. "Please hurry."

Anan never shifted his eyes from Morea. "Where would we be safe?"

She considered for a moment, straining at the threads of her visionweaving. Then she knew. "The ridge. The top of the ridge."

Anan frowned and for the first time since he challenged Morea, dropped his eyes. Time slowed until he shifted his gaze and studied the ridge surrounding their encampment for several long moments. "We will have no shelter. Spread out on the ridge, we would be vulnerable to a longtooth attack. Are you certain?"

Morea turned inward and saw the weaving had not shifted. "Yes, I'm certain. But we must hurry. It's coming."

"What's coming?" Terja asked. Before Morea could reply, he waved her off. "It doesn't matter. I'll find out one way or another."

Anan turned to Joven and Soneri. "Awaken the people. Everyone must move to the west ridge." He turned to Morea. "The west will suffice? I don't want to split the encampment and our lands are to the west."

Morea nodded and her throat tightened. For the first time she questioned her vision. Studying the faces of each person surrounding her, she made her decision.

"Yes. West will be safe. But we need to move. Now!"

Anan nodded again and the four men scattered through the encampment. Soon fires and torches were being lit as the people collapsed their tents and loaded the drags for the short move.

Morea watched for a few moments before moving to help. Although they were only moving to the ridge top, the steep climb would have to be taken slowly or there would be injuries.

The deep black transitioned to dark gray to signal the end of a difficult night. The stragglers who brought the worst injured entered the edge of the ironwood trees clustered along the valley's spine where they camped a short time ago.

Cries of encouragement came from the people in the lead. Morea heard the notes of desperation in their tone and leaned harder into the drag poles she gripped. The woman beside her paused to peer through the darkness.

"By the First Pair...."

Morea followed the woman's stunned gaze and found the source of the fear in her eyes. A wall of churning water surged between the steep canyon walls. They froze for a moment, overwhelmed by the sight. Morea recovered from her daze first and pressed harder to move their load.

"Hurry! It's a flash flood. It will deepen quickly."

The older woman stared at her, but in an instant water swirled around their feet. Morea grabbed her jacket and shoved her forward. "Go! Or we'll be swept away!"

The woman paused and Morea thought she was going to freeze again. But instead she plunged forward like a kuri with a longtooth in pursuit. Morea had to hurry in order to keep her grip. Her heart pounded as they splashed through the rising water. The trail became steeper and she was relieved to feel the water drop lower on her legs. With another rush forward, they emerged from the frothing water and drew up beside the group ahead of them.

As they stood gasping for breath, the water continued to rise. The darkness multiplied the fear since they could only roughly gauge its growth. But eventually Morea could see the water was getting no deeper. The chilled water lapped around her ankles, but as she scanned their group, she was relieved to see they hadn't lost anyone. The people around her were winded, but all wore looks of relief as they saw the flooded canyon floor.

Morea was spun and grabbed in a tight embrace. It only took a moment to realize it was Soneri. Her carefully controlled emotions rose and the wall they had been shoved behind broke.

"Oh, Soneri. Thank the Firsts. You survived."

"Everyone did, thanks to you." He cocked an eyebrow and glanced at the group of stragglers Morea helped. "Even the ones who were slow and stubborn."

She held him even tighter. The scent of his spicy musk helped calm her. As her emotions settled, someone else slammed into her from the other side.

"Morea! Thank the Twined Ones! You're alive," Joven said.

She chuckled and pressed her lips against his forehead. "Calm yourself, Joven. I'm fine. We were the last drag and other than wet feet, everything is well."

He squeezed her again, grabbed her by the shoulders, and held her at a distance as if to verify her good health. After a moment, he shook his head and released her.

"Anan wants to see you. Personally, I hope it's to tell you how important you are to everyone and how sorry he is for doubting you."

Morea flicked the back of her hand against Joven's chest and smiled. "The day that happens I will know I am being called to the Great Weaving. But I'm certain he has a good reason to want me. Let's not keep him waiting."

They worked their way through the small groups. In places the water churned past only a span or so away. As they made their way to Anan, a light drizzle began and the air grew chilled. The distance to the top of the ridge was greater than Morea had judged. By the time the three of them arrived, the sun had slipped above the eastern horizon.

Joven motioned toward Anan and Terja who he'd spotted standing on a relatively flat spot where their tent had been set up. They were snatching small teaching weavings from the ground and carrying them inside the tent. Joven and Soneri rushed to help while Morea moved aside to give the others room for what they were doing.

Once the tapestries were all safely stored, Terja motioned Morea inside while he held the flap open. "Come in. I apologize for the delay. Anan and I are protective of the Kuri weavings. Anan needs to speak with you."

A knot formed in Morea's stomach as she followed Terja inside. He motioned her to a small fire that was a welcome source of heat. Morea huddled close to the warmth while Anan finished whatever task he had. When he turned, his face was severe, but when his eyes settled on Morea, the tension slipped away and a smile appeared.

"Welcome to today's hero! You saved us all. I don't think anyone would have survived the flood."

Morea dropped her head, bashful at the sudden acclaim. But she was certain the smile covering her face was visible to both men. "I'm glad to be of help."

Anan reached down and lifted Morea's face. "I'm sorry I doubted you. It almost cost everyone their lives."

"Many Talac don't understand visionweaving. Only a few each generation have it," Morea said.

Anan shook his head. "Don't try to remove my blame. But trust me, from this point forward I will consider your visions much more carefully."

"I will try not to let you down, Anan."

CHAPTER FIVE

XAIN STOOD on the bluff overlooking a small canyon. The river running through it was too dangerous to cross until the water level dropped. It churned, the water filled with debris, making it even more deadly. His frustration grew that their progress had been thwarted, again. He paced up and down the edge, knowing there was no safe path close, but needing some way to channel his anger and frustration. His emotions flared to new levels at the snapping cadence of a particular pair of boots.

"Captain, I hope you are here to tell me the scouts have located a route around this swirling mess."

To Kosemi's credit she did not let her nerves show. But Xain knew she wasn't happy with the expedition's progress either, among a list of things she resented. If the truth were told, Xain wasn't very happy about the Ubica Triad being part of the group. They had a reputation for completing the letter of their contracts. Nothing less, and nothing more. For Xain, the issue lay in his lack of knowledge regarding the content of their contract with the High Regent.

"The scouts sent to find safe crossing have not returned."

From Kosemi's reaction each time they dealt with the trio, she didn't know their full assignment either. Much of it was common sense. Xain was certain the two Talac who wiped out all the harvesters but himself and freed the slaves were a target for the Ubica. But the High Regent's mind was a weaving not easily unraveled. Many times there were several tasks assigned to each Ubica contract. Xain had to be certain any targeting him failed.

He realized she was waiting for a response. He studied her for a few moments before continuing. "We can't let them gain even a fingercount of days on us. Find a way, Captain."

Kosemi's expression twisted. "I will not jeopardize my soldiers. You are not the commander of this expedition."

Xain faced the hardened woman with a feral expression of his own. "We both know if you don't listen to me the trip will be a failure. So,

31

Captain, when I tell you we'll be across the river tonight, you will find a way to make it happen."

She spat on the ground between them. "I will not let you destroy this company like you did last time, Talac."

Anger rose in Xain. "Geir was in charge of the slavers, not I. I was a lowly Talac pleasure slave Geir brought to service him."

There was a flash of movement, and the tip of Kosemi's knife pierced the skin of his throat.

His gaze met hers. "Are you going to kill me, Captain? Because I'm the only one who can guide you. And without completing their contract, the Ubica will not return with you. How are you going to explain to the High Regent that you killed your only hope of success?"

"I despise you. Let me make that clear. If I could, your blood would be soaking into this godforsaken Talac soil already. But you are right. I need the information you have. Make no mistake, you are not in charge. If you put my soldiers in danger—I will cut open your fur-covered body like you were a grazer at the slaughter."

Xain's eyes narrowed as he became furious "I will tell you this, Kosemi. I am the least of your problems. This group of Talac hasn't realized we're trailing them. When they do, life becomes much more difficult—and infinitely more dangerous."

She flicked her knife away, leaving a lightly bleeding line through the velvet covering his neck. Xain never flinched; he'd experienced much worse. After a moment, she rammed the knife into its leather sheath. He waited a heartbeat, but then pressed forward. "The river is rising. Soon it will be several days' travel before we can cross. We have no choices here."

Without a word she turned and made her way to her tent. As she slipped through the flap she muttered, "We have choices. We will choose how many of my century are lost."

THE SUN was only just visible through the trees in the small glade forming the eastern side of the Varas encampment. The rows of small tents were tinted with the sun's rays, but the scene was not what Xain wanted. He fought to control his fury as he watched the relaxed movements of Kosemi's guards rather than them moving with a sense of urgency. His expression made even the hardened soldiers give him a wide berth. His hand rested on the handle of his long knife, the one concession made to Xain's status, and value. The captain had taken it away and dulled it before returning it. But she did not seem to realize it was a spiritknife and that he was perfectly capable of giving it an edge that would satisfy the most demanding of her trainers, which he had done.

Xain froze in place at the next sound. Longtooth.

The hissing call of the ferocious animals sent a chill up his spine. He envisioned the saliva dripping from incisors as long as his hand while their long tails lashed back and forth as the pack worked themselves into a feeding frenzy. He forced himself into action through his fear, wishing he still had matama in his kilt. He'd give a lot at this moment to have that Twins-damned spinner under his control. It would be worth almost anything to be able to spin a barrier.

He motioned to a soldier who was close. "You. We need to secure the grounds. That's a pack of longtooth looking for an easy meal."

The young man glanced at him and responded. "We have orders from the captain, sir. You would need to talk with her."

Xain started to argue but realized it would do him no good. This was not Geir's ragtag group of slavers. He may not like Kosemi, but she kept order in her troops and none of them would intentionally disobey. Something he would need to work on before they closed with the Talac.

Another blood-chilling hiss filled the darkening space around him and settled the discussion. He spun on his heel and sprinted toward the captain's tent. As he approached the flap, two burly guards blocked his entrance. Xain might tower over them, as any Talac would over a Varas, but these two were several times more muscular than him. Besides being physically intimidating, they were both wielding battle-axes, and he was certain they were experts with the weapons. The entire century seemed to be the best soldiers the High Regent could buy, steal, or bully from his landsmen.

"I need to see Kosemi," Xain demanded.

"Captain Kosemi is currently occupied. I can relay a message," one guard said.

Another hissing howl echoed from the hills surrounding them. "Do you hear that? That's a pack of longtooth in full hunting fervor. Does she wish to find out how many Varas it takes to satisfy the hunger of a feeding pack?"

Their faces locked and they glanced at each other. "We'll let the captain know."

Panic filled Xain and his voice rose. "We need to create a formation. There could be several fingercounts of them in this pack." He paused for a moment before going on. "Sometimes they combine bands to hunt— larger prey."

The guards were fidgeting under Xain's hard gaze when the tent flap opened and one of Kosemi's squad leaders appeared. Xain recoiled. He'd known before they started that this would be futile. But he had begun this warning. If they chose not to listen—well there would be fewer hungry longtooth afterward.

Without preamble, he spoke. "We've been targeted by a hunting pack of longtooth. We must get the troops ready for their attack."

The scowl on the squad leader's face deepened as she waved dismissively. "The century has always proven effective in protecting itself. We do not need the help of a furred animal."

Xain started to speak again, but found himself looking at the back of a receding Varas uniform. His jaw clenched at the words that drifted back to him. "Go back and hide, Talac. The century will protect you."

Indignant fury boiled up inside Xain. He considered sinking his knife deep in the squad leader but knew it would be a death sentence, the most painful that could be devised. Xain knew this, because he'd been the one to deliver similar punishments on Geir's behalf. His teeth clamped tight as he turned and rushed to his own tent.

One part of the insinuation had been true: Xain must defend himself. Stepping into his dimly lit tent, he blinked a few times while his eyes adjusted. Once he could see, he began to prepare. Moving quickly, he snatched up two crossbows he kept close at all times. Next he grabbed his matching set of long knives, a gift from Geir. He paused briefly as he thought about Geir and the horrible ways the Talac would pay for killing him. He missed the man, even if he had been manipulating Geir, using his addiction to sex with pelted Talac.

Xain trembled. The largest predators on the savanna had targeted this group. The danger was obvious as the pack began to call to each other. A shiver of dread rippled through him as the vocalizations became more frequent. He knew it wouldn't be long before the pack began its attack.

He stepped out of his tent and studied the area, running to the trees on their western flank to search for a defensible spot. He found a trio of large ironwood trees to protect his back. Now he had a fighting chance of survival.

"What are we hearing, Xain?"

He tensed for a heartbeat before recognizing Gurvan's voice. He'd forgotten the assassin trio in his haste. "Longtooth. They have targeted the camp as prey. The Varas don't believe they are a threat."

Gurvan studied him for a moment as the volume of the predator's cries increased to a level even the Varas couldn't ignore. "What would you recommend, Talac?"

Xain sighed in relief. His chances of surviving just increased considerably. "We must guard each other. Their normal prey is daggerhorn, which have poisonous horns. They are climbers too. So keep an eye for an attack from the trees above."

Gurvan turned to the other two and began spitting orders. No questions were asked; they simply moved into position. Their dusky skin hid them in the failing light. Oka armed himself with throwing spikes and Daya moved to cover their rear flank. Gurvan pulled a sword from the sheath at his side. The chime of the expertly forged blade reverberated in the darkness.

A grim smile crossed Xain's lips. *I might survive this.*

A very human scream filled the night, quickly followed by a second. The longtooth were feeding.

Turmoil erupted. Xain jumped at each noise, human or animal. Screams of injured longtooth seemed to be gaining in number as he realized something was lighting the area around them. It took a moment to identify the illumination as coming from Oka. He turned to Gurvan and their gazes met.

"Oka is our Forge. His light can be manifest. It would serve to make him a target against men, but the animals should fear the fire."

Xain stared at the young man's face. His eyes glowed as bright as a small campfire. But as Xain watched, he realized even his skin emitted a faint glow. Another agonizing scream came from the side and wrenched him to the present.

"They come," said Gurvan.

Xain snapped up a crossbow and launched a quarrel at the flash of ivory when a tawny-colored longtooth leapt at the group. The air around them exploded with its howl of pain when Xain's quarrel took it full in the chest. Oka appeared at his side and flung a pair of spikes. Both sank deep into the animal, which dropped to the ground.

Two more appeared and were dealt with instantly by the other Ubica. The events blurred from there on for Xain. The assassins fought with grim determination. Xain lost count of how many lethal spikes left the hands of the Ubica they called the Forge. Xain launched his share of crossbow bolts as the other two kept the creatures from coming too close to the four of them with sword and war hammer. The sounds of attack intensified and adrenaline filled Xain's being. Both he and the Ubica had injuries, but the battle rush kept the wounds from slowing them.

At last, several moments passed without another animal launching at them. The pain of Xain's injuries began to creep into his body. A shift in weight sent a bolt of agony racing through him and a gasp escaped between his teeth.

He realized two Ubica were holding up the third—their light source. The sounds of battle were gone, replaced by the moans and cries for help that filled the air. Glancing to the assassins, he met eyes with Gurvan. "Our Forge has overextended himself. But it seems we have defeated the animals."

Xain nodded slowly. "At least for now. Depending on how much we reduced their numbers, they might return. It's hard to tell how many we have lost."

The Ubica cocked his head for a moment, his form disappearing against the darkness surrounding them. After a short time, his focus returned to Xain. "Many have been injured, some have died. Other injuries sound fatal."

Xain decided being cooperative would be in his best interest at this moment. He turned to the Ubica. "Do you require help?"

"From a Talac with no matama? What could you do for our Triad?"

Xain studied the man carefully. He was surprised the assassins had so much information about the secretive Talac. He started to speak but was cut off.

"We are not the mindless spike aimed at a victim. We are hired for our expertise. We are not at war with the Talac. But we gathered as much information as possible to ensure our success. As for us, our injuries are minor, and Oka needs only to rest. We will guard him through the night." He nodded toward Xain. "You were raked by the animal's claws. You should seek a healer."

The moons appeared through the clouds, and he could clearly see the blood soaking his velvet in many places. The claws had gotten past the assassins more often than he realized. But Xain had experienced far worse. Before Geir bought him from the Varas pleasure house, he'd been injured in the name of twisted thrills. Without another word, he turned and made his way slowly back to his shelter.

Tomorrow would be long.

CHAPTER SIX

TERJA STOOD at Anan's shoulder as they studied the path before them. The route they'd hoped to take was impassable. The barrens were a maze of valleys and canyons, some connected, others not. The Meke might have a reason for their unusual configuration, but Terja didn't know. The rain that caused the flash flood seemed to have been widespread in the region, flooding many trails and washing out others. He crossed his arms and sighed.

"We can't pass here."

"No," Anan said. "We would never get the drags through this. Joven and Soneri scouted out what would be a day's travel up and down stream. We were fortunate to be on the west side of the canyon when it flooded. At least we were able to come a few days farther. It gets no better."

Terja let his arms drop to his side and heaved in a deep breath. "Could we weave the trail to make it passable? Maybe you could make travel on them safe."

Anan considered for a moment before slowly shaking his head. "No. I might be able to make the mudflats passable, but not running water. I know of no weaves that will solidify water."

Terja chewed his lip for a moment. "What about an appeal to Iceweaver? We are moving into her season. She could freeze the water."

With no hesitation, Anan emphatically shook his head. "No, Iceweaver will have her turn at us soon enough. But I will not call her down from the Ais Mountains. I gladly leave Iceweaver for the Meke clan."

"What did Joven and Soneri find?"

"To the south there are three rivers joining into one that is massive, and far too dangerous to attempt to cross." Anan paused for a moment before continuing. "We must find another way."

Floodwaters were roiling beneath them, and Terja could feel the power through his feet. The sounds of the flooded barrens became heavy before Terja spoke again. "We have another issue too. I've spun the last of the deathspinner silk. We have been very careful with it, only using it for healing and the guardian web each evening. Gathering the matama after each day's travel as people relive their journey is not difficult, but without the deathspinner silk to store it, I cannot spin the matama."

Anan twisted his lips as he studied Terja as if the answer to his questions resided in his twining mate. Terja became concerned when Anan started to speak again. "We can't complete the journey across the grasslands without the silk. But I know of no colonies in our route."

Terja inhaled deeply and then let the breath slowly leak out. "I know of one. But we will have to travel through Meke territory."

"They are Talac. Why should they object?"

"I've been told the Meke are… unusual."

"You were told the spellweavers were beneath you too. You discovered how wrong that training had been."

Terja couldn't keep from smiling and caressing Anan's cheek. "Yes, my handsome spellweaver. I have learned how wrong the spellspinners were who told me you were beneath me as a mate. The depth of their error was unbelievable." Terja couldn't help but trace his finger over the pattern in the velvet covering Anan's cheek.

Anan grasped Terja's hand and lifted it to his lips to kiss. When he lowered it from his mouth, there was a twinkle in his deep brown eyes. "I'm glad you discovered the truth. I'm happy both of us discovered the truth." He turned to the impassible stretch ahead of them and sighed again. "So where in the Meke lands are we to find a deathspinner colony?"

"The barrens."

Anan studied him for a moment before shaking his head. "They couldn't be somewhere easier, like the court of the High Regent?"

Terja couldn't keep from smirking. But he knew Anan needed an answer. Once he was certain he could keep the chuckle from his voice, he replied, "The barrens are not as bad as you think. The Meke frequent them. My teachers were adamant there is a deathspinner colony in the depths of its canyons. It will also be far enough to allow us to continue our trip west. The rivers should be frozen soon, and we can make the drags into sleds that will work through the winter travels."

Anan threw up his hands as he studied their blocked back trail. "We have few choices. We must find a way through the barrens and to the winter village. If we don't get there soon, it won't matter. This group can't survive Iceweaver's season on the savanna without help."

Terja stared into the distance, trying to hide his apprehension. Then a familiar comfort flowed through their mating bond. His concerns lessened as he grinned at Anan. He bumped against his twining in a familiar gesture of comfort. "That's cheating you know. Using our connection to calm me."

Anan pulled him against his chest, tucking Terja under his chin. They stood in silence, their emotions flowing between the two of them, making words unnecessary.

"I need to speak with you."

The pair turned to find Morea standing behind them. A ripple of apprehension flowed from Anan along their connection. He took a deep breath before speaking. "Another vision?"

"Yes," she said. "It was vivid. Anan, it was as if I were there—"

He waved her into silence. "Just tell me. Then we will work from there."

"The Varas are tracking us, many fingercounts of them. Xain is also working with them again."

A chill ran through Terja at the traitor's name. The last time he and Anan had seen the man, he had disappeared. Anan was convinced Xain had found a way to move using rips in the weave of reality. Terja wished he were as certain. Regardless, he'd hoped he'd seen the last of the treacherous man. Xain had the unnatural ability to steal matama from other Talac, and used it to aid the Varas in attacking several Talac clans and taking captives for the pleasure houses.

"That's not the worst of it…." She dropped her eyes, obviously hesitant to share this final piece of information.

"Morea," Anan asked, "what could possibly be worse than what you described?"

Never lifting her eyes, she said, "They also have a trio of the assassins…."

"A Ubica Triad?"

She nodded in agreement, seemingly unable to form words.

Anan turned to him, but for once Terja was speechless. After a few moments, Anan got out, "They hired Ubica to track us down and kill us?"

Terja considered the question for a moment. Soneri had guessed they might, but deep in his weaving, he had hoped the golden one was wrong. "How bad is that? I know of the assassins from the Ironworker tribe, but it's been generations since they have set foot on the grasslands."

"They are skilled, dangerous and tenacious. I've also been told each Triad is a family group."

"Why would that matter?" Morea asked.

Anan stared at her, focusing his frustration, until Terja thought she was going to curl into a ball. He turned to Anan and lifted a brow. "Tell her. It's a legitimate question."

Anan glared at him for a moment before Terja cut his eyes back to the girl. Anan twisted his lips and looked like he'd eaten something green and sour. "It's simple. You fight harder to protect someone who is family. The training for soldiers makes them feel that way about each other. But the Triad is an even stronger bond."

"But regardless, we must discover if the Varas are pursuing us. If they are, our time is pressed even shorter."

JOVEN EASED away from the brush where he and Soneri were hiding. They had discovered the Varas encampment in one of the canyons left dry by the floods. Soneri found the enemy several fingerwidths ago as they assembled their camp for evening. Once they'd located the extensive thicket that should easily hide them, they studied the encampment.

Bile filled Joven's mouth at the sight of so many Varas. He bit back a yelp when Soneri draped a hand over his shoulder. He lay beside Joven and scanned the area. After a few moments, Joven calmed his pounding heart and fixed the encampment in his memory. Anan sent them on this scouting mission based on Morea's visionweaving. It seemed she had been right again.

He had just begun to crawl to the ridge when he spotted a familiar figure emerge from a large tent toward one end of the encampment.

"Xain," he hissed.

Soneri slapped a hand over Joven's mouth. He tensed for a moment, but knew his silence was critical. Once he relaxed, Soneri slipped his hand away. He glanced at the gold-velveted man and nodded in acknowledgment. He would preserve their silence. Their gazes shifted back to the Varas camp in time for Xain to disappear into another tent.

Soneri motioned him away from the ridge. Moving cautiously, they left the guardian bushes, careful to avoid the hand-long lethal thorns. Traveling on a barely passable game trail, they retreated a fingercount of spans away to a shallow cave situated among the boulders of a long ago landslide. The maze of sharp hills was far enough to remove the danger of someone hearing them. Even so, they kept their voices low as they discussed what to do next.

"We need to go immediately. Anan and Terja need to know the Varas are only a few days' journey behind us," said Joven.

"Yes, you're right. But first we need to give them a reason to slow their pace. I think traps would work, similar to the ones Terja and Anan did. Even if we kill no Varas, they will think we have planted traps and snares all along the path. We need to make our trail harder to find."

"We have drags and people who still cannot complete a day's journey. How could we hide that kind of trail?"

"We could hide it with a weaving. I'm sure we could do it between the two of us."

Joven motioned to their kilts. "Our spell panels are almost empty. Remember, Terja told us we are dangerously low of deathspinner silk. So he has nothing to spin the matama into."

Soneri studied first his spell panels and then Joven's. "You're right. Our panels are almost empty. We can't weave the spells we need."

Soneri let out a muffled scream when a Varas quarrel appeared in his shoulder. Joven froze for a moment as a crimson stain formed where the arrow had pierced Soneri's shoulder. Then he dropped behind a boulder in time to hear the hiss of a second arrow in the space where he'd been standing.

"It's Talac! Fire! Kill them."

The Varas voices mobilized Joven. He shoved down the panic and swung his sling. He exposed himself no more than he was forced to and snapped the first missile at the group. A moment later, he heard a satisfying crunch as an attacker crumbled onto the forest floor. Without thinking, he dropped another pellet into the sling and snapped it forward.

"Take cover! The Twins-damned Talac are armed."

Joven smirked. *Did the Varas think we would be unarmed?* But his humor washed away when he glanced at Soneri. The big man had crawled to shelter between another pair of boulders and had an arrow notched in his bow. But Joven's concern was in the amount of blood he had lost. The velvet covering half his torso was soaked. But he had a grim expression on his face that Jovan had no problem interpreting. Both had suffered under the hand of the Varas slavers and only through the efforts of Anan and Terja had they escaped and released all the others. Neither intended to be taken alive.

Another bolt shot past, and this time it left a cut along Joven's side. The pain raced through him, but he forced it aside as he tried to deal with the attackers. There was movement from Soneri, and Joven caught his glance. Soneri tensed, arched upward, and released his arrow. The effort left him gasping in pain, but it reduced their attackers to three.

The closest of the trio drew his long knife and charged. Joven scrambled for a weapon, knowing his sling was useless at such close range. He grabbed a fist-sized rock and held it ready. This would be a fight to the death, and he refused to be unprepared. The Varas roared as he swung at Joven. He tensed, poised to deflect the knife thrust. The Varas drew back to deliver the fatal blow to Joven, and froze. Joven braced himself, not understanding what was happening. Then the Varas dropped to his knees, impaled on Soneri's bladed staff. The point buried deep in the Varas's torso. Soneri yanked out the weapon, stepped between Joven and the Varas, and in a barely visible move, sliced through the soldier's throat. With a gurgle, the attacker crumpled into a pile.

Soneri collapsed against the rock and gestured toward the two rapidly disappearing Varas. "Can't escape!"

In a smooth motion, Joven loaded and spun his sling. After one fierce revolution, he released the pellet. The Varas tripped and sprawled on the ground. Without a pause, Joven shifted his aim to the last retreating Varas.

The distance was much farther than he would normally attempt, but he had no choice. He spun the armed sling over his head several times, launching it with all the force he could muster. The pellet flew in an arc across the intervening distance. Joven's heart sank when it clipped the man's shoulder, but he continued running.

Grim determination filled Joven as he ran after the Varas. He prepared for a final attempt to silence the last sentry when the surrounding country filled with the hissing call of a longtooth. It was close. Joven's skin crawled as he dropped to one knee and scanned for the lethal animal.

The cry came again, but now there was no doubt as to its intent. It was close and moving. It had targeted the Varas as its prey.

Joven stayed still as the beast launched itself from high in a northern featherleaf tree and landed on the Varas. The sounds of bones breaking filled Joven's ears. The scream from the fleeing Varas ended abruptly when jaws capable of crushing the femur of a snowgrazer closed around the back of his neck. A moment later the body went limp in the animal's jaws.

The longtooth's green eyes skirted over him, leaving Jovan with a sense of dismissal. The victor straddled its prey and dragged the body into the heavy brush, disappearing in an instant. Jovan backed away slowly, keeping his sling at the ready. He knew Terja had killed longtooth with the weapon, but Joven had less confidence in his own ability.

Once he could hear Soneri's shallow breathing, he let himself relax. The relief was short-lived when he found his friend with his back against the boulder and drenched in blood. His gaze snapped to Soneri's face and his gut twisted. The man's expression clearly acknowledged his end.

"Soneri…."

He shook his head at Joven and motioned. "I'm bleeding to death. If you pull out the bolt, it will only happen faster. There is not enough matama left to weave the healing needed either." Soneri swallowed hard. "We need to say our good-byes."

Joven's mind raced through the healing training he had been getting from Anan. He knew their matama was limited, but would never forgive himself if he didn't try.

"No. There is more we can do. We have not yet exhausted our matama strips completely."

"Joven, it's—"

"No! Let me think."

Soneri leaned against the boulder, his eyes fluttering closed. Joven knelt beside him and scrutinized the wound. The arrow's iron head created damage that bled profusely. Determination filled him as he gathered the matama from their almost bare spell panels. Not all of Soneri's strips were filled, but there was little he could do about that with no spellspinner to gather matama. He began weaving the invisible green threads and built a web that barely curled around the quarrel's shaft. When he was certain the threads were placed to the best of his ability, he pushed it gently with his spellweaving and it merged with the wood.

Joven's heart dropped. Had he lost the weaving? He allowed himself to be tugged into the wound, and the carnage from the crossbow bolt seemed beyond his ability to heal. A heartbeat later, he realized most of the damage could be dealt with by Soneri's own system. He needed to find the injury sending Soneri to the Great Weaving.

He plunged forward, frantically searching for the critical information. It seemed as if an entire season cycle had occurred, but only a few beats of his heart passed before he found it.

The quarrel head had severed one of the large blood pathways that traveled down his arm. At first Joven thought it was cut through—unrepairable. Then he realized it was not as damaged as he'd feared.

Focused on this task beyond anything he'd done before, he pulled their matama together and created the weaving to repair the severed artery. The final threads fought against Joven's will as he built the healing. Several times the weaving seemed on the edge of unraveling, but Joven's efforts were rewarded when the final thread dropped into place. An instant later he released the weaving and the fibers began to wind themselves shut. Joven focused on the healing, garnering each tiny scrap of energy from the matama they had. Joven sighed as the last fragment flowed into place.

He drifted from the healing, giving himself a few moments before he looked again at Soneri's shoulder. He dribbled water from their carrier and wiped it gently with a bit of his kilt. He sat waiting, holding his breath at the fear he hadn't stopped the bleeding. After several long moments, the blood stopped oozing from around the shaft and he allowed himself to breathe a sigh of relief. When he looked up, Soneri's eyes fluttered open.

"What did you do? We had no matama left."

Relief flooded Joven. "There was some matama, only very little. Anan has been showing me how to work with bits. Apparently I learned more than I realized."

Soneri looked at the wooden shaft protruding from his shoulder and then glanced at the sun. "We have to take out the quarrel. I'll never survive the return trip otherwise."

Doubt gripped Joven. He reached to touch the blood soaked wound and jerked back in surprise.

"What's wrong?" Soneri asked.

"Nothing. I'm just exhausted."

"What?"

"A delusion…."

Soneri grimaced. "Stop. Tell me what you saw. We don't have time to be evasive."

A flush of heat traveled up Joven's neck. He tensed, and then gasped as his own injury reminded him of its existence. Knowing Soneri was right, he tried to explain.

"There's a—thread—between us." *How can I see a mating bond? We have performed no mating rituals. We've not even been intimate. It's not possible.*

Soneri studied him for a few moments before beginning to chuckle. Joven's jaw dropped as he stared at the man. After a few moments, Soneri gasped and grabbed his shoulder. "Please. Don't make me laugh. It makes it hurt worse."

Confused, Joven continued to try and work out what was happening. When Soneri continued to smile, Joven's indignation rose.

"You think I lie?"

"No, not at all. I'm laughing that you have not seen the thread before, or heard Terja and Anan talk about it. It's grown since the battle with the Varas slavers."

Joven stood with his jaw open. *How could I have missed the connection for more than a full moon's cycle?* "But I never…. You never?"

"There was no reason to look, no reason to discuss it, until now. I found it after I overheard Terja talking to Anan about it."

"What did they say? Are they offended we didn't follow clan tradition?"

Soneri laughed again and grabbed his arm as a hiss escaped between his teeth. He turned to Joven with a slight smile. "No, they are not. Did you not realize their connection is not one of tradition either? This can be discussed later. We must leave, and I can't do so with a quarrel embedded in my chest. You must take it out."

Joven broke into a cold sweat and his hands trembled as he reached for the shaft. He reached closer, but before he touched it, Soneri grabbed his wrists. "Not as a twining mate. Do what Anan taught you. Cut off the head and pull out the shaft as quickly as possible."

The shaking of Joven's hands became worse. "What if I tear the artery and start the bleeding again? I have no way to stop it."

Soneri caressed his face and smiled gently. "I'm a gold-touched Talac. It's a miracle I have lived this long given what my skin is worth to the Varas. If I die at least you can do my unraveling and send me to the Great Weaving. I don't want my skin to be the bedding for some high order Varas."

He slapped Joven lightly on the cheek. "We've talked far too long. Do it."

Joven shoved the part of him gibbering with fear into a deep crevasse and began to work. His obsidian blade cut the shaft as close to Soneri's chest as possible. The big man's jaw tensed as he clenched his teeth. A few moments later, Joven dropped the iron to the ground.

Soneri held out his hand. "Oh, no. I want that. I plan to return it to the Varas."

Joven retrieved the short length of shaft with the iron head. He snapped it off and handed the head to Soneri, who tucked it away in the pouch at his side. He turned to Joven and nodded. "All right. Do it. Do not be hesitant!"

He nodded at the instructions from Soneri and moved behind him. He grabbed the shaft tightly and braced himself against his twining. Resolved to finish his work, he gathered his courage and then yanked as hard as he could. There was a moment of resistance, then it broke free. Soneri slid off the boulder and a groan escaped his clenched teeth from the pain.

Joven threw the wooden shaft into the brush as he turned to check on Soneri. Quickly evaluating each wound, he was relieved to find only a faint trickle of blood, which came to a stop as he watched. He pulled two coils woven of kuri fiber from his bag and covered each wound with the absorbent material. Once he was satisfied with his work, he turned back to his twining.

"It seems there was no more damage inside. We should leave before the scouts are missed."

Without a word, Soneri struggled to stand. Joven slipped under his uninjured arm and helped him. At first, each step seemed to fill Soneri with pain, but then he walked with something closer to his normal speed. Joven moved beside him to lend support if needed.

The sun had dipped into the edge of the grasslands when Soneri came to a stop and wavered. Joven caught him and lowered him to the ground. He immediately checked the wounds, something Soneri had waved him away from doing since they began traveling. He peeled away the wraps and was relieved that although they were far from blood-free, the severe bleeding seemed to have stopped.

He cleaned the wounds carefully, wishing he had the matama left to do a more complete healing. But as Anan had pointed out time and again, the patient's body was capable of impressive repair, with no help from the healing webs.

Once the wound was repacked, Joven squatted on his heels to survey Soneri's other wounds. He frowned slightly but knew of nothing else he could do.

"How does it look?"

"Better. Well, at least no worse. It's seeping blood but there is no sign of wound poisoning. But a half day of walking has kept it from closing as it should."

"It will have time now. I can go no farther."

Joven glanced around them. They were on the beginning of the featureless grasslands, but there were a few trees young enough to have escaped the infrequent fires. The combination of purging fire and low rainfall kept the grasslands as they were.

"There isn't much to use as shelter."

"Then we spend the night here."

Joven studied their surroundings for several moments and noticed a ripple in the waist-high sea of grasses. He motioned to Soneri.

"I see something. Let me go check."

Soneri reclined on his elbows and motioned with his chin to Joven. "Go. I promise I will be here when you return."

Joven trotted toward the anomaly, shading his eyes against the crimson sun dyeing everything in shades of red. As he moved closer, he came upon a dry streambed, his sandals skidding on the loose shale. A short distance farther and he found what he had seen, an outcropping of rock whose base formed a flat depression. Guardian bushes filled the other openings. As he surveyed the formation, it became obvious others had used this space. The outcropping would be much more protective than sleeping in the open. He might even be able to find a guardian bush to fill the remaining opening.

Joven knew one thing: the longtooth's attack on the Varas scout had made him appreciate any type of shelter. He didn't want to awaken from sleep to a set of powerful jaws closing on his throat.

He sped to where he had left Soneri and was relieved to find him seated and slowly taking sips of water. Joven squatted beside him and let a smile creep across his face.

"I found a place to camp. It's a short walk to the north. I believe you can cover the distance easily."

"Almost any place would be more defensible than here. That longtooth left me feeling happy to have any type of protection."

Joven chuckled. "My thoughts exactly. Let's go. It will be dark soon."

Soneri pressed himself upward. Joven could see the muscles in his face ripple as he tried to hide the pain. His knuckles were white around the bladed staff he used for support.

This was going to be a long night.

CHAPTER SEVEN

THE SENTRIES' bodies were arranged in a row outside the captain's tent, except for one. They hadn't recovered the final sentry. Each corpse was wrapped in the red cloak that apparently every Varas soldier carried with them. Rain, snow, and burial, Oka couldn't find much logic in the Varas's ideas.

He stood to one side, his face a mask of indifference, as the captain and Xain blamed each other for the deaths. He didn't understand the reason for the argument. It was obvious what happened. But apparently these two must assign blame.

"How could Talac have gotten through your precious highly trained soldiers, killed an entire sentry group within a short distance of camp, and taken one as captive?" Xain said, waving his hands in the air to punctuate his words.

Captain Kosemi's face was the color of fresh blood and oddly similar to the appearance of victims of a specific Ubica poison. But he knew the captain hadn't been poisoned. She wasn't in the High Regent's contract. Ubica did not kill innocents unless they endangered the forging. Anyone outside of the contract was an innocent.

"You are the Talac expert. How did a force large enough to wipe out a sentry group get this close? You said the Talac we are pursuing were injured and most were crippled," Kosemi said.

Xain inhaled to continue when Gurvan stepped between them. Oka was shocked. Gurvan had told him to keep his observations to himself. But now he stepped into the argument.

"There were two men, Captain. And your missing man—I would think he is filling the belly of the animals who attacked us two days ago. One of the Talac took a bolt."

"How do you know all this? My trackers found nothing more than a flurry of activity," Kosemi asked.

Gurvan held out his hand and Daya placed a wooden shaft in it. He passed it to the Varas captain. She studied it for a moment before returning her gaze to the Ubica. "It was cut and covered with blood on the shaft's lower part. Talac do not use crossbow, so the wounded must be a Talac.

"The number—there are only two pair of feet in sandals, the remainder are in Varas issue boots. So two Talac, one injured, killed your scouts."

Oka lifted an eyebrow at Gurvan's phrasing. He was not casting the Varas in a favorable light, but Oka wasn't certain the Varas knew that.

"What about the missing scout? What makes you think it was one of the animals who attacked us?"

"That required no effort. The predator waited high in the featherleaf trees. The bark shows where it took time to sharpen its claws. If it was the same as the ones who attacked us, death was quick."

The captain began pacing, her hands clasped behind her back. "We must overtake them. They will warn the others."

Xain shook his head. "The main group will already know. They would have sent one of the two who have a strange connection. They can communicate through the tie. Besides, we are in Talac territory now. Even with one injured, it's unlikely we would find them in this sea of grass."

"These Twins-damned animals! I will hunt them down and send them all to the Red Twins."

"No. You will not."

She glared at Xain. "Slave, exactly what would keep me from doing so? I am certain you are not saying you would stop me."

"The High Regent has been promised Talac for the pleasure houses. Even more importantly, he was assured the sun-drenched Talac would join his stable of personal slaves. Either requires living Talac." Xain smirked at the captain. "The sun-drenched one is a huge brutish animal."

"The golden-furred one is the injured one." Before the question could be raised, Gurvan gave them the reason he had the information. "Daya found hairs from him on the quarrel."

Kosemi broke her glare with Xain and turned to Gurvan. "Can you catch them?"

Oka tensed. The conversation was taking a direction outside their contract and their honor code. He flexed his arm and a spike dropped from his sleeve and into his hand. A repeated motion on his other side yielded a similar result. He moved so he was certain he could hit both the captain and Xain, and waited.

"We are able." Gurvan crossed his arms and locked eyes with the captain.

Her returned gaze was heated. "But you will not...."

"No. It was not in the contract. These are likely innocents. It is forbidden to kill innocents."

"Innocents? How could you call them innocents? They killed Varas soldiers."

"Anyone not under contract is an innocent. It is stated in the Great Smith's code of honor."

Oka relaxed and tucked his spikes into his sleeves when Kosemi threw up her hands. "I'm surrounded by superstitious primitives! The Red Twins must be punishing me for something from a former life."

She stood for a moment and then turned to one of her sergeants. "Bury the casualties. Secure graves too. I don't want those animals unearthing the bodies."

The soldiers closest began to move the corpses away to be interred. Oka waited until the area had cleared when he noticed Gurvan had not moved, and Daya was beside him. The two were talking softly, but he couldn't make out what was being said. He wasn't sure if he was being excluded intentionally, or if it was just happenstance.

He began to slowly move away when Gurvan lifted his head and motioned Oka closer. He felt a strange combination of elation at their acceptance, and fear he'd done something wrong again. He'd learned moons ago that Gurvan's expression gave little clue as to his thoughts. He covered the distance between them as quickly as he could without making his haste obvious to the Varas. He stopped within reach, indicating the trust he had for the other two of his Triad.

"Gurvan?"

The larger man slipped his hand around Oka's neck and touched their foreheads together in a gesture of familiarity that surprised him. A rare warmth slipped through him as their breaths mingled. He closed his eyes and let himself dream of the warm sea-laden air of their homeland. But the moment passed quickly and Gurvan released him.

He glanced at Daya and received a faint smile from their Hammer before repeating his question. "Gurvan, what is your request? I did as you said, but did arm myself. My apologies if that was improper."

"Oka, relax. You did exactly as you should have done. I'm glad to have a Forge ready to defend me. But I thought you might have questions."

"Yes. You did what you warned me against."

Gurvan considered Oka's question. A moment passed before he simply nodded and shrugged. "I have been observing the Talac and the Varas captain. They are enemies, but do not declare an honor duel. Neither of them can see what is so close."

"You took a chance that could have been detrimental to our contract. With people who have no contract with us. Why?"

Gurvan's brow creased as he stared into the distance before addressing Oka's question. "This forging has more layers than the most finely wrought blade. Their battle with each other helps us, but cannot go too far. The contract language is specific, and the direct instructions from the High Regent even more so."

Oka dropped his gaze to the ground. "Of course, Gurvan. Excuse me for questioning your reasons."

Daya smiled and squeezed his arm. "You have every right to question him. You *should* question him. Otherwise he will become full of himself, and I would have to do all the work."

Daya's assessment shook Oka. *I am expected to question the Anvil?* The idea that he would, and should, challenge Gurvan was outside his experience. With his former Triad, his opinion had been neither wanted nor appreciated. He studied each man carefully, but they seemed sincere. He began to accept the truth of their words, and the tension flowed from him like a cleansing rain from the storm season.

"All right. I will ask. But you need to remember you requested I bring my questions to the Triad. I...." His gaze flitted from one to the other, afraid he had spoken too much.

Gurvan released him but stayed close. "I swear by the Holy Triad, we are sincere with our words. We want your questions. It might save our lives."

Oka cocked his head thoughtfully before motioning to the soldiers surrounding them. "Are they not concerned? Even after their cadre of sentries were wiped out?"

Gurvan sighed softly. "They think they are hunting something with no more intelligence than a springtail. It is dangerous to underestimate an enemy. The Ubica know much of the Talac. The Varas will regret their misjudgments. They have weavers that rival the best of our smiths. They are not a people to trifle with."

Oka waited for a moment to see if more details were forthcoming. When he was certain there was no more information, he found there was one remaining question. "If the Talac are such fierce adversaries, why did we accept a contract against them?"

Gurvan and Daya glanced at each other. When they looked back, frowns filled their faces. "The Ubica seldom reject a contract. And this one was very lucrative."

Oka took in the information and stood silent for a few moments. The other two seemed to read it as the end of his questions and moved to their tent. A heartbeat or two later, Oka fell in step behind them.

JOVEN WOKE with a start, the open plains surrounding them filled with the first kiss of morning. The grasslands were swathed in layers of gray gradually lightening as the morning stirred to life. *I can't believe I fell asleep. I was on guard duty and Soneri needs rest.* Today they would catch up with the other Kuri and deliver their news. They had been setting traps in the Varas's path, hoping to slow their enemies down. But Joven had no way to gauge how effective their efforts had been.

Soneri's gravelly voice drifted from their shared bedding. "Sleeping later today?"

Joven dropped his head in shame. "I'm afraid I fell asleep. I'm sorry, Soneri."

A gleaming white smile appeared on Soneri's blond face. "You can only do so much. I shouldn't tease. I've been awake since moons' set." His bladed staff appeared in his muscular hand.

"At least one of us was awake. I promise to do better."

Soneri patted his shoulder. "Do what you can. I ask no more of anyone."

Joven studied what few landmarks existed in this part of the grasslands and rose to his feet. "We should catch up with the others by midday. How is your shoulder?"

54

"Useless, and painful. But it seems to be healing, if slowly."

"Real healers will check it once we find them."

He cocked an eyebrow at Joven. "A real healer has been taking care of the injury. I have no complaints."

His ears burned at the compliment. He could feel the sincerity coming over their connection. He wasn't certain what Soneri felt from him. They had not discussed the connection between them.... Their focus was on survival at this point. He hoped their work on the back trail would force the Varas to a slower pace.

He realized Soneri was struggling to stand. He offered a hand and silently enjoyed the rush of pleasure from the touch. Once Soneri was on his feet, he noted, as he had often before, how the man towered over him. But he reveled in the big man's presence. Their gazes locked for a moment and Soneri smiled.

"We should start our travel. With no matama we can't create a weaving to check our back trail. We must assume they are coming as rapidly as possible."

Joven nodded and quickly filled their two woven packs with the gear they had. He considered taking the time to set another trap, but decided it would not be worth the effort.

As if he could read Joven's thoughts, Soneri said, "It wouldn't be worth it to set a trap. They are difficult to create without being able to use matama in the triggers, and we don't have that time any longer. But I'm sure Terja and Anan will have ideas on how to slow them."

Joven took a moment to hide where they had slept while Soneri made his way at a steady pace following the path left by the other Talac. Joven quickly moved to catch up once he had disguised where they had slept. Soneri shot him a smile as the two made their way north.

JOVEN STOPPED and shaded his eyes against the midday sun. "I thought we would have found them by now."

Soneri studied the area and nodded. "I did too. Maybe I am a greater handicap than we realized."

Suddenly there was a high-pitched squeal of delight. A figure raced toward them, moving in bounds across the never-ending grass. In a heartbeat, Joven recognized Morea.

He raced to meet her, grabbing her in a tight embrace. After a moment or two, she began to squirm and batted at his arm. "Let me go, you big brute! I can't breathe."

He chuckled but let go of her. She returned his look of joy and reached up to give him a quick kiss on the cheek. Retaining her grip on him, she looked as Soneri made his way closer. She covered her mouth in horror when he was close enough for her to realize he was injured.

"What happened? How bad is it?"

"Varas sentries found us and thought I needed ventilation. Fortunately Joven was there and kept me alive."

"And a longtooth helped us out too," Joven added.

"Let me see," she said.

Joven dropped his head. "I couldn't do too much. We had only a tiny amount of matama left on our spell panels."

"He kept me from bleeding to death, which I would have done if he hadn't been able to use the matama we had to stop the bleeding."

Morea scanned the wound and then grabbed Joven in another tight hug. "You did great! Your weaving looks like Anan's. I'm so proud of you."

Joven smiled bashfully at Morea. The feeling of success was new to him, but one he could rapidly learn to enjoy. As they spoke, he caught movement from the corner of his eye and realized Anan and Terja had joined them. As they stepped close, he moved to allow them into the circle of friends.

"What did you find?" Anan asked.

Soneri motioned to Joven, who made a slight nod of acknowledgment. Turning to their leaders, he gave them his well-rehearsed summary of their trip.

"The Varas are behind us and it is a much larger group than the slavers. They seemed to be trained soldiers. We didn't escape unnoticed, though. A sentry unit attacked us before we could get away."

Anan's gaze shifted to Soneri. "You were injured?"

"Yes, the first shot went through my right shoulder. Joven saved me."

Joven started to argue, but Soneri waved him into silence. "He took down several Varas with his sling. I was bleeding out and he wove a healing. He kept me alive."

Soneri pulled his clothing away from the wound, and Anan held his hand close, almost touching it. Joven watched his teacher create a weaving to check the injury. He waited anxiously for the assessment. It came quickly in the form of a smile from Anan.

"Nice work. I couldn't have done better."

"He did it with bits of matama too small for my ability," Soneri noted.

"That kind of skill might be what saves us." Anan turned to Joven. "What else did you see?"

"The rest of the news is worse. Xain is with them, and doesn't seem to be as a slave—"

Anan stopped him and motioned. "Xain? You're certain?"

"Very sure. I was the focus of his special ability when I was a captive. I would know him from any distance. But that's not the worst news."

"It gets worse? First Twining protect us. What is it?"

"They have a Ubica Triad."

"A full Triad? You're certain?"

"Yes. Their darker skin and obsidian hair makes them easy to spot among the Varas. They are as tall as Soneri too. They fit every description I've heard of the Ubica."

Soneri motioned toward them. "It was Ubica. My family traveled huge distances, sometimes off the grasslands. We have traded with the Ubica before. These were the Ironsmith's people. I'm fairly certain they were a full Triad. Three males. The Forge had his hair up in the traditional topknot. He will keep throwing spikes in it."

Anan expelled a gust of breath and shook his head. "This makes it harder. The Varas alone pursuing us was bad enough, but Xain and the Triad—we have no means of escape but through the barrens."

XAIN STARED at the body laid on the ground before them. It was obvious that they had stumbled into another Talac death trap and the darkness of today's sky helped hide the triggers. He turned to Kosemi. "Now are you ready to let me search the trail? They are only using tiny drops of weaving in the triggers, if any. It's so small an amount that it's difficult to sense. They are incredibly problematic to find, but I can do better than your soldiers."

Kosemi rounded on Xain and snarled. "You think you can do better? Fine. We will use you to discover them. You are more expendable than my soldiers."

"We will help."

Both Xain and Kosemi looked at the Ubica. It wasn't their usual spokesman. This was Oka, the Ubica with eyes the color of amber. There was no dissension from the others. Actually the other two flanked the younger one in support. Xain studied them for a moment before asking *the* question.

"What would make you any better than her soldiers?"

A dark eyebrow moved slowly up his forehead as a smirk formed on his lips. "The Ubica are masters at traps and locks. We doubt the Talac can make any that one of us cannot identify before it is tripped."

"Why have you decided to help now?"

"Because we have been watching you. If we do not help, there will not be enough Varas left to overcome the Talac. Already you have lost close to a quarter of your soldiers. If you lose many more, we may find it impossible to complete our contract."

Xain considered for a moment, but Kosemi was the one who spoke.

"We do not need your assistance. My soldiers are well trained and can deflect any attempt from the Talac."

Oka nudged the body in front of him. With two lengths of wood driven through its chest, only an idiot would not know the cause of his death. He shifted his gaze to the captain. "It appears they cannot."

Kosemi's face flushed deep red and her hand tightened on the hilt of her long knife. Oka studied her for a moment. "Do you wish a demonstration?" he asked.

"What do you mean by 'a demonstration'?" she asked.

"Order your soldiers to stay exactly as they are…."

"What are you saying?"

"Do it. We're wasting time," Oka said.

Her jaw clenched as she glared. But a moment later, she turned to her troops. "Everyone stand down. We apparently have a lesson to learn from the assa—from the Ubica."

Soft murmurs flowed from the curious soldiers, but they did as ordered. Oka flexed his arm slightly and Xain caught a quick glimmer in his palm. Before the discussion could continue, the young man drew back and flicked his arm forward. A throwing spike buried itself into an ironwood tree, severing a vine smaller than Xain's smallest finger. What followed was both terrifying and impressive.

A tree, slightly smaller than Oka's wrist, snapped forward with more force than a Varas slaver's whip. The snap at the end released a handful of guardian bush thorns to spray across the foliage opposite them. One of the troops reached to touch a thorn embedded in a tree close to him.

"If you want to see another fingerspan of this day, I wouldn't touch that. It's a guardian thorn and will stop your breathing."

Oka turned to the captain. "If you still believe our services are unnecessary, we withdraw our offer of assistance."

The glare from Kosemi was more poisonous than the thorns Oka just released. "Ubica, you are with the forward guard."

She stormed away without another word. Xain crossed his arms and watched with amusement as the soldiers quietly waited for the Ubica to tell them what was safe. It was obvious that some were too frightened to move.

Gurvan spoke to the soldiers. "We found no other triggers and believe this area to be safe. We do not think they would have taken the time to create others."

Most of the troops relaxed at least marginally, but Xain spotted the small muscular sergeant fingering the handle of his whip, his symbol of rank. He couldn't help but be reminded of the butcher Kotu who had tortured so many before the Talac killed him, which sent a cold chill through him. This one needed to be watched.

He realized the Ubica Triad had not left, but instead stood watching him. As soon as he caught their gaze he walked to them. "I know you can't need my help. What is your question?"

"We have the Ubica's knowledge of the Talac, but it has been generations since a Triad was sent against them. What can you tell us?"

Xain grimaced and dismissed the idea with a wave of his hand. "They are nothing more than primitive herdsmen. The spellweavers and spellspinners despise each other. But they are valuable to the Varas as pleasure slaves."

"This is all known, as we told you before. What else can you share that will help in finishing our contract?"

Xain clenched his jaw and looked away for a moment before answering the question. Turning back Xain's mouth was a thin line and his brows knit together. "You should understand the leaders are a mated pair, a spellweaver and spellspinner. And in spite of the fact that their twining is forbidden, they have a blessed connection. They were able to unweave the Ubica locks the slavers used. They destroyed my plans, and I will have vengeance against them."

"Why are you willing to work against your people?" Oka asked.

"You have my upstanding Talac parents to thank for that. They sold me as a young boy to the Varas. The pleasure houses bid high for me because I fulfilled so many exotic tastes. But the men who used me didn't think me capable of speech. When you relegate someone to the role of a pet, they hear quite a lot. I became determined to live and take out my revenge on the people from whom my parents came."

The Ubica bowed slightly, never taking his eyes from Xain. "Thank you for the information. It was highly informative."

OKA WOULD have paced if the confines of their tent allowed it. As it was his flames were barely suppressed enough to keep the fire from his eyes. He had again overstepped his role, and he chastised himself for his lack of discipline. His frustration built until the words came spilling out. "I hope I did not create more problems. What if we miss a Talac snare?"

Daya put his hand on Oka's shoulder. "Your words were right. They would have wiped themselves out before we caught up with the Talac—and made our contract more difficult to fulfill."

When Daya leaned in and kissed his neck, Oka froze. He knew the Triads that formed matings were common. There had been no Triad mating before for Oka. He'd shared intimacies with Ata and Lanvi. But they had never given him the choices Daya and Gurvan presented to him. He wasn't certain how he felt about sharing himself. *Perhaps there is something wrong with me. Am I damaged?* He closed his eyes and tried to relax.

Daya's scent crept into his nostrils. He had enjoyed sharing with his previous Triad. But he felt distant from the process. He had reacted the same way each time, by allowing them to do whatever they desired.

He tried not to think about his past and live only in what Daya was doing now. Oka tried to send his thoughts to something pleasant, but his body grew more and more tense.

Daya's kisses and touch slowed, coming to a stop. As he stepped back, Oka's eyes flew open. What he found surprised him; his Triad both watched him closely, and their expressions were… unreadable. Daya glanced at Gurvan who nodded.

"Oka," Gurvan began, "you have your own will. We would never force ourselves on you. You and you alone decide what you want to share. We are a Triad, but we are not a mated Triad. The mating requires all of us to be committed to the final forging. That includes you. Trust us. We want only the best for you. This is a new Triad and we must find our roles. Today was a first step. We agreed with your words. Daya was just showing you his affection, nothing more. But when he realized it created discomfort for you, he stopped.

"It will be as the Holy Triad wills it. Nothing less, nothing more. But in this moment, we have committed ourselves to protecting the Varas, and the traitorous Xain. The Talac know their lands better than we. This will not be easy."

The others returned to their tasks and Oka was glad the awkward moment passed. He sorted through his belongings and began to arm himself for what lay ahead. Knives were quickly honed with a whetstone to an even sharper edge. Most of his blades were carefully tucked away in his robes, while a select few were sprinkled in strategic locations.

He smiled as he pulled a set of spikes from his pack. They were his favorite weapons. They were made from a triple-fingercount of layers by a master weaponsmith. A wound from these could not be healed by any means Oka knew.

He twisted his black hair into a long-practiced Forge knot and laced in the spikes. He ran through a few basic stances until he was comfortable that everything was settled into place. Once he had completed his preparations, he turned to find Gurvan and Daya waiting quietly.

He flushed slightly and started to apologize. Before he could even begin, Daya motioned him into silence. "It's always a pleasure to watch you arm yourself. It's a graceful dance ritual that only you hear the music to."

Oka flushed, but this time his head didn't dip.

CHAPTER EIGHT

ANAN STARED at the inhospitable terrain in front of them and the endless grasslands surrounding them. For as far as he could see the land was filled with deep canyons, tall spires, and steep buttes. Each formation ran from base to tip with thick bands in all the colors of the earth. They had reached the barrens' eastern edge.

"First Twining protect us. How are we going to make our way through this? Even the Meke avoid it when they can," Anan said.

Terja and Morea silently studied the lands before them, but the expression on their faces was difficult to distinguish. Finally Morea spoke.

"It's beautiful."

"The deathspinner valley in the Kuri territory was beautiful too. But it didn't keep them from being one of the most dangerous animals in our lands," Anan said.

"Life is dangerous, and finite. This is beautiful, but probably deadly too," Morea said.

He shifted his attention to Terja. "Any idea where this mysterious colony of deathspinners is?"

Terja slowly shook his head as he scanned the horizon. "I'm afraid not. I was only told the colony in the barrens was unique."

Anan's gaze snapped to Terja. "Unique? You didn't say anything about it being unique before."

Terja's mouth formed a hard line. "There was no point. It's the only colony within a fingercount of days' travel even if we did not have the injured to slow us down. We had no choice. We have little deathspinner silk remaining, and I'm sure the Varas are moving faster than we are. You were right to believe the Varas were behind us, so what other choice did we have?"

Morea took charge of the silence that followed. "Silk isn't the only thing we are lacking. We have little food. I find it difficult to believe the land we are about to enter has no animals larger than a slither. But we are on the prairie's edge and should be able to refill our larders."

Anan's eyes narrowed as he studied Morea. "You have woven more visions. What have you seen?"

Terja lifted his eyebrows at Anan. "Why are you asking her again?"

"Because I am listening to everyone. I will then take what is said and make a plan that is in our best interest. Morea's visions are always open to interpretation, but the foreshadowed thread might help save a life. Everything must be considered." He paused and looked at the young woman. "You are right about the supplies. We must hunt or we will never leave the barrens."

Before they could discuss it any further, a strong wind from the north swirled around them. It found each bit of exposed skin and every loose seam to send a chill through them. The scent of winter came to Anan in the sudden gust. He turned to his companions with a rueful smile. "I think Iceweaver is giving us warning. She will soon be storming down from the Ais Mountains. We must gather food. Those well enough will make a last push to harvest food for winter. The others will travel as deep into the barrens as they can. The hunters can travel fast enough to catch up, and we will not lose precious traveling time. Be certain to leave travel cairns for us so we are not wandering aimlessly."

Anan nodded to several of the group. "I will stay and hunt. Joven, you stay with me. Terja, Soneri, and Morea: you will guide the clan. That will—"

"No."

Anan stopped and stared at Morea. "What do you mean, no?"

"I'm going with you. I'm as skilled with a sling as Joven, learning other weapons, and better at spellweaving." She gave them a hard look. "You know I'm right."

"Morea, it's just—"

"No 'Oh Morea.' This is not a battle against the Varas. And just how well did it work last time for me to be hidden? About as well as tossing a springtail to a pack of longtooth. I refuse to be the springtail again."

Anan considered for a moment, and then seemed to deflate. With a gesture of defeat, he quirked a smile at Morea. "All right, I surrender. Morea, you stay with the hunters. Joven will help with the band of injured Talac."

His visage became sterner as he turned to Morea. "You will be hunting springtail, and not because you are fragile. You are the least experienced hunter and not as skilled with the heavier weapons. Mistakes from inexperience leave a clan with empty bellies."

Morea nodded and remained silent. But Anan didn't miss the smirk.

TERJA CURLED tight against Anan. The summer tents were woven to allow the air through the walls and now they were using them as if they were the thick winter shelters made of felted kuri fiber. They would have been sufficient for a passing cold spell, but Iceweaver had settled into the barrens. They had moved beyond the lands where they might find a grove of trees to slow the winds. Now they were enduring the full force of Iceweaver's breath. He and Anan covered themselves with anything that would help keep in the warmth. But Terja didn't mind the opportunity to cuddle tight against his twining mate.

"You press any harder and you will be inside my velvet with me."

Terja chuckled and shifted slightly. "You could wrap yourself around me you know. You're the one with the warm velvet covering. I'm just a lowly, bareskinned spinner."

"A spinner who has managed to get everyone in the camp to feel pity for him and give us any spare blankets or rugs they found when we scavenged the slavers' camp. You're incorrigible."

Terja feigned offense. "The things you say about me. Those were freely offered. I never asked for any gifts. It would have been rude to reject them."

"I would hazard to say some are regretting their generosity at this point. Most of their tents are the same summer weave as ours."

Terja's lips twisted and he pulled back from Anan for a moment. Then he sighed and dropped next to him. "You've succeeded. I feel guilty now. I'll return all the things we were given. But you're going to keep me warm even if it means you have to lay on top of me for the entire trip."

Anan chuckled softly and rotated in the bed so he held Terja against him. Terja wiggled against the warmth of Anan's body. "I don't care what you say. Your velvet is getting thicker. I'm so jealous. I could use a pelt."

Anan curled down, taking Terja's earlobe between his teeth. The wash of pleasure through their mating bond was comforting. Its undertones were also a clear indication they hadn't been together like this for far too long.

He released Terja's ear and planted a line of soft kisses along the edge of his jaw. Terja sighed again and turned his head so their eyes met. "Anan, I'm certainly not complaining, but is this a good idea?"

He ran his tongue down Terja's neck and flicked it in the small hollow at its base. Terja arched his body against his mate and luxuriated in the sensations still so new to him. He landed another light kiss before pulling back, his hand resting on Anan's chest.

Terja enjoyed the delightful texture under his hands. His fingers skimmed over Anan's muscular body as he leaned in for a kiss. As they separated Anan leaned closer and whispered.

"To answer your questions: no, velvet does not get thicker in the Iceweaver's season. First Twining made us using themselves as models, not a springtail. And so far as it being a good idea—I think it's a wonderful idea any time we can be together."

Terja slipped his fingers over Anan's face, and the sensation had him close to a contented moan. They leaned toward each other and their lips met. The warmth pulsed through Terja and his body responded. But Anan was delighting in ways to tease Terja.

"There was a time then you had no use for a spellweaver. I believe you'd told me you would mate with a rattleback before you would with me."

"I think you are exaggerating. But you also had some serious doubts about being with a bare-skinned spellspinner."

Anan chuckled deeply and shook his head. "I have no idea what you are talking about."

Terja slid across him and sealed their lips together. He pulled the layers of coverings around them and captured Anan's face between his hands. He released himself to Terja's explorations, one moment tender and soft, the next urgent and filled with passion. The matama from the two of them filled the tent, the precious corcra being in the majority. In spite of the passion-filled moment, Anan broke their sensuous dance and looked to Terja.

"Should we be gathering the corcra? For the deathspinners?"

Terja looked at him with an expression clearly filled with disbelief. "Now? You want to discuss deathspinners? Are my talents lost?"

Anan tensed, glancing around the room as if he were a trapped springtail. "No! This is wonderful. It just occurred to me. That's all."

"Then the answer is no, we do not need corcra stored. We don't have the silk to store it in, and we need more healing colors than anything else." Terja narrowed his eyes and glared at Anan. "Any other command discussion we need to have?"

Anan clasped his hands around the back of Terja's head and cradled it gently. He pulled his twining closer until their lips were crushed against each other. Anan ran his tongue along the edges of Terja's mouth, and the low heat it created left Terja swimming in pleasure. When they separated, both of them were panting as if they had just run from a pack of longtooth.

"I have no more questions," Anan said. "Are there any you'd like to ask of me?"

Terja pulled their faces together and began their kiss where he had left off. Their tongues darted quickly, pressing hard against each other as their passion grew. Terja luxuriated in the sensation of Anan's velvet against his bare skin, and from the expression woven across Anan's face, the pleasure was mutual.

He stared at the man he loved, gently tracing his fingertips across his face as if to memorize its content. Combing through the long strands of hair across his head, before slipping lower to enjoy the sensation of bare skin over hard muscle.

Anan pinned Terja under him, and they kissed urgently, each seeming to need the gift of pleasure the other provided. He flicked his tongue between Terja's lips until he eased them open under the onslaught. Anan's tongue slipped in the slight opening and began to explore. As the pull of attraction built, their actions became more passionate, more insistent. *It has been far too long.*

Terja slipped his hands down Anan's torso, loving the familiar heat from the touch. The need grew as Terja's hand slipped lower. He chewed the lobe of Terja's ear and moaned when he slipped his fingers under Anan's kilt.

"You're starting something."

Terja pushed Anan to his back and crawled on top. The sensation of the two of them rubbing against each other filled Anan with desire. Terja's hands seemed everywhere. He groaned at the touch. His muscles tensed in a ripple as Terja's hand wrapped around the base of his stiff cock.

"Oh, by First Weaver. That feels so good. Why have we waited so long?"

"We seemed to be busy saving everyone."

"Yeah, that must be it," Anan chuckled but then quickly shifted to enjoying their intimacy.

Terja slipped lower, kissing down his torso. Each of the spellspinner's touches brought out louder cries of desire for his twining. Terja's lips touched his pelvis and he arched his back and sighed.

"Anan! Terja! We need to talk with you."

Terja's head popped up and their eyes locked. It was Morea, and it didn't sound as if she were alone. The disappointment washed over Terja as if he'd bitten into a bad piece of daggerhorn. Anan grabbed him under the arms and pulled him in for a final kiss. Terja wriggled over him, not helping his obvious arousal.

"Anan?"

"Strands," he muttered under his breath as he straightened the kilt around his waist. As he slipped his arm into the short jacket he'd fashioned from some of the tent scraps, he growled out, "We're here, Morea. Give us a moment. It's cold."

They both wore expressions of disappointment as they quickly dressed. When they passed each other, Anan grabbed Terja by the jaw and kissed him hard. In a need-filled whisper he said, "This isn't over."

THE TENT flap popped with an odd rhythm as Morea studied the map. Anan had lit the fire in an attempt to warm the tent he and Terja shared, but everyone wore as many layers of clothing as they could manage. But he hadn't asked them to gather tonight to discuss the cold.

The map gave all the details he could scratch on the small piece of hide. Anan looked at Soneri, and then Morea. "You spotted snowgrazers and they're close?"

Soneri studied the map for a moment and then stabbed his finger in a spot north of where they were now. "Here. This is where I saw the tracks. And it's a large herd. Many fingercounts."

"When did you find them?"

"Earlier today. I was one of the hunters sent out. I decided to focus north and came across the path of a large herd."

"You're sure it was snowgrazers? Maybe it was just daggerhorns?" Anan asked.

Soneri cut his gaze toward their leader. "Have you ever seen the trail left by a snowgrazer drove?"

Anan turned, his lips forming a tight line, and glared at Soneri. "Do you think—"

Morea put her hand on Anan's shoulder and squeezed. When their leader paused for a moment, she addressed Soneri's question. "The Kuri are too far south. Snowgrazers do not like the heat of our region. They sometimes come during the Iceweaver's season. But the blizzards she sends generally keep all life huddled in their burrows."

Soneri returned to the most important focus. "If we could take down even a pair, it would feed us until we arrive at the winter village."

"And you are proposing we hunt them? Only a few of our group have any kind of weapon. At least a strong bow would be required before even considering it. We have only mine, and eager as I might be to add to our meat supply, I would not face a drove with only a single bow and a few slings. It would be a sacrifice to the plains, and I have no intentions of fulfilling that role."

Morea scrutinized Anan for a moment before speaking "We have other bows. Not as many as one would like, but more than you think."

"How do we have bows? Where did they come from? Only my weapons and those of Terja survived."

Anan caught Terja's scent when he moved closer. Anan drew some comfort from the hand resting on his shoulder. With the touch the promise of their unfinished intimacy flowed across their connection. He glanced back and was surprised to find a slight smirk on Terja's lips.

"What?" asked Anan.

"We do have bows. Almost a fingercount. We didn't want to tell you until they were finished and we knew they were without flaws."

"It would be helpful for me to have known all our options. It would have been especially beneficial to know we had archers. Can they even shoot a bow? It's not a sling, you know."

"They all have experience with a bow."

"How were they trained so quickly? The wood should have been seasoned, shaved to shape, wrapped—even a master bowweaver would need several moons' cycles to complete one bow."

"I assure you. They are sound bows. Fine ironwood bows that would take down even a snowgrazer."

Anan spun to find a Talac he'd missed in his original inventory of the group. A young man stood before him, perhaps closer to Terja's age than his own. But Anan could not remember seeing this man before. He looked in far too good of health to have been a slaver's captive. He'd already dealt with one traitorous Talac, and it had almost cost them their lives. He would not let it happen again.

"Your face is not familiar. How could I have missed you?"

"I am Ite. Perhaps this will help your memories."

Ite removed his wrap and the crisscross of scars was almost artful in its hideousness. The thick ridges trailed down his abdomen. A few scars were still tinged with red, but all appeared to be healing.

With no emotion, he began to untie his kilt as a sense of dread flowed into an icy knot in Anan's stomach. The memory came quickly, and he wanted more than anything to stop what was about to be displayed, but he stood frozen as if he were filled with deathspinner venom.

When the spiraling cloth fell to the ground, he remembered.

It took a moment longer for Terja to realize, and then he gasped.

"You needed proof I was not another Xain, but rather suffered as being one of his playthings. This should be proof."

Bile filled Anan's throat and the memories came flooding back. He hadn't thought this one had survived.

"Put your kilt on, Ite. You have far more than made your point."

"So you remember the gelded Talac now and trust him to make the bows you need?"

Terja met his gaze without flinching. "You were horribly injured when we worked on you. And we did more than one weaving. Your wounds left you swollen and bruised. Many with far less severe injuries are now part of the Great Weaving. No slight was intended."

Ite sighed and replaced his clothing. Once he had accomplished the task, he looked again at the small group. "You will have to overlook my behavior from time to time. My… injuries… are not something I have come to terms with."

Anan recovered, to a degree, from the shock. "You have a multitude of reasons to hate the Varas. Could you tell me how you are making seasoned bows so quickly? How did you hide the practice you say you've gotten?"

This time he shrugged and seemed to relax. "Just as you heal. I am a true bowweaver and use the blue and green matama to shape the things of nature. The bow is ironwood, and I would challenge you to find a better one." He motioned to the spellspinner. "We practiced when you and Terja were scouting. He made sure we had a fingermark or so each time. He didn't want you disappointed if the idea didn't work."

Ite passed a bow to Anan and motioned him to try it. Anan drew back carefully, still distrustful of a bow he was unfamiliar with. But its draw was as even and sweet as any he had tried before. His old bow fit him perfectly and was battle tested, but Ite's bow was a temptation.

He slowly released the sinew bowstring. He slid the tips of his fingers along its face and let a few threads of matama weave themselves into the grain. Solid and true. He was ready to admit his suspicions were unfounded.

"The bows are amazing. Terja and I found the arrowweavers' cache after the Varas destroyed our summer camp and captured spellweavers for pleasure slaves. So we have many well-prepared shafts. How long before we can begin the hunt? I'm sure the traps sprinkled on our trail by Joven and Soneri have slowed them. But they have Ubica with them. They will be highly skilled at traps too. The hunt needs to happen tomorrow, or we might be facing the Varas."

Ite considered for a moment before nodding. "We can fill the quivers, on one condition."

Anan sighed with yet another bargaining chip being played. "What?"

"I will be one of the hunters."

He started to argue that Ite was too valuable to risk in a hunt against a snowgrazer herd, but then he caught Morea's gaze and her uplifted brow. He was concerned about the outcome, but they didn't have the time for another argument, which would likely go poorly, regardless of his wishes.

Anan threw up his hands. "Yes. Fine. My carefully crafted plans might as well be a springtail in heat for all they are considered. You can hunt, and my guess is you have a bow perfectly suited for Morea."

He glanced over to catch Morea's smile and nodded. "Just as I thought. I suppose Soneri also has a bow and will not be traveling with the clan to offer protection."

"One bow is mine. But I've loaned it to another hunter. Your plan is solid. I am not needed on the hunt."

"At least one person is following my plan. So we have hunters armed with solid bows. Is there anything else that must be discussed tonight? Or can I get a little sleep before beginning this latest challenge?" Anan said.

Hesitant glances darted between all of them and Anan rolled his eyes. "I'll build up the fire."

THEY KNELT in the waist-high grass and tried not to shiver. The thick winter gear they would typically have donned was carefully stored in their winter homes. So the Talac were improvising, including Anan and Terja. The long thick hair covering the snowgrazers was another reason they needed today's hunt to be successful.

He glanced across the open grasslands, white in today's coating of frost. Anan could see the lumbering masses moving closer. The sight twisted his gut until he feared he would lose what little he'd eaten before leaving their camp. These were the animals capable of fighting off a pack of longtooth. Weighing as much as a fingercount of Talac, and sporting awl-sharp horns close to the length of Anan's forearm, they were formidable quarry.

All of this, combined with being highly aggressive and protective... they were a prey seldom hunted. Usually more hunters died than did snowgrazers. But they had no choice. He knew most other quarry on the plains had either migrated or taken to deep burrows already.

Of one thing he felt certain. They would be doing an unraveling for someone tonight.

"I've been told they memorize the scent of those who attack them and hunt them down in retribution," Morea said.

Anan turned toward her. "I pray to the First Twining that you're wrong. Focus on one of the calves. Your bow is the lightest. We will take down the mother. She will never leave her offspring."

"Yes, I've been watching. There is a calf wandering closer to us. I think the first shot may be mine."

"Focus on the target. I'm sure you will be successful." *And I will have an arrow ready in case you miss.*

Now that he knew which animal Morea targeted, he watched it and its mother too. She seemed young, more likely to let her calf wander. She was also one of the largest females, close in size to the males.

Suddenly one brute threw his muzzle into the air and bugled. The sound sent a chill through him and he questioned their plan. These were far larger than any animal he had ever hunted. The daggerhorn might have venom in their horns, but these animals were more lethally armed than any of the hunters. Their reputation was not one to be trifled with either. They were more likely to charge the hunters than run from them.

A booming call sounded from the opposite side of the herd. The reverberations made the earlier cry sound positively juvenile. Morea and Ite crawled beside him. Concern colored both their faces.

"What was that? We aren't hunting that creature are we?" Morea asked.

A faint smile tugged at Anan's lips. "That was the herd master. And no, I'd like to stay as far away from him as possible."

"Will he come charging over here when we start?" asked Ite.

Anan considered for a moment. "I don't think so. He will call the herd to him. Which might actually make this hunt easier." He motioned to the two hunters. "Get to your positions. With luck they won't detect us until it's too late. But the grassland's winds can be unpredictable."

He watched as the two moved back to their spots before checking their quarry's location. This time he didn't risk lifting his head above the grass, but sent out a thread of inquiry. The strand passed through the cow and calf much quicker than he'd thought, and the bull that had sounded a call from this side was not as far away as Anan had hoped. But it was too late to change plans.

A fitful breeze curled around him and a few heartbeats later there was a warning snort from the cow. Another moment and they would be charging the hunters. It was time.

Anan signaled, and the other hunters rose above the grass as one and began firing. Morea's first shot was perfectly placed, and Ite's fletching appeared beside it a moment later. The calf bawled from pain and its mother charged them.

Abandoning the need for secrecy, Anan stood and drew his first arrow. After taking an instant to aim, he released. It passed his cheek with a hiss and appeared a moment later buried to the fletching in the cow's side. Arrows from several other hunters appeared in quick succession. But the deeply buried shafts seemed to have no effect as she charged to her shakily standing calf. Her trumpeted challenge filled the air.

"The cow! Aim for the cow!" Anan yelled.

A flight of arrows were released and most seemed to find their target in the massive animal. The calf had fallen, fatally wounded. The cow nudged it with her muzzle, trying to get it back to its feet. She swung her horns in a lethal sweep to keep them away.

He drew another shaft, sighted, then released. His arrow became two as Morea shot her last arrow. Both buried themselves high in the cow's chest. There was another low call, and Anan began to think they might finish this hunt without any injured Talac.

"Stay back. Her wounds are fatal. As long as we don't press her, she may go down where she stands."

Anan sensed relief traveling through the group as they started to relax.

A bellow sounded from one side, followed by a chilling scream that had to be from a hunter. Anan leapt toward the sound, hoping to save the man. He raced across a low ridge to find his worst nightmare. The bull had circled and returned to help the cow. He'd found their small group and impaled one hunter.

The man's gaze locked on Anan for an instant, and then he shuddered as life left his body. Anan set his teeth and let fly with another arrow, burying it deep between the bull's ribs. The huge male shook the body free, the forearm-long curved horns dripping blood, and turned on the hunters.

"Run! We cannot take this one down," Anan said as he pulled another arrow from his quiver. The bull charged as he released. He tossed his bow to the side and grabbed his warriorglass sword in both hands. The jagged black blades lining both sides glistened in the weak sunlight.

He sent a message of comfort to Terja along their connection as he prepared himself for death. He hoped his sacrifice would give the others enough time to escape. There was no time to prepare or have regrets. The snowgrazer was only a few spans away and racing toward Anan.

Adrenaline flooded his system and events seemed to slow. The bull lowered his head as he rushed to close the distance.

Suddenly his system flooded with raw matama, seeming to burn new threads through him. As it ripped open his spellsight, Terja commanded him.

Live!

He wove a barrier so familiar it required no thought. It covered the spans of grass between them and disappeared to Anan's spellsight. And nothing happened.

Anan tensed as the bull ran and he could see only one, impossibly difficult, way to escape. He ran directly at the bull, screaming his battle cry. As the animal swung his head for the fatal blow, Anan jumped.

At such close quarters the reach of the bull's horns meant little, and besides, Anan had reach too.

He twisted in midair and came down on the bull's neck with a double-handed blow. The sword bit in deeply. A gift of the First Twining when they declared bloodweaving, it had proved its worth more times than Anan could count. Its bite was again deep and vicious, but it seemed to only anger the behemoth.

Anan landed and took up a guard stance as he tried to catch his breath. He waited for the next attack, unwilling to guess its outcome. Blood laced through the bull's spittle as it roared another challenge. But this time the prairie resisted his efforts. He was amazed to see the blades of grass weave themselves around its immense legs. Fingercount after fingercount of tough plants tied the animal in place.

An arrow hissed past and buried itself in the snowgrazer's rib cage. Anan felt certain the bellow that resulted would bring the entire herd to its defense. Twisting close, he used the distractions to dance under the animal's neck and buried the warriorglass blades deep in its throat.

This time the wound he left was not inconsequential. Blood drenched his side as the thick arteries emptied. But the animal was not dead and seemed determined to take Anan with him to the Great Weaving. With a final lunge, he hooked the tip of his horn into Anan's side and ran it to his shoulder.

The two separated.

Both fell to the ground, still.

ANAN GROANED at the wash of pain from his side as his eyes fluttered open. He glanced about and realized they had moved him back to last night's campsite. The tent surrounding them was a combination of several layers, as were the coverings on the bed he rested upon.

"Oh, thanks be to First Weaver. He's alive," Morea said.

Anan stared at the young woman for a moment before pushing himself up into a sitting position and meeting the eyes around him. He was relieved that it appeared he hadn't lost any others. Ite was huddled as close to him as Morea, and Anan could feel the sensitive trickle of matama as the young man reversed the damage caused by the snowgrazer.

At that thought, he spun to Morea. "The bull—what—where?"

A white grin exploded across her face. "He was dead from your last sword strike before he hit the ground. Unfortunately, you had to get in his way."

Anan started to stand and gasped. He looked down at his well-wrapped torso. "How bad was it?"

"Nothing major. But he scored along several ribs. You will not be pulling your bow for several days."

"Did you—"

"Yes. Of course we got your bow. Ite has it stored away."

"What about the weaving of thanks? And the...."

"Both were kept until your healing was woven. We can begin now."

Two of the hunters brought a grass wrapped bundle and sat it down in front of Anan. They peeled back the covering to reveal a huge piece of uncooked meat. He looked at Ite this time for confirmation.

"Yes, it's the liver from the male. There's no question that he was the most formidable."

Anan nodded and pulled his obsidian blade from its sheath. The stone knife sliced through the flesh with ease. Anan picked up the piece and reverently brought it to his mouth and began to chew. The mineral-rich meat was delicious, filling the craving Anan had barely acknowledged.

Anan turned his gaze skyward. "Thank you, First Twining. Those who offered their life to feed the Kuri are appreciated."

The other hunters dropped their heads in silence for a moment. Once all were finished, Anan motioned toward the food.

"Eat. It's warm and delicious."

Morea carved off a bite and popped it into her mouth. "Wonderful. It's truly delightful."

Anan ate another slice of liver but his eyes began to wander.

"Eat. At dusk we will do the unraveling."

"What a horrible way to die."

Morea studied him for a moment before replying. "There are worse. He was free and doing what he loved. I remember him from our capture. He never thought he would see the grasslands again. For him, life as a slave would have been much worse than what happened." She turned to Anan. "It was as I saw in my visionweaving. I saw a vicious animal whose fangs were as large as a forearm and covered with blood. The snowgrazers' horns looked like that."

They sat quietly, finishing their meal. Once it ended, they worked together to prepare the valuable meat. The animals were skinned quickly, cut into manageable pieces, and strapped to the drags they brought for this purpose. Once the work had been assigned, Anan stepped away to use his connection with Terja so he knew what had happened.

Terja had been demanding news, bombarding his twining along their connection. Anan had been dealing with white-hot anger since he'd regained consciousness. But Anan knew it was all due to fear. A cold, deep, overwhelming fear. He knew the emotion. He'd experienced similar terror when he lost Silbre. He was glad he couldn't hear Terja's voice. His reprimand would be intense enough when Anan returned.

But he could at least let Terja know he was well. He studied the area in the fading sunlight and found a protected swale where the others could hear him if something happened. He opened himself to the life weavings surrounding him, and then located the intricately braided connection between him and Terja. He gently flowed into the connection so as not to shock his twining. But when he did, it felt as if he'd plunged himself into a colony of sparrow hornets. The sensations flooding their connection were anything but calm.

This was from a twining who was angry enough to make the Varas look like amateurs with their whips. Terja's fury was enough to ignite the prairie, and Anan had no idea how to calm him. But he considered his options and sent the pain from his wound along the connection, together with the joy of having lived.

The flood of anger stopped.

The connection became hazy for a moment, something that had only happened a few times, usually after something tragic. Then the strong sense of apology oozed to Anan. He could easily envision Terja's expression. One thought occurred to Anan, and he had no intentions of sharing it with Terja at this point, but this was the farthest they'd tested their connection. It wasn't unusual for the bonds to stretch as far as one could walk in a day. But the connection between the two of them was composed of most of the colors of matama and made from more threads than the finest Talac teaching weavings.

But First Twining blessed their union, in spite of Terja's fear that they hadn't performed the proper ceremonies. Deep inside, Anan wondered if Terja didn't still hold strands of the idea that the spellspinners and spellweavers shouldn't be twined. But that issue seemed to have passed.

The emotions shared over their connection soothed each other. Soon Anan felt as if they were intertwined in an intimate embrace. One he wished would never end. But even from this distance, he could hear the other hunters preparing the animals taken.

They would also perform the unraveling for the fallen hunter. As many Talac as he'd sent to the Great Weaving, one might think he would be impervious to more feelings of loss. But it couldn't be further from the truth. Maybe it was because he knew more intimately what was required of the weaver each time. At least this time it wasn't friends, family—or his mate.

Terja sensed the sadness and pushed another caress of support through their connection. With a promise of being reunited soon, Anan returned to help with preparing the meat for travel. The drags made it possible to get the supplies to the remaining Kuri clan. Even the calf required more than a single drag.

The fleeing Talac needed the food they had taken, but it would not be an easy journey.

By dusk they had everything ready. Anan studied the well-secured bundles and nodded. Had this been a normal hunt, everything would have been used, nothing wasted. But weight was a factor that might mean the difference between life and death. This meant some parts were left for the longtooths.

With his inspection of the final drag, he turned to the task none were relishing. The body had been cleaned and prepared for the ritual by two friends. Anan always regretted they hadn't been able to do the same when they did the unraveling for most of the Kuri village. He shoved the past behind him. Over the past few moons, he'd developed the ability to a point finer than the covering of a needle bush.

One hunter looked far more stricken. *Strands. Have I lost half of a twining pair?*

Without a word, he motioned a fingercount of hunters to circle the fallen man. Anan pulled matama from the spell panels on his kilt, slowly weaving the spell of unraveling. The air thickened with the same gray strands of release while he wove the too-familiar pattern. Once the weaving was completed, he released the finely woven spell.

The power flowed together and the hunter's essence began to slip away. The scene became filled with haze as the strands escaped to join the Great Weaving.

Anan sensed the final thread's release and heaviness filled him. Each new loss took from him. They had to return to the Kuri village. He needed to walk through the winter grasslands without the worry of pursuing Varas. He'd done as First Weaver asked after he'd declared a bloodweaving. But he would not be sad for them to finish the threads of vendetta.

He came back to the ritual as the threads began to spread and separate. The swirl of colors slowly disappeared while the first threads began to fade into the night sky. Time passed slowly until the final few strands disappeared.

Anan took a step forward, knelt, and looked at the grass the body had lain upon. The slightly flattened foliage was the only sign anything had been there. A hunter stepped beside him and stood quietly. After a moment Anan looked up when a tear splashed on his forearm.

He saw a face twisted in grief staring at him. There was no sound, only the soft drip of tears as they ran down well-worn trails through his face velvet. Anan rose quietly and stood offering silent support.

"Sikari was a wonderful twining mate. We'd known each other since we were kits. When we realized we had fallen for each other, we formed a mezi pair. He kept me alive through—what happened with the slavers. He always said we would escape."

He wiped tears from his face. "I'm sorry. I know I am not the only one to lose loved ones. Some have lost much worse than me."

"Mourn your twining. When the time comes, send a blessing to First Twining in his name. You will never forget him. But you must be the strong one now. Others depend on you. It will take all of us to get to the Kuri lands."

He nodded and wiped his arm across his eyes. Then he turned and fixed his gaze on Anan. "I'm ready to do my share."

Anan clasped him on the shoulder. "Pedi, I never had a doubt. Come. Let us return to the others. The moons are bright tonight, so we will try to close the distance."

They made their way to the group to find everything prepared. Each took the handles of a drag in their hands and began their arduous trip.

CHAPTER NINE

OKA STOOD at the edge of the tree line. Before him lay an ocean of grass that stretched to the west as far as he could see. Somewhere ahead of them were a group of Talac, two of whom they had sworn to send to the next life. He wondered at times if they were really doing the work of the Ancients.

The others of his Triad began to prepare for the day. The sun had almost been in its lodging for the night yesterday when they had discovered the remains of three herd animals that had recently been taken.

He walked back to the door flap, took a piece of trail ration from his robes, and began chewing it as the sun rose above the eastern horizon. He was no happier about the cold than Daya, who he could hear grumbling in the tent. The previous night had left him chilled to the bone, and frost still covered everything within sight.

Daya ducked through the opening and pulled his robes tight around him. "By the Triad of Ancients, it's so cold."

Oka glanced at him and smiled, trying to project more confidence than he felt. "The Varas say it gets much worse. Snow coming down so thick you cannot see your hand in front of your eyes. Be glad the Varas did at least bring winter tents. The weavers' shelters are whatever they scavenged."

Xain rounded the corner and growled at them. "Worry less about the Talac and more about yourself. If you don't do what you were hired to do, your bodies will be thrown into the brush as longtooth food."

Anger roiled inside Oka, and he spun to Xain. As they glared at each other, he could sense the fire coming to his eyes. "Is that a challenge, Talac? Do you feel that you can punish a Triad?"

Xain stepped forward, but as he did Gurvan and Daya moved beside Oka. The Talac dropped his gaze. But the Ubica stood unmoving until he retreated a few steps.

"Ubica. Report," the captain said in her familiar clipped voice.

He sighed. *Could one more person try to tell my Triad how to do our job? We are not mercenaries for the Varas.* Just as he readied himself to educate the captain about the value of Ubica to her mission, a muscular hand grasped his shoulder and squeezed lightly. Immediately the solidity of the Anvil filled him, giving an outlet to his fire. A breath or two later, he was prepared to deal with Kosemi.

"It's a hunting party. They took down three animals the Talac call snowgrazers. We also believe one hunter was killed. They are still several days ahead of us."

"One died?" Xain asked.

Oka turned to the traitor, leaning on the foundation Gurvan provided. "We believe so, yes."

"Was there a body or not? Why is this question so difficult for you to answer?" Kosemi asked.

Oka stiffened but tried to explain. "If any Talac dies, there is never a body. Their weaving has similarities to Ubica forge work. We don't know as much about this part of their death rites. Old writings speak of the plainsmen and their forging that returns the body to the aether."

"Good. One less slave to recapture. But what are these animals they hunted?" asked Captain Kosemi.

"They are snowgrazers. They typically live in the mountains inhabited by the Talac." He nudged a massive leg bone. "They weigh many times a single Ubica. It appears they killed three. It should fill their larder for some time to come."

"This pace is too slow. We must move faster."

"If we move faster, more traps will be missed. You will lose more soldiers," Oka said.

The captain's hand tightened around the pommel of her long knife. He smiled at the idea that she could threaten him. He didn't even bother to drop a blade into position. But he knew he should try to quench the anger filling her.

"Captain, we are moving as quickly as possible. Their traps are not impossible to disarm, but they are not the work of children."

The captain's jaw tensed several times before she spoke. "Prepare to go, then. We need to cover as much distance as possible before we stop for the night." She glared at her soldiers when they only stared at her. Her frustration peaked. "Now! Move! Or by the Bloody Twins I will use the slaver's whip on all of you." The encampment swung into action and soon was making their way along the trail of the Talac.

The day that followed pressed the troops hard; Kosemi seemed determined to overtake the Talac on that single day. By the time they stopped, the soldiers were exhausted and moving at a crawl.

Kosemi glanced to the west at the rapidly disappearing sun. "We will stop here for the night. I would meet with the Ubica at dusk."

The Triad glanced at each other as the soldiers set up tents in the waist-high grass. The captain's tent went up first, and she disappeared inside as quickly as it was completed.

Oka turned to the others of his Triad. "These grounds are indefensible. If we are attacked by another pack of longtooth or the Talac return, no one will survive."

"Sometimes the gods protect idiots," Daya said.

"Not ours!" Oka said.

The other two chuckled softly. "True, Forge. True," Gurvan said.

"Regardless, this is where we are stopping for this day. We need to find a place to get at least some rest. You both know as well as I do, the Talac traps are getting more difficult to find and dismantle. Their spell forgings are becoming more complex with each passing day. But we need to locate our lodging where we can defend ourselves."

"Putting our shelter as far as possible from where they are cutting salted meat from the larder would be a wonderful start," Oka said.

Daya chuckled and pointed to a place in the prairie where the grass was much shorter, only to their ankles, for several body-lengths in each direction. "I'd feel better without the tent around us, but each night seems colder than the one before."

Oka shivered. "If it is colder than last night, how are we going to keep warm?"

"Pitch the tent and huddle together. We have few other choices," Daya said.

Oka sighed and then smiled crookedly at the others. "I will sleep in the center then. You two brutes can warm me."

Daya grinned lecherously at Oka. "Oh my Forge, you give us much more heat than we could possibly return. You turn iron molten."

Oka's face flushed hot at the compliment, but he did not return the banter. "We should prepare. The captain requested our presence at dusk."

The trio laid out their bedding, carefully considering all the ways they might be attacked. There was little natural cover in this area, but they used what they could. Their small camp was practically invisible unless someone was to stumble across it.

Oka inspected their work before turning to the others. "I think we are as ready as possible. We should meet with the captain."

"Yes, it's time to begin that part of the contract. The most lethal trap of all begins to fall into place now," said Gurvan.

Daya nodded solemnly while Oka resisted the urge to ask questions about Gurvan's statement. Regardless, Oka felt secure in his Triad as they followed Gurvan to the captain's tent. Oka trailed slightly behind the other two, hoping to be able to watch and learn. But as they reached their destination, Daya and Gurvan parted and motioned him between them.

"This is an equal Triad. You cannot slip into a lesser role. You are doing well. This is no different. We support each other. Details can be hammered out before tempering," said Daya.

Hesitation filled Oka, but he fought to hide it. A moment later he nodded, accepting what came next. They stepped into the torchlight beside the well-guarded door.

"Well-lit targets. Have they never heard of Talac longbows?" Gurvan said.

Oka struggled to keep a grin from his face. For such a solemn person, he was learning Gurvan had a wicked sense of humor. But his expression never varied as they halted outside the reach of the guards' long knives—and well within the distance at which Oka could bury a throwing blade in their throats.

"The captain requested our presence," Oka said.

The guard clenched his fist around his knife hilt and glared at them for a moment. He glanced at the other guard, who tensed but nodded. "Wait here."

He disappeared inside the tent flap. Oka twitched his arm and released one of the throwing pins dipped in daggerhorn venom into his palm. The instantly reacting poison would paralyze its victim in a heartbeat.

Daya's fingertip caressed his knuckle. He glanced over, ready to be reprimanded. But instead, he received a wink. So startled he almost dropped the tiny piece of metal, he gathered his wits and stood ready. The guard reappeared a few moments later and held the entrance open.

Gurvan moved between him and Daya as they entered the shelter. Their eyes took a moment to adjust to the multitude of lanterns lighting the space as if it were midday. Kosemi leaned over an elaborately embellished table flanked by her three sergeants. Oka slid his feet an imperceptible amount, but it placed him in a better position to use both the pin held between his fingers and the throwing knives hidden on his person. A thought suddenly occurred to him. *They didn't search us. Each of the Triad members carries a blade of some sort. How foolish.*

The captain glared at them from beneath dense eyebrows before motioning to the others. "Leave us. I need to speak with our Ubica allies."

A wash of bile filled the back of Oka's throat at the captain's words. The Ubica were not Varas allies. By the Great Forge, that would never happen. The Holy Triad would desert them if they were to be that foolish. The Ubica could be hired, but an alliance was something of a different order.

Let the Varas think what they will. I would sooner lose my entire Triad than be their ally.

There was an almost imperceptible tap on his boot. Oka snapped back into the present. He was there to learn. He must focus on the words being said, and the answers, which were not always spoken.

He studied the face of the Varas before them, using his years of training to categorize those around him. One of the most deadly weapons available to the Ubica was their vast library of knowledge. The Ubica were meticulous scribes and it was evident in the information they had on each client and target. As their information on the Varas filtered through Oka, he brought the captain in an even tighter focus.

Without turning, he heard the flap being laced closed. There was the sound of heavy boots moving away, and then silence. Kosemi cocked her head for a moment before centering her attention on them.

"It's time to execute the contract. I want Xain eliminated before he costs me more soldiers."

Gurvan inclined his head slightly. "I'm so sorry, Captain. But we cannot comply with your wishes at this time."

Her face became redder than a ripe bloodfruit. The hand she'd rested lightly on the hilt of her sword tightened until her knuckles drained white. Oka readied himself, but only watched.

"Please check the contract you were given by the High Regent. The same stipulation is hammered into it as every other agreement. The task will be completed at the discretion of the assigned Triad." He glanced at Oka and Daya. "We agree it is not in the best interest of the overall contract to eliminate Xain at this time."

The captain looked stricken, and furious. She leaned across the desk, her voice becoming low and threatening. "You will do as I say or…."

Oka eased slightly forward as Gurvan locked eyes with Kosemi for several long moments. This time Oka knew what was asked of him. Far from unpleasant, it was a task he relished. As Forge, the fire of their Triad always burned inside him. But typically he held it to safe levels. Now he would release some of that power.

The layers of fire built with each heartbeat, and by the time she looked back at Oka, he was ready. He fanned the fire as high as he dared, then opened his eyes.

The captain took a step backward and gasped. "What's wrong with his eyes? They're on fire."

"Oka is our Forge. Do you dare threaten the force behind what you see?"

The captain hesitated and Gurvan pressed his point. "The Ubica Triads are well known. There are reasons we are so highly sought. The power of our Forges is one of them. A Forge as strong as Oka could turn you to ash. Also know that a Triad will protect itself against anyone who threatens it."

The captain's face had the expression of someone who had just eaten rancid meat. She turned an unnatural color and seemed to shake slightly. Oka glanced around the room. *I don't believe the precious rugs on her floor would survive the release of my fire.* But Oka kept his face in a carefully neutral expression. He did not wish to be the speaker at this point. Gurvan played the role with great competency.

The tension between Gurvan and Kosemi grew until even Daya shifted the grip he had on his war hammer. Such a reaction from the person who was typically the least prone to taking offense concerned Oka.

"All right. I see no choices here beyond those you've given me. But rest assured, the High Regent will hear about this."

"Once we've fulfilled all the requirements of the High Regent's contract, he will not care about the timing."

Kosemi's expression clearly said they had made an enemy. *I wonder why Gurvan handled the situation as he did.* She was still the commander of a century of soldiers. Although the number under her command was much less than they'd had when they started. Even with the Triad searching for traps, the Varas continued to fall victim.

Kosemi motioned them out. "Go. I have no use for you."

They turned to exit, leaving their backs unguarded. A twitch traveled down Oka's spine. He almost turned at one point, expecting the bite of iron in his back. But they moved at an easy pace, as if simply shopping in the bazaar.

Oka wanted nothing more than to bury a few blades in that woman. *That would lack honor. I refuse to act with dishonor. Daya and Gurvan share my views. What* I have *heard from them over the previous days has changed my assessment. We are following the teachings of the Master Smiths.* He locked himself into position at Gurvan's right, as was tradition. If he died due to treachery, it would not be because of his shortcomings.

As they neared the tent flap, Oka heard the fastenings being unlaced and saw an opening appear in the tent. They slipped through it without a moment's hesitation and returned directly to their separate encampment. Once he was certain they were out of earshot, he whispered. "What was the purpose of that meeting? We've made an enemy of the Varas captain. You also overstated my ability. I cannot turn someone into ash."

"Kosemi was always one of the barriers to this mission. It was time she learned the truth. And I am well aware of your abilities, but the Varas are not."

"But now she will assign some of her people to follow us."

"And if they are watching us...."

Oka considered Gurvan's statement for a moment. "If they are watching us, someone else is not being watched."

Oka stopped in midstep and stared at Gurvan's receding back. The big man turned his head and winked.

CHAPTER TEN

TERJA WATCHED as their small encampment began to break down for travel. They had awoken to their first snow. The people around him wrapped themselves with anything that might help keep them warm. They looked more like refugees than a traveling group of Talac.

Which, when Terja thought about it, was really closer to the truth.

A younger member, who still struggled to heal, was wrapped firmly in the bull snowgrazer's pelt. The long wool almost touched the ground as he walked past. Terja's gaze caught his eye, and he waved slightly and smiled. Terja was amazed at what a little comfort could do to raise someone's spirits.

"Asha, how are you today?"

The small man stopped and shifted the pelt around him. "I'm warm. This pelt is amazing. Even with the fast tanning, it's the best piece of clothing I've ever had."

Terja grinned as he studied the half-tanned hide. It was far from acceptable for even a novice hidespinner. But in their current situation, it was probably the most valuable item in camp. He waved on the enthusiastic youth, noting his pace was much improved from even a few days earlier. Some captives would never recover their ability to walk after Xain had cut their heels. Many that did survive would find walking difficult for the rest of their lives, and the handful of the worst damaged still rode on the drags.

He was pleased to see Asha take up a small drag and make his way to the edge of the camp.

"He's growing stronger."

Terja glanced to one side and found Anan watching the young man. "I didn't think he'd survive." He turned again to Terja. "I'm glad I was wrong."

"It's not over yet. But that almost-green hide seems to be a lifeline for him."

Anan broke into a smile. "It's not just that hide. It's who he shares it with at night."

Terja furrowed his brows and studied Anan for several moments. "What do you mean?"

"I think our young Morea has found herself a twining."

Terja's eyebrows shot upward. "Is there a thread between them? When did this happen? Why did I not know?"

"Calm yourself. It's too new for you to be bothered with. And I had to search for their strand. It's almost invisible. But it's there. If you look close enough."

Terja shook his head. "How can a twining form in the middle of all this turmoil? Going straight into Iceweaver's embrace; chased by a century of Varas; and low on deathspinner silk. Yet somehow they find love."

"As I recall, we found a much stronger twining under worse conditions. Never underestimate the Firsts. Also, I thought we were close to the deathspinner colony, which would solve one of our problems."

Terja smirked slightly and shrugged. "Yes, I might have exaggerated that part. But it is true that we only have a few days left before the spell panels will be empty."

"Where are the deathspinners?"

"It's difficult to say. But I think we should arrive at the colony by dusk today."

Anan studied the land around them. The high spires of rock and clay punctuated the deep arroyos between them. "This landscape is stark even by the standards of someone who has spent their lives on the grasslands. How could a colony survive without the featherleaf trees to support the complex sheets of webbing? What would support their deadly architecture?" He paused for a moment before giving Terja a tentative smile. "Our discussion isn't going to get us there faster. The earliest risers have already begun their day's travel. We need to set an example."

Terja turned to the task and soon they were at the head of the procession. The gnawing cold kept the focus on travel, and hard labor helped keep them warm. He glanced over once to see Morea and Asha chatting. The shy smiles and soft chuckles warmed his heart.

The trail they were following swung upward at a steep angle and stretched out for a double fingercount of spans. The summit twisted around a butte that emptied into the largest canyon he'd seen yet. But what forced a gasp from him was the content—a huge deathspinner colony. The ghost-white webbing covered every tree, rock, and formation. The land for as far as he could see had the same covering. With the scene in front of him, he wondered where in this desolate country could they possibly find enough prey to feed a colony this large.

"What do they eat?" Anan asked quietly.

Terja smiled; their minds were on similar tracks. He looked closely and realized these deathspinners didn't simply have the sheets of webbing covering everything. Instead there was a maze of tunnels incorporated into the sheets of silk.

He noticed a couple of things as he studied the webs. No deathspinners were in sight, none. That was different from the colonies he'd dealt with in the past. Also, and even more troubling, he couldn't see the nest where the eggs of silk were found. But in this maze of web and rock, it could be just around the next turn in the trail.

"They're closed."

Terja glanced over toward Anan as a sense of dread filled him. "What's closed?"

"The tunnels, or tubes or whatever you call them. They're sealed shut. None of the creatures are outside."

Terja nodded, the clues beginning to mount. "It's to keep them warm. Otherwise the cold would make them sluggish or dormant like the little orb weavers do at home.

"Even though we can't see anything, I still wouldn't walk onto the webbing." Terja reached down with his toe and touched the thin finger of web in front of him. It moved, but only reluctantly. "At least it doesn't track us. But I still don't want us setting camp close to them."

Anan gave him an almost comical expression. "You think we shouldn't sleep close to a strange colony of the most dangerous animal on the grasslands?"

Heat flashed through Terja and he dropped his gaze. "I suppose that was a foolish statement. I apologize."

Anan actually chuckled out loud this time. "It wasn't foolish, just not as considered as most things you say. And my words made you angry, which wasn't my intent."

Terja ignored Anan's comment as he intently studied the scene before them. "These are deathspinners. But we need to find the eggs before we start a trek across the barrens."

He glanced over to see Soneri and Joven coming toward them. They appeared intent on delivering their news.

"The colony is huge. It completely blocks the trails to the south. We have no choice but to go deeper into Iceweaver's realm," Soneri said.

"I'm not surprised. This is a strange weaving even for the deathspinners," Anan said. "But we have not been able to find their eggs. I wish there was a way to see over into their territory."

Joven and Soneri exchanged glances and then turned to the older two with a smile. "We might have a solution. Joven and I have been working on ways to improve our scouting in the barrens. Climbing a tree certainly isn't a choice."

"So we've worked on something to help," Joven chimed in. They stared at each other for a moment before Terja motioned to them.

"Well? What is it?"

Several more Kuri stepped forward. The group pulled a large weaving free and moved until they stretched it tight. Joven stepped backward a few spans, and then sprinted toward Soneri. They were close to a collision when Joven jumped into Soneri's intertwined fingers. The big man heaved Joven onto the weaving. The others moved in unison and leaned backward, pulling the weaving tight. Joven bounced and then shot skyward, gracefully launched several spans into the sky. They repeated it again, tossing Joven even higher.

"The first few times Joven found it difficult to keep upright, but eventually found his balance, and with everyone's help we could send him much higher than any other way."

Terja looked at the two. It would have never occurred to him to do what the younger men had accomplished. He heard a familiar deep chuckle and surprise became part of Terja's current mix of emotions. He shot Anan a glance to see what happened, but the laughter only grew. After waiting an instant, he couldn't contain his question.

"By First Spinner, what are you finding so funny?"

Anan motioned his hand toward the pair. "These two have worked out a method to be as tall as many men, and to do it in a few moments. They look like the traveling performers that wander the savanna."

Terja considered for a moment, then began laughing also. "We are both insane. We have a massive deathspinner colony ahead of us, and Varas behind us. And we are standing here acting like two kits who have snuck into the sweets cache."

"We've earned the right to a few moments of laughter. Even if it's at the antics performed by these two."

Terja stared up at Joven, who tried to hide his smirk. "What did you see? Are there any caches of silk eggs?"

Terja tensed and seemed to infect the others too. They tossed Joven skyward several more times. At each apex, he gazed intently, seeing what he might discover. As Terja's patience stretched to its limits, the young man's bounces slowed and he jumped from the fabric. He turned toward Terja and his twining.

"I don't see anything. There are a few places where the tunnels seem to merge, but that's it."

"Did you see any deathspinners?" Anan asked.

Joven shifted his focus to Anan. "Something is moving inside the tunnels. But I can't tell what. Only that the shapes are traveling together."

"Strands! What are we going to do? We don't have time to learn about these cousins to our deathspinners," Terja said.

"We will create the corcra threads on what silk we have left and hope it works. There are no other choices."

Soneri smiled slightly. "Now you can do what you've been trying to do for many nights."

The heat rushed across Terja's face and when he glanced toward his twining, Anan's hands hid most of his. Feeling defensive about their privacy, Terja turned to Soneri.

"Before, there was no choice and few people knew what we were doing. Now—" He gave Joven a significant look. "—the corcra is common knowledge. Yes, I would enjoy time with my twining. But this way is nothing but duty."

Neither young man could meet his gaze. A quick check found Anan wearing a smirk. He'd gotten his point across, but now they needed to work out a way to gather silk. Another thought occurred to him.

"What do they eat? Has anyone seen them feeding?"

"I haven't even seen a deathspinner outside of the tunnels. The game in this area is not in great supply," Anan said.

"Me either. I see a few bones, but they are scarce," Joven said.

"What size?" Anan asked.

"What?"

"Size. What size are the bones? Big, little, what?"

Joven considered for a moment. "Nothing as large as the snowgrazers. A few as small as springtail. More that could be from a daggerhorn or longtooth."

"Any the size from a person?"

Terja shuddered slightly at the thought, but Joven didn't appear repulsed by the possibility. "Maybe. The webbing is thick. I couldn't see anything more than shapes."

Anan sighed before giving Terja a crooked smile. "I think we need to weave a plea to First Twining tonight."

Terja wrinkled his brow for a moment before he understood, and his face flashed red. In a moment he regained his balance and replied. "Yes, they'd said we could contact them again. I don't see what they can tell us. One must use caution when appealing to the gods, or even the avatars of the gods. We are still under a bloodweaving that must be fulfilled."

At the reminder of the stakes, the other three nodded gravely in recognition. What had been a round of teasing at his and Anan's expense evaporated like morning fog on a hot summer day. Soneri and Joven both started to speak, and stopped. After a few aborted attempts, they turned and left Terja and Anan to their own thoughts.

After a heartbeat of quiet, Terja looked to Anan. "I know it was to silence them, but it might be to our benefit to appeal to the First Twining for insight on what is ahead of us."

Anan nodded. "I agree. If they don't appear? Well, it leaves us no worse off than we are now."

Terja considered Anan's statement carefully before deciding he shouldn't add anything further. He could see a number of ways a meeting with the gods could go badly. But there was no reason to point that out to Anan. A few quiet moments passed before they left to gather what they would need.

TERJA KNOTTED the last cordage tie for the ground-hugging tent they'd found. Or rather it had found them. Word spread through the Talac and everything they needed appeared. Asha had even donated his precious pelt for them. Terja swore each and every thing would be returned.

The tent went up quickly, which Terja appreciated in the growing wind. Anan used a rock to hammer in the last support peg and then the two dove quickly into the secure enclosure. They started a small fire that warmed the air appreciably. He sat for a moment as the wisps of smoke made their way out the almost-invisible smoke hole. They settled warmly into the pelt that spread across one side of the tent. They sat quietly, awkward with each other for the first time in moons. But as the heat filled the room, Terja began to relax.

"The fire's nice. I didn't realize how cold it was until I was warm again."

Anan smiled at him. "I know. I feel the cold too, and I don't have bare skin. At least my velvet helps."

"Come here. I'd like to feel your warm furry body against me. It's been far too long since we've had time alone."

Anan settled beside him and took his twining in his arms. They sat without speaking as the wind howled outside the walls of their tent. Terja wriggled out of his tunic and laid it to one side before curling into Anan's embrace. He closed his eyes and let himself imagine they were in the Talac homeland and could be a normal couple. For just this moment he didn't want to think of anything other than the comfort of Anan's embrace, his spellweaver scent, and the wish for someone to care for him. At his core, he knew it wouldn't last long, but he let himself swim in its depths.

Anan began to move, and Terja grabbed his wrists and held him tight. "No, just a moment longer. I don't want to think about the tasks ahead of us."

He caught a wisp of Anan's scent as his breath curled around them. "We have to start. We have a lot to do in a single night."

"I know."

"Let's begin with our call. We will have to wait for their reply, and that could take more time than we would like."

"They answered quickly enough in the past," Terja grumbled.

"And we were glad they did. Before it felt like we were two kits playing hero. Now I feel older than the Ais Mountains."

"You look about as happy as Iceweaver too."

Anan pulled him closer and tucked his chin against Terja's neck. They lay like that for a moment with Terja enjoying being filled with contentment. But he knew this wasn't who they were. As much as they wanted to be Anan and Terja, newly twined of the Kuri clan, they were not. They were the rescuers of the Talac taken by slavers. They solved the puzzle to unlocking the Ubica cuffs. It was the two of them who'd gotten the ragged group to the barrens. This might not be as they wished it, but it was their truth.

He squirmed against Anan, drawing more comfort from his twining. Terja could see why Asha treasured the snowgrazer pelt. It was as soft as kuri fiber, but even warmer. After a moment, feeling returned to his fingers and toes for the first time today. But he knew Anan was correct. They had a duty to fulfill, regardless if it made them uncomfortable. He sat upright with a sigh.

"You finally agree with me," Anan said.

"You know, for an uncultured weaver you are far too perceptive," Terja said.

"And for an arrogant spinner you have good insight. And it is time to weave the call to First Twining."

Terja knelt beside the fire, feeding it small twigs until it crackled happily. While he built up the hearth for their long night, Anan wove a protective shell around them. Terja gnawed on his lip as the colors disappeared from the spell panels on their kilts and the fiber supporting it vanished with a puff of dust.

Once the spell settled onto the weave of their tent, the rustling winds decreased and the shelter warmed even more. Anan settled into place and wove the ritual's most important part—the call to First Twining. The spell weaving flowed around them, the weaving intertwining with the threads of the tent until a wall of kuri fiber and matama surrounded them. Both men made shallow cuts across their palms and added their blood to the call. Terja braced himself. First Weaver and First Spinner had a tendency to arrive in the guise of the largest pair of deathspinners he had ever seen.

Anan put in the compact weaving's final strands and then cut the ephemeral warps to release it. While he couldn't create the weaving, Terja could appreciate the use Anan made of the carefully spun matama threads. In a heartbeat or two, it disappeared even to his spellsight. Their gazes met and Terja shrugged. "Now we wait."

Terja had scarcely moved when a thread making up the tent began to glow. Starting low, the silvery light raced over their heads to disappear into the earth on the opposite side.

"Strands! Already?"

Anan cocked his head. "Apparently we will not be waiting long."

They watched as another thread, perpendicular to the first, repeated the performance. Additional strands frosted with silver darted like a swarm of sparrow hornets until the interior was filled with a soft glow. Terja stared at the shell now surrounding them. He turned to Anan with amazement. "We are sealed off. Listen, complete silence."

Anan nodded and studied the walls surrounding them. Terja could sense Anan's unease through their connection. Once he inspected the entire perimeter, Anan turned to Terja. "How are they coming, I wonder? There is nothing for them to appear from."

Terja was considering Anan's question when a tiny crawler scurried across their bedding. Anan reached down to swat it, but Terja grabbed his wrist. "Wait. What does it remind you of?"

"A crawler. It reminds me of a crawler, and that we don't have the matama left to keep them under control like we should."

"No. Look close."

Anan leaned nearer while Terja kept his grip. If he was right, the last thing they needed was for Anan to flick it away. A heartbeat later he got his confirmation, and Anan relaxed in his grip.

"They look like tiny deathspinners. Half the size of my fingernail but marked exactly as First Weaver was."

Terja motioned toward the thin stream of red-marked creatures that flowed through their tent. "And those look like First Spinner. I think we have the answer to how First Twining are going to appear this time."

Anan's nostrils flared and he drew back as their bedding became covered with small crawling animals. Terja struggled to keep the apprehension under control as a few crossed his bare skin, sending a distinct sensation through his body. He sensed the panic flowing through their connection from Anan, but he was certain he sent off equal amounts. The two types began to congregate opposite them.

Terja tried to watch, but the seething mass had much of the same effect as when First Twining appeared to them when they called bloodweaving. When First Twining had transformed those times, the sight made Terja's eyes run like a spring freshet. As the individual forms began to merge, he turned away. A few heartbeats later, he heard an oddly familiar voice that seemed to echo through the enclosure and turned to find First Twining standing before them.

"Greetings, kits. You have called us again. This time to take advantage of our offer to serve as guides through the rest of your journey?"

Terja glanced over at Anan and found him equally spellbound. They turned to the figure without being able to form words.

A chiming laugh came from the opposite side of the tent and Terja's gaze snapped there to find a chuckling First Spinner. "I told you they would still be in awe of us, twining. But each time they put out the call, they have faced us. One reason the Blessed Ones answered their web of request."

First Weaver nodded as he turned to the pair. "My twining is right to correct me. Kits, we are here to give what help we can. You have no reason to fear us. But we are also not the Blessed Ones, and our help is limited. What you have resolved thus far was from your own abilities."

Terja cleared his throat as he tried to bring his thoughts into cohesive speech. "But you did help us. There were changes, more complex spellweavings. Before we could not—but then."

"The bloodweaving has a power of its own. Those abilities were granted from the vendetta you pledged in rescuing the living Kuri. But it was still in each of you. The bloodweaving brings out those skills you already possess; nothing new is created."

"So my healing ability, and the way Terja found a way to spin a wound closed. We would have found them at some point?" Anan asked.

First Weaver stared at them for a moment before giving them an answer—of sorts. "We cannot see how things would have gone. But you have called us here—for what purpose?"

Terja was somewhat startled at the abrupt change in focus. But one didn't question the gods' will. "We lack deathspinner silk. There is a large colony a short walk from here. It is wide enough that avoiding it will take us another day into Meke lands—and those of Iceweaver." He paused and glanced at Anan who gave him a nod he interpreted as supportive. Given permission he picked up the thread of his story. "We've never seen a colony this large. But more troublesome, these deathspinners live in tunnels, and we aren't certain we found the main nest. We think it is where the tunnels merge, but are not positive."

The pairing stared at each other, and Terja could almost feel the thoughts and emotions being exchanged in that instant. But however packed with information, the interaction was brief before they turned to the young twining. "What you described is a deathspinner colony; rest assured they are every bit as deadly as those you experienced before. But over more high summers than anyone can count, the influence of Iceweaver has—changed—them. We can tell you the animals are similar, but the specifics of their uniqueness are not known to us."

"Can you tell us if they have silk?" Terja asked.

First Spinner shrugged his shoulders. "Of some type, yes. Of the type you need? We do not know."

Terja let out a sigh of exasperation before looking at Anan. "What are we going to do?"

First Twining seemed to expand, becoming larger for a few heartbeats. Terja blinked and they were back to the same size as they had been earlier. *The stress is causing me to have delusions.* But when they spoke again, their voices were deep and their resonance filled Terja.

"You have woven the bloodweaving together. We told you moons ago that the majority of those who weave the tapestry do not live to see its completion. You have made it further than most. Are you doubting your ability to complete the last portion of the weaving?"

Terja felt as if the snowgrazer bull had gored him. He couldn't catch his breath as First Weaver's words filled him until it seemed he would burst. He looked at Anan to find an expression that echoed his feelings. He turned back to try to give words to his emotions and was relieved to hear Anan's subdued response.

"Firsts, we know the weaving we laid the warp for is still not complete. The Kuri are not home. We have not completed our pledge. But…."

When Anan drifted off, Terja picked up the thread of their response. "It's not us we worry about. We have many people. Some still injured, and there are others that will never completely recover. They deserve to reach home. We—" He glanced at Anan and got another almost imperceptible nod. "We don't matter. We are only seeking a way to save those people who are looking to us for leadership." Terja was overwhelmed with desperation at the thought of the people he'd come to care for. "We don't know how to get them home."

First Spinner locked eyes with Terja.

"Did you know how you were going to harvest the silk from the Kuri deathspinners?"

"No. But we had the teaching tapestries. We worked it out."

"And Xain? You were prepared for a Talac traitor?"

"Well… no. But we worked together and found the pathway through the Ubica locks."

"But of course you were prepared for the trap woven into the kit's body that almost resulted in the death of your twining?"

"Of course not. There was no way to—" He cocked an eyebrow and smirked at First Spinner. "You're right. We will find a way home."

First Spinner nodded knowingly. "It will not be easy, and not everyone will survive, but you must trust your twining."

Terja sensed a light caress through his connection with Anan and knew they were there for each other. When their focus returned to the Talac gods, they were beginning to dissolve into the army of tiny deathspinners. But as they slipped away, First Twining's voices echoed through him.

You must support each other. Some of the future paths you might take are dark and difficult. No path is without peril. But you must trust each other.

A moment passed and then Terja was filled with a softly humorous chuckle. *We will leave you the reinforced shelter until dawn. It will make your duty more… pleasurable.*

A flash of heat shot across Terja's skin as embarrassment filled his system. But the comfort became real when Anan reached over to pull him close. "They mean no harm. It will keep us warmer than the tent would have otherwise. Even with the snowgrazer pelt, the tent would have been frigid tonight."

The last of the tiny creatures disappeared into the bedding before Terja looked up again and grimaced at Anan. "Usually I would be making every effort to eliminate such creatures."

Anan chuckled as the final tiny beings scurried away. "Normally I would be helping you. But I don't think trying to smash the bits of First Twining would be to our advantage."

Terja started to reply when he felt soft lips press against his neck and deliver a kiss. A sliver of lightning shot through his body, and he sighed softly. When Anan's teeth scraped across his skin, the moans deepened. After a moment, Terja began to pant softly and leaned away from Anan's gentle attention.

"I think we should wait until First Twining is gone before we begin," Terja said.

Anan chuckled and ran his fingers through the thick hair on Terja's head. "I'm fairly certain they can check on us at any point. Leaving the tent with their blessing tells me they are not offended by our actions. More approving, would be my thought." He pulled Terja close and kissed his cheek.

Terja trembled when Anan's tongue flicked against his bare cheek and it again set his body to shivering gently. Anan tilted his head and put a row of careful kisses along Terja's neck. The heat from Anan's touch began to bring a hot flush to Terja's cheek. He slipped off Anan's tunic and then tossed it to one side. He let his hands trail down Anan's torso, closing his eyes to relish the sensation of Anan's velvet under his hands. The multitude of hairs pricking his skin set his lust on fire, and he reached a new level of desire for his twining. He grabbed Anan's shoulders and pushed him onto the bedding. With a lustful glance at Anan, Terja stripped off his kilt to toss it aside. He lunged forward and kissed down Anan's neck while grinding his bare body against his mate.

The two masculine hands caressing him only added to Terja's hunger. His desire built until he would have mated with Anan at the sun's zenith with the entire clan watching. Terja smirked lustfully at Anan as he nipped up and down his neck.

His work had its effect as Anan's hardness pressed against the thick fabric of his own kilt. Terja lifted himself upward and ground his now-hard shaft against Anan. Terja gasped for air and was close to his limits. He pinned his twining beneath him.

"Stop. I'm so close. I don't want to—" Terja lost his focus as Anan ground against him. He grabbed the top of Anan's kilt and rolled them so they lay side by side. He quickly unlaced his twining's kilt and let it fall away. He wrapped his fingers around the base of Anan's hard shaft and squeezed.

Anan squirmed and released Terja, allowing him the brief relief he needed to keep from plunging over the edge too quickly. Once his breathing slowed, he ran his free hand over Anan while stroking his hard member. Terja leaned forward and flicked his tongue over Anan's nipple. He sucked it between his lips, teasing it until Anan arched upward.

Terja spent long moments enjoying the pleasure he received from Anan's growing lust. Their bodies ground against each other as Terja slipped lower. He flicked his tongue out, tasting and sensing the masculine body beside him. Anan's velvet caressed his tongue as he moved closer and closer to his goal. He eased down Terja's torso until he reached his target. He ran his hands over Anan's taut waist and then leaned in to kiss the tip of his leaking shaft.

The tastes and scents surrounded him as Terja inhaled deeply. His body responded as it always did, and Terja relaxed in their bond. He had no intention of fighting the wonderful sensations floating through him. He moved until he was less than a fingerwidth from Anan's stone-hard shaft. The heady aroma urged him onward, and he moved slowly closer until his lips slipped over the crown.

"Oh strands! That feels amazing."

Terja sensed the flow of ecstasy between them and ran his tongue slowly along Anan's sensitive cock. Another loud moan filled the tent as he worked to find whatever gave Anan the most pleasure. Soon his twining writhed on the bedding and Terja felt certain his cries were being heard for many spans around them. But at this point, Terja would have fought off an entire pack of longtooth had they attacked the two of them.

He let Anan slip from between his lips and lapped at the distended tip for a moment before Anan grabbed his head and held it still.

"You have me so close. I can't hold out much longer."

Terja braced his tongue against the base of Anan's shaft. Then he slowly eased along the underside of the hard flesh, flicking back and forth as he moved with teasing slowness to the tip.

"Oh gods! I'm—"

Terja recognized the signs and plunged his mouth over the end of Anan's length. Muscles tightened through Anan's body and the first jet filled Terja's mouth. Each contraction pumped Terja full again. After close to a fingercount of times, Anan slumped into their bedding, gasping for air. Terja swallowed and curled against him, tracing the intricate patterns in his velvet. As they both cooled down, Terja pulled the pelt over them and cuddled against Anan's side.

His hand slipped over Terja's torso and caressed him gently. "That was amazing. I can't remember the last time I felt this good."

Terja's body pulsed with desire for his twining. He could feel their matama poised to join as was needed. His desire built with each moment. Terja traced his finger lower until he found his goal. Teasing Anan, Terja eased his finger through the trench formed by Anan's muscular butt. With each pass, Terja pressed his finger deeper until Anan had pulled his heels to his hips. His lust soared like a red-winged diver stooping a springtail. With his next pass, Anan gasped and then moaned softly as Terja sank his finger deep inside.

Terja trembled as he began working the finger as his pleasure built. Time ceased to matter as Terja explored his twining with first one and then more fingers. Anan bucked and thrashed under him until Terja could wait no longer. He moved between Anan's widespread legs, pressed his stone-hard length against Anan's opening until he slipped inside. He pressed deeper until his pelvis ground against Anan.

"Terja. Oh gods," Anan cried.

Lost in the moment's intimacy, Terja moved himself in and then out of Anan as his opening tightened and the heat flooded his body. His passion built until they called to each other as Terja slammed against Anan. His breath coming in gasps, Terja strained to pleasure Anan again even as he reached the edge. Releasing the last shred of restraint remaining to him, he slammed in hard and grabbed Anan's arms.

His entire body shook as his ecstasy built past the point of no return. With a final push, Terja plunged over the last restraint. His body trembled as he emptied himself, transforming the matama surrounding them to the corcra they needed. As the tension left him, Terja lay down on the bed beside Anan. After tucking the bedding around them, he leaned in and kissed a still-panting Anan.

"That was worth all the fears and embarrassment I imagined," Terja said.

Anan returned his kiss and then chuckled as he nibbled at Terja's ear. "It is always good to share myself with you. But I think we should gather what corcra we can before it fades."

Terja nodded and let his spinner sight slip into place. As always, the space around them swam with the purple matama. With long-practiced focus, he began to spin it with the bits of deathspinner silk still remaining. But as Terja spun, he noticed the loose fibers from the snowgrazer pelt were floating close enough to become part of the spinning. After restarting a few times, Terja snorted with frustration and leaned against Anan.

"What's wrong?"

"Fibers from the pelt keep floating into the spinning. I can't seem to keep them out. I've tried every method I can think of."

"What happens if they stay?"

"I don't know. It's not as if we have snowgrazer fiber to work with in Kuri territory."

"Let me try something," Anan said as he held out his hand.

Terja picked up the small ball of fluff that was becoming the bane of his existence and quickly spun it into a fine thread several fingerlengths long. That bit of thread he handed to Anan.

He studied it for a moment and then began to weave. The corcra was plainly visible to Terja, but he wasn't certain what Anan wove. A moment passed before Anan released the spell with a flick of his fingers. It spread through the tent with a slow ripple to settle and then fade.

"What did you do? Did it work?" asked Terja.

"Ever since you talked about First Twining being like crawlers…."

Terja chuckled. "You've been itching too. Did it work?"

Anan studied the area around them intently. "I think so. But the first visitors might have cleared them for us. Regardless, the snowgrazer fiber didn't seem to change anything in the weaving. I think so long as we are careful, the spinnings you're doing can be woven."

Terja nodded and then focused on his work again. He was careful to keep out most of the snowgrazer fiber, but it was impossible to ban it completely. But regardless of the impurities, the corcra spun a strong thread. It took more time than he would have liked, but he did eventually have a small winding of threads in every shade of purple. He studied them for a moment before passing them along to his twining.

"I couldn't keep out all the snowgrazer strands, but it seems to be sufficiently strong."

Anan tugged at one of the fibers. "It feels perfect. We should have plenty for me to create the spell panels from. Hopefully it will be enough."

A sharp snip of doubt wore at the edge of Terja's thoughts. "Do we have enough? That colony is huge. What if we can't get them all asleep? We haven't seen any food animals either. Last time we spread the sleep matama over a pair of springtail."

Anan laid his hand on Terja's shoulder, and his tension immediately lessened. "We don't know the answers. But we haven't through most of this. Let us sleep tonight and by nightfall tomorrow, we will know more than we do now."

Terja folded against Anan who pulled him tight against his chest. "Come. We have the rest of the night to ourselves. I can think of ways to take advantage of our time."

He moved deeper into Anan's arms and sighed. "I think that sounds like a wonderful idea." He leaned up and kissed Anan softly before drifting off.

CHAPTER ELEVEN

TERJA WOKE to a chill that permeated his entire body. He and Anan had burrowed themselves into their bedding, topped by the snowgrazer pelt. He pressed himself against Anan's warm chest and sighed with contentment. After a moment passed, he pulled Anan's arm over him for another layer of heat. As he waited to thaw, he studied the interior of their tent.

His breath, as well as Anan's, created small puffs of white and a layer of frost covered the inside of the tent. Terja marveled at the twinkling crystalline exhibition until his twining began to move. To add to the cold, it had snowed too, and the accumulation had settled in each ripple of the tent's covering.

"First snow of the season. Iceweaver is early in her work this year," Anan said.

He ventured a hand from beneath the layers of bedding to poke at the side of the tent. The frost on the tent's interior flew away with little effort from Terja while the white powder on the exterior slid down like a miniature avalanche.

"Strands! It should not be dust snow this early."

"We're much closer to the Ais Mountains. And First Weaver told us Iceweaver ruled over this part of the Talac lands more than anywhere else," Anan said.

"I had hoped she would be lenient with our group."

Anan turned his gaze toward Terja and chuckled. "Iceweaver is never lenient. Ask the Meke. They know her best of us all."

Terja sighed and pressed against Anan, unwilling to think of anything beyond their immediate comfort.

"We can't hide in here all day," Anan said.

"Are you certain?"

He glanced over his shoulder to catch Anan grinning at him and Terja began to chuckle. Then a strong gust hit the side of the tent and set

104

the fabric popping. The disturbed rime fell across them like a miniature snowstorm. Terja shivered at the cold and curled into a ball.

"I hate winter. It's so cold," said Terja.

Anan shook his head and chuckled slightly. "Winter village is colder than this. This year you're experiencing it through a thin tent rather than a lodge of thick earth. It makes a lot of difference."

Terja slipped his hand out of the bedding and grabbed what clothing he could reach. He pulled them into the folds with him and Anan.

"Strands!" Anan squeaked. "Those are cold."

"And who was just telling me it would be much colder at winter village?"

"Yes, and we'll have daggerhorn fur and thick sheets woven from kuri fiber. I'll be warm as a high summer day. But now we're trying to make do with what we've scrounged."

Terja nodded slowly in agreement. But he knew there was nothing he could do to change their situation. Reaching into the bedding, he dragged their semithawed clothing to them.

He pulled them on as quickly as possible, but the cold still soaked into his body and left him chilled. He waited until Anan had dressed before wrapping the snowgrazer pelt around himself. Anan met his glance with a cocked eyebrow. Terja pulled the skin tighter and turned away. He couldn't keep himself from looking at Anan.

"Why are you staring at me like that?"

"Just finding all this funny for some odd reason. You know it would be warmer if you had some velvet on your bare body."

"We did once, in the beyond times."

"What are you talking about? Spellspinners have always been as hairless as a shardfish," Anan said.

Terja shook his head. "No, I will tell you how the Talac gained their velvet."

Anan grinned at him. "You are just trying to avoid leaving our bed."

"Maybe. But will you listen?"

Anan nodded, "Yes, of course. Spin your tale."

Terja settled into storytelling position. He wanted to weave his legend with all the force of the best of Iceweaver's storytellers. When he was satisfied everything was ready, he flipped the pelt around his body and settled in his spot.

"In the beyond times, the Talac were all smooth-skinned like the spellspinners. The people did not have the markings we now have. Each Talac looked much like any other. The clans did not exist. The Talac wandered on the edges of the grasslands. This was during the times before our earth-covered winter homes."

Terja paused for a breath, excited to see Anan had settled into the traditional seated position for the listener. He focused on telling the story for his mate.

"The Talac enjoyed this time of plenty and easily lived from one hunt to the next. We did not have the skills to preserve foods as we do now. Those were taught to us later by the First Twining. The people happily lived this way for many generations.

"But then the seasons changed over a fingercount of cycles until a time came when Iceweaver's power was such that the snows reached the same height as the older kits. A blizzard grew on the grasslands until the people could see little beyond the tent next to them. Their food was diminished and bellies tightened until the youngest kits cried themselves to sleep at night.

"Egbon and Jaa, the elder twining of the village, knew they must do something, or the Talac would be lost. Together they wove a spell to protect the people from the bitter cold. They wove matama from everyone into the magic.

"At first their weaving held against the fierce winds. The last of the matama was added and the protection stayed fast. But before they could relax, the wind doubled in strength. The weaving rippled and lashed in the high winds until they could both sense rips in the fabric. They tried to close the rents, but the wind was too strong. Soon it was frayed and being carried away.

"Fear filled the pair as a tent toppled and the Talac inside ran for protection. They turned to each other, knowing they must make a plea to Iceweaver. They called to her with the last of their matama and then stood, buffeted by the winds. The cold penetrated their layers of clothing until they both thought they would freeze."

Terja paused for a drink from their water skin. He smiled as Anan became impatient at the delay. When it seemed he could stand no more, Anan blurted out, "What happened?"

"Yes, there is more to the story." Terja smiled around the water skin as he took another sip.

"Well? Finish it."

"All right, if you wish," Terja said. "The storm roared around them as one by one their shelters collapsed under the fierce blizzard. The numbing cold filled Egbon until he sank to the ground, unable to move. Jaa felt the Talac who could still move fight their way to his side. They began spinning the storm's matama. As they battled Iceweaver, one of the Talac helping Jaa dropped to the ground as the last heat left his body. Jaa couldn't spare the time to mourn his friend as he rapidly lost his own heat.

"As the last matama swirled into a pure white thread, the connection between the two of them plied together. The main cord shot over the remaining encampment. A heartbeat later, weft threads arched in perpendicular lines to the first. Soon a loose web was domed over them, breaking the worst of the blizzard. The pair battled the strength of the tempest until the winds began to calm.

"During this time some of the fallen Talac revived. Jaa sensed Egbon beside him and they merged their skills until the spell covering them was almost solid. They relaxed against each other for a moment, thinking they had saved at least some of their people.

"But suddenly the weaving was shredded to nothing more than scraps of fabric and thread. Jaa and Egbon braced themselves against the winds, but none came. Instead a woman stood, tall even for the Meke. She was dressed in layers of white and blue."

"That is how Iceweaver is described in our stories too," Anan said.

Terja lifted an eyebrow at his twining. "Do you want to hear the tale?"

"Sorry, of course I want to hear it."

"Very well. The visitor was Iceweaver, as you guessed. And neither man could gauge her mood. After a moment of silence, a brittle voice carried across the winds.

"'You have challenged my lands, and survived. But from this day forward your people will be divided. Those that spun the matama of my storm will keep their bare skin while those that fell to the side will have the pattern of the winter winds in their velvet, which will protect them from the cold.'

"'Your magic will also be divided. The Talac with velvet will only be able to weave, while the stronger ones who could spin the matama will always be the creators of thread for the spellweavings.'

"With that, a strong wind blew, and Iceweaver disappeared into the growing light. Jaa turned to Egbon and found his mate was covered with a fine coating of velvet.

"That is how spellweavers came to have velvet while we spellspinners kept our smooth skin."

Once Terja had finished, Anan uncoiled from his sitting position and smiled. After a moment, Terja couldn't wait any longer. "What? Did you not enjoy the tale?"

"No. That wasn't it at all. It was a wonderful story."

"Then why do you tease me with your smile?"

"Well… the spellweaver version is slightly different."

"How?" Terja asked.

"Are you certain you want to know?"

"Of course I do. I am not a kit who can't stand something different."

Anan chuckled and shook his head. "Only a few moons ago you were exactly that kit."

Terja began feeling exasperated with his twining. "Tell me."

Anan shrugged. "In our story, velvet was the reward to the spellweavers."

"That makes no sense."

"Whether it makes sense to you or not, it is the version taught over the spellweavers' fires."

Terja's lips formed a small thin line and he turned to begin putting away the bedding and getting ready to break camp. He was almost finished when a touch caressed his shoulder and a wave of intimacy flowed from his connection with Anan. A moment passed and he breathed out a sigh and shook his head.

"I'm being unreasonable. I don't know why it bothered me."

Anan shrugged. "You've had a lot of changes in a few moons. We both have. We've learned the divide between the weavers and spinners was not what it seemed."

"I understand. It seems there are times when I come across the old beliefs again. Whether velvet was a reward or consolation doesn't matter. My twining fits me perfectly," Terja said.

"Let me help you finish. When the sun is at its highest point, we will need to be ready to gather the deathspinner silk."

A knot of trepidation grew in Terja's gut, but he turned back to packing their supplies, dreading the day ahead of them.

ANAN SAT just outside the edge of the webbing. The steady wind had swept the dusting of snow into the recesses, leaving the grounds to look like a mottled daggerhorn pelt. But the current stillness had removed the cold bite and as the sun moved to its apex, the filtered sunlight began to brighten. Focusing on the colony, he carefully wove the sleeping spell they'd used before to harvest silk. He would feel better if all the elements they needed were coming together with fewer problems.

He knew he could create the webbing they needed, but it had to be attached to a live animal to entice the web dwellers to feast on it. They'd used a pair of springtail that had stumbled into the webbing last time, but in the few days they had been here, he'd yet to see an animal become entrapped.

They knew this might be a problem, so he'd sent Soneri and Joven to trap something they could use as bait. So far there had been no word from the pair, and he worried. They didn't have another day to wait, and without more silk they had no way to create the spellweavings they needed against the Varas, and especially the Ubica.

"I hear something."

Anan glanced at Morea. "What?"

Her face twisted in concentration and confusion. "It sounds like a daggerhorn."

"A daggerhorn? Why would one be running toward us? We haven't even seen signs of them since we entered the barrens."

She shrugged and strained to listen again. After a moment she shook her head. "It sounds like a daggerhorn to me. And it's coming fast."

He considered for a moment and then glanced at Terja. "Could they be driving one?"

Terja threw up his hands. "Perhaps. I don't know. How could they drive a daggerhorn?"

Anan wove a spell so light that it barely existed and sent it echoing through the canyons and buttes surrounding them. He cast it as far as possible and found them at the edge of his reach. The two men did seem to be driving a daggerhorn before them. But the two Talac were moving in an oddly familiar pattern. Then it dawned on him.

"Longtooth. They are chasing the daggerhorn with the hunting calls of a longtooth pack." Without hesitation he spun and shouted to the Talac close to him. "Hurry! Climb to the rim of the two large canyons that feed into the deathspinners. Once it's passed, add to the pack calls. It will need to be completely panicked when it reaches the valley."

He grabbed Terja and pulled him along as he raced to the butte closest to the edge of the webbing. Terja yanked himself free and Anan stumbled to a halt and spun to find Terja already running toward him.

"I can run faster if you aren't pulling me!"

Anan grinned but reached the edge of the butte a step behind Terja. Anan took a moment to view the web-covered arena. Sheets of webbing covered everything, giving the landscape a frost-coated appearance. The blue-white coating thickened in places to form the tubes, reminding Anan of arteries threading their way through the body.

"Anan, what's your plan?" Terja asked.

Anan quickly twined the last threads of corcra into the weaving, and it was ready. The distance the web had to travel was much farther than he could throw. Their success would depend on Terja's skill with his sling.

"The spell's ready. I want you to use your sling. But our timing has to be perfect."

"Our timing always has to be perfect. It will be again. Where is the daggerhorn?"

Anan dipped into spellsight. The daggerhorn was close. It would appear in the rightmost canyon in a few heartbeats. He turned to tell Terja when he heard the snort of a daggerhorn buck in full rut. He yanked his obsidian sword free as he spun to face an enraged stag. *How did it get up here? One prick from those poisonous horns will end either of us.* A heartbeat later his twining was at his side, sling in one hand and First Twining-gifted shield in the other.

The stag's nostrils were bloodred, his eyes almost all whites. He snorted, his breath shooting from his nose like a hot spring. Anan's heart raced as the daggerhorn charged them with his head dropped low. Anan jumped to one side and began to execute a spinning chop with his sword. He realized they couldn't kill this animal. He was their bait, and if they didn't get the deathspinner silk, the Kuri's chance of surviving was nil.

"Don't kill him!" Anan yelled out to Terja. There was no time to explain. Hopefully their connection was enough. He twisted his arms to blunt his attack. The wooden flat of the sword slammed against the animal's shoulders with enough impact to rattle through Anan's arms. The buck swung his horns at Anan as he staggered back, missing his throat by the thickness of a fingernail. The daggerhorn's head swung again as Anan struggled to avoid it a second time. Just as he thought he was going to be impaled, something slammed into the animal from the other side.

He scrambled away in the instant it was distracted, ripped his ironwood bow from his shoulder, and held it like a club. In a moment of silence, he saw Terja pound against the animal with the flat of his shield. They used their twining connection to synchronize their attack and slammed against the animal from both sides. The impact shook the stag. Cries of a hunting longtooth pack filled the air around them, and the buck lunged from the butte to plunge into the vast webbing of the deathspinners.

"Now! Throw it over the buck while it's deep in the webs."

Terja prepared himself as Anan tried to control his emotions. He wanted to yell out for him to throw the weaving already, but the sling was not his weapon.

Anan had almost given up hope when Terja began to swing his sling loaded with the matama-spun silk. It cut an arc through the air what seemed to be a fingercount of times before he released it into the deep blue sky. Anan's spell set it to slowly unfurl, covering more and more area, until it was a sparkling net stretching for spans around the wildly panicked daggerhorn.

Anan felt a moment of horror as it settled over the animal and its horns became entangled in the gossamer threads. His chest tightened as it fought the restraint. But the edges were sinking into the thick webbing that stretched around it. With a fierce bellow, it fell to its knees and its flailing gradually weakened. A few heartbeats later the stag lay on the ground, its sides heaving.

"Look."

Anan followed the motion of Terja's chin toward the tubes. Large dark shapes shot through them at amazing speeds. Soon the tunnels were filled with dim forms, giving the appearance of being filled with blood. The first deathspinners reached the daggerhorn, and fangs as long as his finger pierced the tubes and sank into the heaving animal as it bellowed in fear and pain.

Abruptly the bugling ended and the valley became silent but for the scraping of a multitude of deathspinner feet.

Just before the daggerhorn disappeared under thick webbing, Anan lifted his longbow, drew an arrow to his ear, and released it. It sank into the daggerhorn's body, relieving it of the agonizing, lingering death it was doomed to from the deathspinners. Terja glanced up when Anan handed him his bow.

"I have the same request as before. If something happens, at least give me the same mercy I gave the daggerhorn."

Terja swallowed several times before he nodded, slipping the quiver over one shoulder and lofting the bow. "As you wish, Anan. But we have done this before. I see no issues."

Anan nodded, focused on the fastest route to the nexus of tunnels they guessed was the central nest. It was dangerously close to the slowing deathspinners. But guesswork was put aside as motion within the tubes came to a stop.

"Quickly. We don't know how long we have." Anan shrugged on the carrying basket and tossed off all but the barest minimum of clothing. The chilled air bit at his patches of exposed velvet as they moved to the edge of the webbing. Pausing, he studied the colony closely and found no movement. Turning to Terja he started to speak, but instead cupped Terja's face and kissed him lightly.

"Remember your promise. I don't want to suffer through a moon of the deathspinners feeding on me."

He turned at Terja's nod and trotted toward his destination. The floating deathspinner web sheets clung to his feet and legs, making travel more difficult. But Anan pressed onward, avoiding the small outcroppings of rock scattered through the valley, determined to reach their goal. They chose the location where they'd thought he had the best chance of success.

His progress seemed like a crawl and Anan felt as if he was getting no closer. Gasping for air, he pumped his legs as hard as possible across the empty space. Suddenly he slid to a stop, almost falling as he came abruptly upon the cluster of tunnels. After pulling his obsidian knife from its sheath, he slashed at the webbing. The resilient material fought back for a heartbeat, then parted with a release of warm air from inside.

The stench that surrounded him left Anan retching as his senses rebelled. In a moment, he emptied the contents of his stomach, before peering into the opening. What he saw was a multitude of infant deathspinners, and no eggs for silk. The immature deathspinners poured from the cut he'd made as he backed away.

Anan spun, moving at full speed from his first step. The webbing that was a slight hindrance on his way in became grasping tendrils that threatened to pull him into the mass of glimmering white. Then he saw his worst nightmare; some adult deathspinners were awake, and between him and the open ground, with Terja frantically urging him onward.

He pounded to the edge of the ground webbing, his mind frantic for escape. A small part of him huddled in fear, but Anan refused to give up. When he was a few spans from the foremost of the animals, he tensed his muscles to attempt a jump.

As his body uncoiled, a burst of energy surged through him, almost throwing him over the clicking embodiment of death. Landing farther away than he'd ever expected, he raced for the boundary of the colony, where Terja hysterically called to him.

A fierce pain exploded from Anan's thigh. It was as if a roaring bonfire had been embedded into his leg. He stumbled, hope dashed as the fangs of a second deathspinner sank almost a fingerlength into his calf. The pain from the two bites was indescribable.

Falling he screamed at Terja. "Now! Give me mercy! By the Twined Ones, shoot!"

Anan's world dimmed as Terja nocked an arrow and drew to his cheek. He released just as Anan's world went black.

TERJA'S CHEST seized as Anan pitched forward with two deathspinners attached. He knew what he should do, what Anan had made him promise to do, but he couldn't. There had to be another way. He had a fast heartbeat to decide. He couldn't live with himself if he didn't try to rescue his twining.

He calmed himself as if it were another practice session with Anan, slipped the arrow from the quiver, and snapped the nock onto the multistrand bowstring. After pulling it back to his ear, he released.

He was transfixed as it spiraled to his target, the fletching creating the blur of color he followed. A heartbeat later it pierced the center of his target, and the deathspinner attached to Anan's thigh burst like a ripe hollowfruit. He quickly shot again with equally successful results.

"Anan!" he yelled. "Get up! Run!"

He paused for a moment before tossing the bow and quiver to Soneri. With a nod of acknowledgment, he sprinted toward Anan, not certain of what he would do. He hoped he hadn't relegated both of them to death from these animals. He reached Anan before the wave of deathspinners, but found him unconscious. He grabbed a limp arm and frantically dragged him out of the colony. But he realized the deathspinners would reach them long before he could find the edge.

In a move of desperation, he froze, braced himself, and began spinning. Webbing, grass, deathspinners, anything he could sense was twisted into the thread of desperation he battled to create. The struggle shifted back and forth as he strained to save himself and his twining. He pulled matama from the barrens themselves until something shifted and he was able to clear a path out of the colony.

He pulled his love across the deep red, pebble-strewn ground. Fatigue was setting in when he was suddenly thrown across someone's shoulder, bone and sinew plowing into his gut as they pounded for the colony boundary. Through his haze Terja realized he'd lost Anan and started to struggle. *I have to get Anan out.*

"Stop moving! They have Anan and are ahead of us."

He recognized Soneri's voice and went limp. A few moments later, he was deposited on the ground, with Anan beside him.

Morea checked Anan to see if she could help, but the look of panic on her face was a clear answer. "He's not breathing. I can't hear his heart."

Terja scrambled closer, but already knew his twining was alive, if only barely. Otherwise their connection wouldn't still exist. With Morea's help, he rolled Anan to his stomach and examined the bites. They were crusted with black and oozing a deep red fluid only a few shades lighter. Terja pressed on either side of the wound, and a flood of tainted blood escaped. He turned to Morea.

"How bad is it?"

Her breath came in gasps as she stepped back, her panic building. Terja knew what her fear would do to the already failing weaving. He gave her a moment, but all she did was stare helplessly at the growing wounds.

"Morea! What do we need to do? If we lose Anan, the rescue is doomed."

She nodded and placed her hands on Anan. Several agonizingly slow moments passed as he waited, needing to do something, but not certain what it might be. She jerked from her spellsight and Terja's hopes sank at the look of desperation on her face.

"His muscles are melting. The venom can't be stopped. It keeps getting bigger."

"Can I spin it?"

"Deathspinner venom? Are you crazy? It would kill both of you."

"If Anan dies, I don't want to go on living anyway." Finished with pointless discussion, Terja settled in for an extended battle. His sight focused around them and he spread his hands over the wound on Anan's thigh. The hole was larger than his finger, and he could tell the venom was doing exactly as Morea had described. The bottom was dangerously close to the big artery in Anan's leg. If it opened, Anan would bleed to death before anything could be done. Locking his focus on that critical point, he let his spinning sink inside and begin to unravel the venom's weaving.

Colors different than anything Terja had ever handled swirled in a dancing pattern that fought each time he struggled to move it away. In his determination, he again reached for matama. Joven and Soneri gripped his shoulders, and he took the energy that was offered.

Time stood still as he created threads unlike any he'd done before. Each matama fiber from the deathspinner was teased away from Anan's life weaving. Terja wiped the sweat from his face as the difficult work took its toll. Terja's fears began to lighten as he pulled the strands of poison. The last spinnable fiber released from Anan's weave and Terja started twisting the open flesh of the wound closed. Keeping strands twisting required Terja's complete focus. A longtooth pack could have attacked at that moment, and he would have been helpless.

Terja studied the spinning he'd just finished to find a minuscule bit of multicolored venom matama. He glanced around and motioned at the spell panel on Soneri's kilt.

"That. Hurry."

Soneri ripped the bit of cloth free and handed it to Terja. The color flooded a few matama-free threads it contained and stopped. Terja studied it for a moment before tossing it to Soneri. "Later. Needs examined."

"Terja, hurry!"

He spun to find Morea cutting away the leggings from Anan's second wound. Terja pressed his fingers against Anan's neck and found a stronger pulse. They had a chance.

Already exhausted, Terja knew there was no choice. He settled in again, but each action seemed to take much longer than before. He was thankful the poison damage wasn't as widespread. Even with the gift of matama from Morea, Joven, and Soneri, the fight was difficult. But while each nail thickness of progress was hard won, they were succeeding.

Long past the point where Terja would have expected his body to shut down in exhaustion, they continued. His fingertips became numb as he reached the end of the healing. This time he was at the true limits of even his gods-assisted strength and slumped onto the ground.

Morea stepped forward and closed the wound with a whisper of spellweaving. He realized Joven stood beside him with the tab of white from before. With a trembling hand, he added the bit of venom matama to the almost colorless woven strip. After tucking it carefully into his pouch, he crawled beside his twining.

Someone covered them with a skin as Terja huddled against him. Anan's pulse was strong, but Terja could sense nothing more than life through their connection. His conscious thought was buried too far for Terja to recover. The deep chill lessened as the thick fur managed to warm them. The fight had exhausted him and the warmth began to seep into his aching muscles.

Anan shifted in his arms.

Terja bolted awake with the surge of life that flooded their connection. He fed what little matama he still controlled into the precious connection with his twining. He swam through Anan's rising consciousness and joy filled him as Anan came closer and closer to awakening. His eyelids fluttered, and then Terja was entranced by the deep brown eyes he stared into.

"Terja? Are we in the Great Weaving?"

A rough chuckle arose from Terja as he pulled them into a fierce embrace. "No, we are still firmly in the barrens."

Anan writhed as Terja pulled him tighter. "Ahh! Stop! I hurt all over."

Terja pulled away, releasing his love. "I'm so sorry. But I thought—"

"It would seem the gods are not ready to bring us to the Great Weaving. But they have managed to leave me as weak as a newborn kit." He paused for a moment and then extended a hand to Terja. "I need to get up. The Varas must be close, and we have no deathspinner silk."

"There were no eggs?"

"None. It looked as if these creatures don't create eggs."

While Terja digested this information, he gripped Anan tightly and helped him stand. He slipped under one arm and then remembered Anan had been bitten in both legs. Anan's jaw clenched as he steadied himself with Terja's help. They paused for several moments before Anan took a step forward.

"Oh First One!" Anan collapsed, trying to support himself on his twining. Terja fought to hold him up for as long as he could, but he dropped with a whoosh of air when Anan landed on top of him.

"Strands! I can't possibly walk any farther."

Soneri appeared and lifted Anan in his arms. As Terja crawled to his feet, Soneri stood holding Anan as if he weighed nothing. Anan met Terja's gaze with a grim expression.

"You're going to have to leave me. The Varas are too close, and I won't be able to walk for a moon."

Terja rolled his eyes at his twining's words. "I will not. And you cannot make such a statement again. Each time you do it, I may spin knots through your velvet. I never left you before when you thought it was grim, and I have no intentions of doing so this time."

"Terja, you have to be reasonable. You can't—"

"No. Our weaving is far from over. If I have to drag you by your legs, I will if it keeps you from becoming a captive of the Varas."

Anan cringed and glanced at his legs. "It might be less painful to surrender to the Varas."

"I think we can find something less painful. But we need to move. The Varas are close to the eastern edge of the barrens," Soneri said. He carried Anan to an area sheltered from the cold breeze and began giving orders. Terja had no problem with the big man taking charge; his attention was on making Anan as comfortable as possible.

In what seemed to be a brief moment, Joven pulled a large drag close to them. Without needing to discuss it, he and Soneri lifted Anan and carefully arranged him in the pile of pelts lining the drag. Terja moved to help pull, but Joven motioned him away. "You are exhausted too, and we only have a short period of daylight left. If I become fatigued, we can switch."

Terja nodded, knowing he couldn't last long with the exhaustion washing over him. He made his way to Anan's side and fell in step beside the prone figure of his twining. A scant moment passed before Anan's hand engulfed his and squeezed.

CHAPTER TWELVE

XAIN STOOD beside a series of spires that populated the canyon's floor. A desolate land with mazes of canyons, littered with dry washes for variety. He'd come to believe he would be better off as Geir's well-kept slave than having spent the past few days battling his way through this horrific landscape. The deep red of exposed clay covered everything—skin, clothing, tents, boots, hair. That the winter wind had shifted, carrying more chill, during the past few days was not helping morale either. It did help that the escapees were setting fewer traps, which the Ubica were finding easily.

"Why are we stopped?" asked Kosemi.

"There was a signal from the advanced group. The troops are using the time to rest. We have been moving at a rapid pace. The fatigue is beginning to show."

"They seem fine," Captain Kosemi said as she motioned to the Ubica with her chin.

Xain tried not to sigh. He needed the support of this infuriating woman. "They are a Ubica Triad. Their training began at birth. You cannot compare even your best troops to them."

The muscles tightened along the captain's jaw. "We will find the escaped slaves. The ringleaders will be executed. I have sworn this to the Burning Twins."

"Exhausting your troops will not be productive."

If her glare had any real power behind it, Xain would have died in that instant. But he stood against her, matching her scowl. A moment passed before she continued.

"We will catch them in a few days. Then we can leave this gods-forsaken land."

"As we get closer we must be more cautious."

Kosemi glowered at him. "Slave, that is common knowledge among those of us trained in the service of the High Regent. You are here only to give us information we might not have collected on our own. I can't imagine how that might be true, but those are my orders."

"Captain! Captain! You need to see what we've found."

They both turned to the soldier, who was gasping for air but still standing at attention. Xain was not feeling particularly generous and took grim delight when Kosemi barked at the reporting soldier. "Why does everything need my supervision? Can nothing be decided without me?"

A look of panic filled the man's face. "I was sent with the message, Captain. I didn't—"

"Where? Show me this terrible problem my officers can't resolve."

The soldier spun and raced back the way he'd come. With a sigh, Kosemi followed at a slower pace. Xain struggled to keep the smirk from his face that would tell the captain he enjoyed her frustration. But a moment later, he followed at a slight distance. *I wonder what they found that was so baffling.*

In a short time, they threaded their way deeper into the maze of earth and rock formations that made up the barrens. A growing sense of foreboding filled Xain at the muttering of the soldiers they were approaching.

As the captain reached the edge of the canyon, she froze in place. Xain joined her and his blood ran cold.

Spread before them for as far as he could see was the webbing of what had to be the largest deathspinner colony he'd ever heard of.

"What in the Red Twins is that?" Kosemi asked.

"A deathspinner colony. We will have to find another route. Check for signs of which trail the slaves took. They would never have tried to go through the colony," Xain said.

"There is no need to search. They hide their trail well. But they have gone north," said Gurvan, who it seemed had followed them.

Xain turned with Kosemi to find the Triad leader. Before Xain could ask the question himself, the captain pressed him. "Why? Winter is coming. They would not go into the fierce weather."

"The Meke clan lives in the Ais Mountains. That is to the north," Gurvan said.

"So we must move faster. If they find help, our mission will be much more difficult," Kosemi said.

"Captain, we have no choice. We can't cross the deathspinners, and your troops are already exhausted."

She spun on Xain, her face the red of a blazing fire. "A cluster of animals will not stop a century of the High Regent."

Shock flooded Xain. By the Twined Ones, she couldn't be saying what he thought. "Captain, we cannot go through the colony. We must go around. It's a deathspinner colony."

Surely she doesn't understand. Or I do not understand. It's deathspinners!

Kosemi turned away from Xain to snap out orders to those soldiers who were nearby. "Prepare the guard. Full battle armor. Spears, long knives, and a shield wall. We will cut through these animals while they huddle from the cold."

"Captain! You can't. These are the most deadly animals living on the Talac grasslands."

She turned with a sneer to Xain. "Stay here until we clear the way. I would expect no less from a traitor. But we will empty this valley and then the captives will be within striking distance."

Filled with shock and disbelief, Xain was speechless as the soldiers followed their orders. He studied the spans and spans of thick webbing. He had to admit, it was different from the other colonies they had seen. As much as he disliked the captain, he hoped he was wrong this time. This could be the end of their quest.

The sun had scarcely moved when the guards created a shield formation. They were armored far beyond what any Talac ever would be, but Xain still felt a haze of doom surrounding them. He cringed and willingly moved away as the soldiers began their advance on the colony, which seemed deserted. But as the first booted foot pressed downward on the edge of the webbing, he caught movement from their depths.

"Captain!" he called out. "The deathspinners are coming!"

She shot him a feral sneer and then shouted, "Battle formation! Forward!"

Xain watched in horror as the spectacle unfolded before him. Dark shapes filled the multitude of tunnels that permeated the layers and layers of silk. The front guards were having difficulty moving as the webbing seemed to bind their legs and feet. Their smooth charge became a stumbling morass as the webbing itself fought back. His blood chilled at the sight of the previously empty tunnels filling with rapidly moving dark shapes. Xain braced himself for the inevitable disaster as the Varas wall challenged the lords of the savanna.

The lead soldier drew back his iron-tipped spear and thrust.

"No!"

A nerve-rending trill filled the air around them. Xain slapped his hands over his ears to deaden the pain. He caught a movement behind him and spun to find the Ubica staring down at him. One of them shook his head and motioned toward the webbing with his chin. Xain snapped back to the growing battle.

The soldier who killed the first deathspinner screamed piteously as a fingercount of the animals sunk their fangs into him again and again. The order and symmetry of the Varas guard shattered under the vicious attack. Men and women littered the ground, their bodies heaving and muscles locked as the poison flooded their systems.

Xain had to give them credit, even if he felt it was a poor choice. They didn't flee at the first deaths, agonizing as they were. He was amazed to hear the captain ordering them forward as she stood outside the webbing. But quickly the front ranks of soldiers were downed, their bodies crawling with the fist-sized animals.

Xain involuntarily took a step away, then another, until Oka stopped him. "You do not need to run any farther. They will not cross the edge of their weavings."

He hardened himself and turned toward the young man. "I am not running. Merely making room for the retreating guard." His eyes flicked to the first wave of soldiers escaping the onslaught. When he turned to the Ubica, a fingerlength knife bit into his throat. He met the dark-skinned man's amber eyes. Xain swallowed hard and slid away as the screams of the dying soldiers filled the air. He'd told Kosemi. The fault did not lie with him.

The century broke, flooding back through the opening they had created, but the ground was littered with troops that had gone into the deathspinner colony and would never return. Clenching his teeth, Xain grabbed a crossbow from one of the men streaming past him and began giving mercy to those who still lived. He quickly ran out of quarrels. When he turned for more, he found the captain pointing a crossbow at his gut. He glared at her as she ground the crossbow butt against her shoulder and took aim.

"You know you need me. I warned you not to try and cross the colony. I am giving mercy to those who deserve it, to those who desperately need it."

Her finger tightened, pressing on the dark metal trigger. But Xain refused to run or beg. He would face his death unlike he'd lived his life. He swallowed as the trigger slammed home, launching the shaft directly at his chest.

His death was sealed.

Then it happened. The Ubica's sword seemed to move of its own volition, carving the bolt into several pieces that clattered to the ground around them. An instant later, Kosemi slumped to the ground. Xain stepped closer to find a fingercount of throwing needles buried in her throat and the side of her face. There was a final shuddering breath and then the body was still.

Xain gathered himself, trying to decide why this had happened. Why had they saved him? He'd done nothing to warrant their intervention. What of the troops? Their captain had just been assassinated. He looked up to find Oka standing a few feet away watching him.

"Throw the body to the creatures. They will dispose of it. Now. While the troops are focused on what just happened."

"Why? What have you done?" Xain asked.

"She jeopardized the completion of our contract. She just killed many troops. With the losses to the Talac traps and much of the guard gone, she was a hindrance."

Xain studied the three emotionless men until they turned as one and climbed the butte. "Wait!" The three stopped, turned toward him, and waited in silence. A moment passed before Xain realized they were granting him an audience.

"I thought you were forbidden by your gods to harm the innocents."

Gurvan studied him for a moment before replying. "She was never an innocent, no more than you."

Xain stood in slack-jawed shock as the three disappeared into the barrens.

THE METALLIC taint of blood twisted with the reek of bowel from the row of covered bodies of those too injured to live, or whom the officer beside him thought would simply slow them down. A last young soldier was dying slowly, with two bite wounds into her midsection. She panted raggedly as she watched the two of them with tears streaming down her cheeks. Xain acknowledged her bravery with a nod before the Varas officer's knife flashed out, and the ground was drenched with the young soldier's blood.

The executioner glanced at Xain. "Is that the last of the marked ones?"

"Yes. The rest should heal quickly. Although many will have much scarring." Xain shook his head. "Nothing I can do to help. Without a spinner, I have no matama. Being able to steal the matama from others doesn't help when there is nothing to steal."

The soldier stopped to watch as two men threw the body into a nearby arroyo. "She was a good soldier." Then the man studied Xain for a moment. "I'm Soja. Now that Kosemi and the other officers are dead, I am the commander. Things will be different now. I have lost too many soldiers."

Xain grabbed the man's shoulder and squeezed, trying to emulate the bonding ritual he'd seen with others. "They were all good men. They paid for Kosemi's mistake. I mourn them all."

Soja nodded in agreement. "I was close enough to hear. I know you told her not to cross the webbing." The soldier's eyes grew hooded as he drank Xain in from head to toe. "I'm making you my special advisor. We obviously need someone who knows the area."

He gave Xain a lecherous grin. "Besides, it's been some time since I've enjoyed a good Talac."

Xain was caught off guard at the response. He studied the man as he walked away. *What does this mean? Have I sold myself to another Geir? How was it that all the other officers were killed?*

His muscles tightened as someone approached him from behind. He was somewhat surprised to find Gurvan watching the new Varas captain make his way through the encampment. Their gazes locked and then the Ubica began to speak.

"We need to leave quickly. The Talac will be moving and hiding their trail as much as possible. They seem to be leaving fewer traps, but that could be a ruse to get us to relax. We can still track them. But we cannot move as rapidly as Kosemi was pushing the troops."

Xain cocked an eyebrow as he studied the Ubica. "You understand I am no more in charge now than before. Soja declared himself commander now and named me as advisor."

And whore?

One of Gurvan's brows slowly slipped upward as he studied Xain. After an uncomfortable silence passed, he began to speak. "We are pleased. Soja will serve our needs, with you to guide him. It serves our contract."

"And if I didn't meet your contract?"

"You are a Talac slave who survived the pleasure houses. We are certain you will work diligently so that doesn't happen."

A cold chill ran through Xain that had nothing to do with the winter storm gathering around them. He struggled to find a response, but nothing could be added. The Ubica were known for the extreme devotion they exhibited to the negotiated contract.

He watched as Soja moved to join them. Without a pause, he spoke to Xain. "I want away from here. It reeks of death and failure."

Oka evaluated Soja as he surveyed the land around them before turning back to Xain and the Triad. "Get ready. I want no more soldiers lost." He included the Ubica in his glare. "You will see to it."

"Yes, Captain. We will be ready to move shortly," Xain said.

The four of them stood in silence until the new captain was out of sight. Oka turned to Xain. "Soja was the only surviving officer. We find that interesting."

"He indicated a taste for Talac from the Varas pleasure houses," Xain said.

Oka never broke his gaze. "There are those among the Ubica whose bodies are their greatest weapon."

Xain nodded slowly. "I'm sure there are."

THE TROOPS moved as far as they could from the site of the massacre and the animals who had killed so many. They found an area more sheltered than they had been able to locate for the last several days. The order had been passed to set up the camp. As the sun slipped behind the horizon, Xain was relieved to see that most of the guard had pitched their shelters and were ready for another cold night. He also saw the dark tent used by the Ubica Triad, separated from the main body of troops.

Soja sought him out as the night haze darkened. He waited as the typically short Varas moved slowly closer. But from Soja's stance he was all business. Xain settled back, ready to play the part of subordinate. Geir had at least prepared him for that role. So, with eyes carefully hooded, he stood and waited.

He drew close to Xain so they would not be overheard. "We can't catch the slaves at this speed."

"And you have an idea?"

The man nodded slowly as he studied Xain. "Send out a small group. They could travel light, move much faster. So they could start harassing the slaves and slow them down until the main body could catch up. Then we could attack as a group."

Xain considered the proposal but saw few flaws with the idea, other than the traps. "The traps they are setting. What about those?"

"I would send one Ubica with the troops."

"Triads do not separate."

Xain shivered to find Oka close enough to overhear their conversation. As he fought to control his emotions, the Ubica continued.

"But your idea is valid. We had decided much the same," Oka said.

Xain glanced at Soja and then motioned Oka closer. They needed to work out the details of this skirmish group.

"So the Ubica would be willing to work as part of an advance group?"

"Yes. We believe it would be in the best interest of our forging with the High Regent. But only a small number. Less than a fingercount of Varas, at the most."

The man's statement did little to allay fears building in Xain. He looked to Soja, who took up the thread of the conversation. "I will select a few who would be successful working with the Ubica. Meet me before moonrise and we will form a plan."

A small smile crossed Xain's lips. "Soon we will have the escaped slaves on their way back to the great river." *And I will have the High Regent's gratitude.*

CHAPTER THIRTEEN

TERJA PACED the confines of their tent. The snap of its ties in the wind served as a counterpoint to his steps. His frustration did little to clear his mind. Anan was reclining, still recovering from his injuries. Terja was glad the bites had healed as quickly as they had, but now his source of frustration was Anan's stubborn single-mindedness.

"How could you not understand her gift? It's no different than ours. Her visionweave saved us from the flash flood. By the First Twining, how can you question her gift when you have been the beneficiary of her skill several times?"

"Spellweavers and spellspinners have existed since the Talac came into this world. Only a few Talac acknowledge visionweavers. Her vision of the flood could have been her spellweaving expanding further than ever before."

"Some Talac don't believe in the deathspinner's silk either, but it is beyond my mind how anyone could not acknowledge something so concrete and easily proved," Terja said.

Anan rubbed his face and sighed. Before he could begin again, Terja lunged into the argument. "Someone will always question even the most obvious of things we live with and can clearly see if you have the will to look. I understand this is something you can't see, that has a warp and weft that shifts depending on the choices we make. But Morea has already saved us once. Don't you think that is enough?"

Anan turned to the young woman who had been standing quietly while they argued. "It's not that I don't trust you, Morea. But I have difficulty accepting that visionweaving is reliable. Terja says it's the same as spellweaving, but it's not. If I weave a spell correctly, then it will be true. But sometimes your visions are right, and at other times what happens is completely different."

"But I've told you—" she began.

127

"Wait. Let me finish," Anan interrupted. "You've told me that your visions sometimes change. Isn't that right?"

Morea inhaled deeply and Terja could tell she was trying to gather her thoughts before she made another futile attempt at changing Anan's mind. He had thought this argument was settled at the flash flood, but Anan had talked himself into doubting her ability. He found Anan's stubbornness surprising. To Terja, her explanations were perfectly logical. But she also refused to change her beliefs to align them more closely to Anan's. They seemed like two pieces of warriorglass battering against each other. Chips might fly with each strike—there was even the possibility of one shattering—but neither would bend.

He shook his head when he realized Morea had started again.

"My teacher always said that with knowledge comes power. If you act on the information, then you change it. The future is mutable. The last time, my vision of people dying didn't happen. Why? Because you made a decision to change a thread of the weaving and the tapestry shifted. This time it could shift again. But—"

"I know. I understand. But I can't make decisions that could affect our lives knowing that it's a guess."

Morea threw up her hands, frustration etched across her face. "They are coming, Anan. In my dream they were riding longtooth and three dark-colored snowgrazers raced at their core. They caught us and it was like a newly knapped obsidian blade cutting through kuri cheese. None of us survived."

Anan slowly ground his hands into his face, and Terja could clearly feel his frustration over their connection. Terja sent a tendril of support and comfort to his twining. He turned to Morea but found himself facing Soneri and Joven. He glanced around, but Morea had disappeared from the tent.

Anan studied the pair and Terja sensed his curiosity. He could tell both were nervous, but it seemed to have nothing to do with the argument they had happened upon. They glanced at each other, and then Joven turned to Anan with a grim expression. "We were checking our back trail. I wove a thread to see what followed us."

Soneri burst into the conversation, seemingly more nervous than Joven. "They're close. Very close. We think they will catch up with us before this day ends."

They glanced at each other, seemingly unwilling to continue.

"What? What else?" Anan said.

"We think the Ubica are with them, but the traitor is not," Soneri said.

"How can you tell?" Terja asked.

"They feel… different. Not seeped in red mud like the Varas, but no taste of summer grasslands like a Talac."

"How many? Is it the entire century?" Anan asked.

Soneri shook his head. "No. Less than a fingercount."

Joven looked hopeful for a moment. "Maybe we've thinned them that much, almost wiping them out. Then we could surround them and rid ourselves of the Varas."

Terja considered for a moment and then shook his head. "The Varas troops would never follow the Ubica. They are no more to be trusted than the Talac pleasure slaves, so far as the Varas care."

"So Xain…."

"He must be dead. The High Regent's guard would never allow themselves to be commanded by a Talac slave. Even when Xain was the one who planned the expedition, he still worked through Geir."

Anan's mouth twisted into a frown. "I'd prefer to see Xain's head separated from his shoulders as proof that he was dead. He avoids death with more dexterity than a springtail during mating season."

"We will plan for the unimaginable then. But right now we have a force of Varas coursing us while we try to put one foot in front of the other in an attempt to escape the barrens," Terja said.

Soneri shot out of the tent to reappear a moment later, carrying the bladed staff Terja had given him. He held it out to Terja. "You will need this. It is woven for you. My father enjoyed the weapon's beauty, and I would do my best to honor his tradition. But I've seen it being used by you and your training shows. It would be a travesty for it not to be with someone trained in its use. You and Anan may be the turning point to save the entire Kuri clan."

Terja took the shaft in his hands, relishing the smooth dense wood. He eased through a practice form he'd learned and his heart pounded with excitement. Anan's approval and pride flowed through their connection and filled Terja with contentment. His spellsight dropped into place, allowing him to feel each fiber that made up the weapon's web and made it possible for Terja to move with a lethal grace no one else ever mastered.

He briefly relived his battle with Xain's lover, Geir. He had enough confidence to realize his staff was more than effective against the iron weapons of the Varas. He turned back to find Morea standing close by, holding his obsidian-edged shield. The gift created by First Twining for him had proven itself several times over. He threaded his arm into the straps of the round shield and thrilled at the comfortable and natural feeling that filled him.

He glanced at Anan and sensed pride radiating from his twining. A sense of contentment filled Terja that he would have thought impossible a few moons earlier. As he double-checked the straps and laced on his sling pouch, he realized the small group around him were all preparing for battle.

Anan forced himself to his feet and pulled his full quiver over his shoulder. He moved with a slight limp but held his bow tightly and studied each person carefully. Terja knew this tiny group was the only hope for the escaping Talac. But a sense of impending disaster filled him as he watched them. His foreboding washed even deeper over him when Morea reappeared carrying her sling.

A sigh escaped from Anan as he turned to the young woman. "I was wrong, Morea. I should have believed your vision. It was just so hard to trust lives with something I can't see myself."

Morea nodded toward Anan in acknowledgment. "I understand, Anan. But now we have to decide how to save the Talac."

"Yes, you're right, and I need you to stay with Ite to move everyone as far as possible. They might need your healing skills."

"They might need yours too, Anan. But you are still leading the people who are being sent to stop the Varas. You are the one looked to for leadership. I'm just a Kuri who survived the Varas slavers. Oh, wait. Everyone here survived the Varas too."

"No. I will not risk taking you, Morea."

"Why? Either Soneri or Joven are more valuable. I'm too small to pull the drags. They are both better spellweavers than I am. And I am just as skilled with a weapon."

Anan pounced on Morea's last statement. "You believe you are as skilled as anyone in the group?"

Morea nodded, obviously not intimidated by Anan. "Yes. I'm as good with my sling as any of you."

"And if you are not?"

"Then I will stay here and help Ite move everyone deeper into the barrens."

Terja started at Anan's next words. "Then I choose Terja. Best two of three throws."

Apprehension grew into a knot inside Terja. "I never said I would compete against Morea. I cannot choose between you."

"Strands! You know you have to do this. You have the most skill with the sling. Morea knew I would choose you." Anan smirked. "She is a visonweaver after all."

Morea touched Terja's shoulder as his panic grew. He turned and met her gaze. "I did know. It required no visionweaver talents. I want to test my skills against you."

Terja nodded reluctant agreement.

"Good. Then let's move outside to settle this contest," Anan said.

They stepped into the windy landscape that was becoming less hospitable with each passing fingermark. Once everyone had moved outside, Anan studied the terrain for targets. A moment or so later, he practically glowed to Terja's sight. "Good. The rock spire on the next butte. Three throws each."

Terja swallowed hard. It was more than a fingercount of spans to the mark Anan had chosen. *That would be a challenging target for anyone. We might both miss it.* He looked at Anan and lifted an eyebrow.

Anan seemed completely oblivious to his message, even though he filled their connection with confidence. But when he glanced at Morea, she appeared composed and returned Terja's stare with a grin.

"Ready, teacher? Your student is feeling like it's a good day to challenge you."

"Let it be noted, I do not agree with this."

"Noted by both of us," Anan said.

Terja glanced toward Morea and received another nod. With a feeling of failure, he turned toward the spire. Terja focused and dropped a pellet into the sling. Blocking out everything but the target, he whipped the weapon with increasing speed. At the moment it felt right, he released. The pellet arched toward its goal as the group watched. To Terja's surprise, he heard the sound of it hitting the rock. He turned to Anan with a quirk to his mouth.

"I think I hit it...."

Anan motioned Morea forward. Terja was proud of his student as she duplicated his movements almost exactly. He couldn't suppress a smile at the sound of her pellet hitting its target. It disappeared when he saw the deepening scowl on Anan's face.

He stepped up and the two of them repeated their movements, with similar results. One turn remained for each of them.

Terja's nerves grew as he readied himself. This time his preparation felt off. He couldn't explain the difference. But he knew it grew in severity with each beat of his heart.

"Morea, you go first this time," Anan said.

Terja turned to Anan in time to catch a glimpse of an expression that he couldn't pinpoint. Even a quick check of their connection told Terja nothing. He wasn't certain what Anan was attempting, but it left a taste he did not like.

Morea stepped forward without a word and went through the movements with a fierce determination. Her sling whined as it cut air and ended with a snap as she released. The stone seemed to move of its own slow volition. Terja had no problem following it through each span of the distance, to hear it hit the target with a satisfying thud.

Terja didn't wait for discussion. He knew it would do nothing but increase his nervous tension. He readied his sling and began—but his apprehension continued to grow. The swing never fell into the comfortable cadence he normally felt. But the moment arrived and he released the sling.

The instant it flew, Terja's concern grew. The stone arced toward the target, and he struggled to keep it in sight. The moment stretched until it was almost beyond Terja's tolerance.

"It's going to hit too," Joven said.

"It's too close to tell. At least, I can't tell," Soneri said.

The pellet shot past the formation and clattered down the other side.

"Strands!" Anan said.

Morea turned toward them, her arms crossed in confidence. "I'm going. No more arguments."

OKA LAY quietly in their shared tent, curled with Daya and Gurvan, with thick blankets covering them all. The relatively milder weather had disappeared in the past few days to be replaced by a building winter storm. He could sense the changes in the weather all day and now it seemed to be accelerating. This, mixed with the events of the last few days, had left him quiet and contemplative. He wished for once that he could forecast the future as easily as he could the weather. But at this moment he was comforted by his position between Gurvan and Daya's muscular bodies. His Forge-graced frame seldom lacked for warmth. It was comfort, not heat, he sought.

Daya curled closer and Oka smiled at the soft sigh that escaped his lips. "If it weren't for you, this would be a truly miserable expedition. Even with our heavy robes, by nightfall I am numb from the cold. You're the only thing that keeps me moving in these forsaken barrens."

"I'm glad you enjoy the heat, Daya. I happily accept my role as Forge for our Triad," Oka said in a whisper.

"You do your duty well. We are proud to have you." Gurvan's deep voice rippled through Oka's whipcord-lean body. He lay quietly for several moments thinking of what their future might hold. The other two men lay immobile, but Oka knew neither of them slept. The tension grew too intense, and Oka couldn't hold in his emotions, and worry, any longer.

"Tomorrow we will find the Talac."

"That is likely," Gurvan said.

"The battle will be fierce. The Varas seem to think the Talac will simply surrender."

Gurvan nodded. "The Varas are wrong. The Talac will fight until none live."

"Then what are we to do? Our forging is clear. We are sworn to protect the innocent."

"Tomorrow will bring choices that are not what we would prefer. But our forging is against only two Talac: the two who released the slaves. All others are innocents. But we are not sworn to protect the innocents from each other. We cannot harm them ourselves."

"That wasn't the forging the High Regent wanted...."

Gurvan tensed behind him. "The High Regent requires caution. But the Ubica has sent out Triads to test young warriors for generations. It was set forth by the Triad of Ancients as a way for our young to learn without killing our own people."

A soft chuckle drifted to Oka before Gurvan continued. "Imagine the heat of our Triads focused on each other. The Triad of Ancients was wise. Now the young are sent as their skill levels dictate. But it is known that our honor is forged before all else."

Oka lay quietly for some time before speaking further. When he did, it was with great sadness. "Ata and Lanvi believed in the honor of the Triad above all else. They died defending that honor... defending me."

Daya put his hand on Oka's shoulder and squeezed. "We knew about your Triad. You do not have to share with us as you did with them. But Gurvan and I want you to know we respect you and care for you. This is our last forging. We would invite you to stay with us."

Oka lurched upward, turning from one to the other. His feelings of desolation had built until they threatened to overwhelm him in recent days. "You can't want me. I'm too damaged for anything other than going from Triad to Triad until the Ancients need raw iron for another forge. I can't seem to bind with any."

"Why do you believe that? Daya and I would gladly welcome you."

"And what if my flaw breaks during battle and both of you are killed because of me? I would send myself to the reforging if that were to happen."

"You are not flawed, Oka. No one's skill is perfect. We all miss our aim from time to time. You are a strong part of the Triad. Daya and I agree, you are a fine Forge for our mating."

The last of his resistance melted away. Gurvan's words brought him the reassurance he needed. He would honor their invitation. But he would forever mourn the loss of his first Triad as his fault. The emotions flowing through him created a confusing mixture of ecstasy and depression. He found himself sinking into an abyss darker than the blackest coal when suddenly he was yanked back to the present.

The heat of a passionate kiss seared his lips, burning through the darkness like a star in the clear sky. Oka let his eyes drift shut as he enjoyed the euphoria of what was happening. The heat built until the kiss came to an end and their lips pulled apart with a slight tug. He eased his eyes open to see Daya's smiling face and beautiful olive skin.

"You were drifting into the cold, Forge. I couldn't let that happen."

Oka locked his eyes on Daya as he ran his tongue over his lips, enjoying the kiss's tingle. He groaned when a large hand pressed against his chest and he turned to see Gurvan. The silence stretched out for several moments before anything more was said. When words did drift from Gurvan, the heat built in their tent.

"We care about you, Oka. You aren't the only one to have lost a part of your Triad. Daya and I lost our Forge too. We also thought we'd never find someone to fill the void left by Satu's death. Our Triad with Satu was not forged and tempered when he died either. But it left us plunged into sorrow." Gurvan's massive hands cradled his face as if it was a newly hatched sunbird. They moved closer together, and the scent of a stoked forge filled the space. He closed his eyes with a sigh as hot lips pressed against his cheek. The trail of tiny kisses Gurvan planted along his neck was like bellows across hot coals. To Oka's surprise, his body began to respond for the first time since the death of his Triad.

Oka dropped into their bedding, his need growing as he watched Gurvan and Daya meet over him in a passionate kiss. The obvious connection between the two of them filled Oka with the desire to be a full part of their Triad. Their fully forged Triad, not just a working grouping.

The kiss continued for a few moments before they separated slowly and they gazed at him. In a synchronized motion, they lay on either side of Oka and wrapped themselves around him until they were a tangle of masculinity. His gaze locked with theirs and concern filled him from each of them. Daya kissed the tip of his ear and whispered. "We would invite you to nikata."

Oka dropped his gaze, afraid of what the invitation of sharing would mean to him. Much to his own shame, he'd never been able to reach full nikata with his former Triad. They had never pressured him for more, although Oka had sensed their disappointment, but he couldn't forge without iron. This time it was different; the reaction of his body was easily matched by the emotions flowing through him. He twisted toward Daya and kissed him with a passion to match any intimacy he'd shared before. Oka's pleasure grew as he pressed harder, pushed his tongue between Daya's lips and then drove deep inside. He gripped the back of Daya's neck as they kissed with a desire he had never experienced before.

Before he could change his mind, Gurvan nipped at the nape of his neck. The combination brought a flush of heat through Oka's body and he began to slowly undulate under the attention of his Triad. Multiple hands stripped him bare. He realized the tent should be freezing cold, but relished the heat of the warm sun that seemed to fill it. With that, he relaxed under the caresses.

Oka was overwhelmed by the need to see and touch the men he was with. He had struggled with his attraction to the pair for so many days, but now he knew there was no need to fight the desire. He slipped his hands over the silky smooth skin on their arms and began tugging at their clothing. A moment later robes were tossed aside and all three had on nothing more than the day they were born. The press of the others against Oka left him breathing hard and desiring more.

His body was transfixed as Gurvan and Daya kissed down opposite sides. They teased him until he writhed from the building desire, close to losing control of himself. They moved away, giving Oka a moment to recover. But then he felt two blasts of hot air across his aching shaft. Before that sensation had more than a heartbeat to register, their tongues darted up and down his length. The frenzy was more than Oka thought he could stand. But as they became more urgent, Oka lost all focus other than the heat of pleasure building inside him.

He curled up and grabbed his mates. The bliss filled him as the sensations built one layer on the next like a finely forged sword. Daya flicked his tongue against the base of Oka's shaft and moved up its length until he reached the tip. Oka's body throbbed with a fire he'd never experienced before. Daya glanced at him—and gasped.

"What? What's wrong?" Oka asked.

"Your eyes," Daya said.

"What about my eyes?"

"Relax, Daya. Our Forge has much heat. We saw it before."

Daya scrunched his brows together for a moment and then his face lit up with a smile. "Ah yes, I remember now. Our young mate *is* a strong Forge."

Oka started to question them, but both returned to working on his shaft and balls, and he quickly forgot everything else. Clear liquid flowed from his tip with each new touch from his lovers. Soon he was slick and hungry. Sinking lower, he grabbed the hard shafts jutting from his mates' groins. Wanting more, he tugged Daya toward him. Oka rose to his elbows, slipped the head of Daya's shaft between his lips, and pumped his head up and down.

As he focused on Daya's pleasure, Gurvan moved lower and sucked one of Oka's balls into his mouth. He worked it slowly until it was coated with spit. Oka's head swam with pleasure as Gurvan released one full orb and took the other in his mouth. Time lost all meaning as Oka received attention from his mates. He was dimly aware when two meaty hands slid up the back of his thighs and curled him forward.

Oka's curiosity as to Gurvan's intent was answered when he pressed his face between Oka's ass cheeks and began licking and probing down the length of his cleft. The wet heat fanned the flames of his need as Oka joined the other two in the forging of their mutual love. He'd never felt this before and his fires roared.

Their mating deepened in ways it would take Oka days to examine in an intelligible manner. Then, in the ultimate action of intimacy, Gurvan's tongue pierced him. He sighed and wisps of steam curled from his mouth as he arched his back to open himself. The teasing exploration continued until he was at the edge, and then it stopped. Frantic, he pulled off Daya and twisted to confront Gurvan.

"No! You stopped! You—"

Oka was silenced with a smirk. "Our metals have not been blended enough for a true forging, and you have not known the heights of pleasure."

With a fluid motion, Gurvan positioned himself. Realization of what was about to happen came to Oka when Gurvan's hard shaft pressed against him. He let out a long moan, which Daya silenced by filling Oka's mouth with his manhood. Oka had a moment of anticipation before the other two moved into action. Gurvan pressed forward, sinking himself deep inside Oka. Daya intertwined his fingers in Oka's hair, which he'd freed of throwing spikes, and began thrusting deep into his mouth.

Swept along like a summer firestorm over the highland grasses, Oka let the others take control. They merged into a single mass of seething smith-hardened muscle with sparks of pleasure showering Oka from every angle. His climax moved closer and closer as their passion grew. Beyond any separate feelings of lust, Oka was surrounded by the molten heat of a fully forged Triad. His body trembled and seized as he plunged into the magma they had created. He began erupting, white lines of scorching pleasure shooting from him. The urgent thrusts against him heightened his desire, and his need.

Simultaneously, Daya and Gurvan pressed in deep and locked their muscles as they reached their individual orgasms. The sensations built inside Oka as his muscles clenched and he plunged into pleasure of a depth he'd never experienced before. Wave after wave of elation washed through his body as he closed his eyes to relish each delicious moment. As his muscles relaxed, his mates eased him onto their bedding. He lay quietly as Daya and Gurvan curled on either side of him, enjoying the dwindling heat of their passion.

Oka shivered when a set of fingertips traced down his ribs. Before he could respond, his world burst into flames. He could see nothing else and started to yell. Gurvan pinned him against the floor as he thrashed wildly, filled with panic. A moment later the flames dropped and Oka's world had changed as his senses filled with the sharp musk of his lovers, and the colors surrounding him were richer. He slowly met Gurvan's gaze.

"What happened? What changed?" Oka asked. Emotions flooded Oka but as he calmed himself, he came to a startling revelation: most of the emotions he felt weren't his. Teetering between hysteria and delight, he turned again to Gurvan.

Still struggling with the sudden event, Oka said. "Anvil to my Forge, your Triad and mate asks you. What blessings have the Ancients bestowed?"

Oka recognized the moment of adjustment by the fact he brought his request for information to such a level of formal speech. They both knew the gravity it signified. He was not surprised that Gurvan took several moments to respond. First, he released Oka and motioned Daya away. With a nod, he began his portion of the ritual.

"Forge to my Anvil, your Triad and mate responds. Our Triad's mating found the blessing of the Ancients, and the Ancient Forge bestowed the final gift of fire to you. To us all." He nodded again, acknowledging his portion.

Oka turned to the naturally quiet Daya to find a smiling, round face. Oka couldn't help but grin back at his joyful lover. It soon became evident that Daya wasn't in the state of mind for the response when he wrapped his fingers around Oka's thick shaft and slid his hand down its length.

"Daya...." came the raspy warning from Gurvan.

"What? I told you Oka was the choice for us. If that forging wasn't one to go into the storytellers' tales, then I should come back as a neutered springtail."

Oka couldn't keep from bursting out in laughter at Daya's irreverence toward the Ubica ritual. Even Gurvan's typically somber expression showed a glimmer of humor. Daya smiled at both of them before letting the emotionless mask all Ubica learned, from the time they could focus, settle back into place. This was the only view shown to outsiders. With this veneer of formality, he began his part in the ritual.

"Forge to my Hammer, your Triad and mate responds. As the ultimate protector of our Triad, I swear by the Ancients to gift the spirit within me, should that prove necessary. I am the first and last level of protection to our group. Outsiders will be deceived by the mass of our Anvil when it is me they should fear."

Oka closed his eyes to study the swirl of feeling inside and this time it had changed. The sensations traveling through his body were ordered, settling like pools of molten iron in a sand casting. His eyes shot open and for a moment the shadow of what he saw lay across Gurvan and Daya.

"You aren't losing your sight," Daya said. "Part of being a true forging is the gift of knowing. From this moment on, you will always know where we are and our emotional state."

Oka paused for a moment, his mouth twisted as he considered this change. "It wasn't like this... before."

"It wasn't a true forged Triad."

Oka snapped his gaze to Daya. "They were—"

"I am passing no judgment. But one of the signs of a forging is the gift of knowing." He paused for a moment before continuing. "We knew it was unlikely your previous Triad was forged. You wouldn't have survived otherwise."

"So this time?"

"If Gurvan and I both die, you will likely die too." Daya hesitated again and then whispered, "We should have explained what you were doing more clearly." Daya glanced at Gurvan who nodded. "This can be broken if you wish."

Oka stared first into Daya's eyes and then Gurvan's before replying. "The loss last time was almost more than I could bear. I wasn't certain I wanted to live past their deaths. I would rather die than go through that again, or worse."

A smile reappeared on Daya's face. "Good. Greetings, forge mate."

CHAPTER FOURTEEN

ANAN CROUCHED against the rocky spire as he scanned the lands surrounding them. He wanted to pace, hoping to release some of the frantic energy building within him. But instead he stayed hidden from sight. The Varas were close, and the packing of those who moved ahead this morning was fueled by desperation. Before the weak sun began to crest on the eastern horizon, all but the selected Talac were making their way as quickly as possible to the west. The sun-dyed threads of clouds twisted behind them, leaving a trail of crimson that Anan hoped wasn't an omen. After the argument last night, he was as ready to move as anyone. But he knew that wasn't the way his weave was threaded.

"It's gotten colder."

Anan glanced to the source of the softly spoken comment and nodded at Terja. "It has. It cuts through the layers of kuri fiber you wrapped me in."

Terja smiled but made no comment as he turned toward the west to see the last drags disappear over the ridge behind them. Anan's attention shifted to the short brush and grass that carpeted the grounds surrounding the outcropping of rock they had chosen as their watch point. The wind whipped around again and Anan tightened the woven piece over his face until only a slit for his eyes remained.

"Iceweaver is readying a storm, and we do not have enough shelter for our people," Anan said.

A soft sigh came from Anan as he considered the mounting impossibility of fulfilling their bloodweaving. "We were so close to escaping into the Kuri lands, but now…."

Anan looked back in surprise at the growl that came from his twining. The fierce anger feeding through their connection left him even more shocked. He snapped his attention toward the source to find an angry Terja. "Don't say that. Ever. We will reach the clan's winter home. We will reach it together. Then we will live the rest of our lives telling the young ones how easy their life is. I have already lost my mother and father, and my mother

I can no longer remember in spite of my best efforts. I have no intention of losing my twining."

In spite of himself, Anan smiled, but it shifted to a grim countenance. He turned toward the darkening eastern sky. "If it is the entire Varas century... I don't see how we can weave this problem in our favor."

The look he received from Terja was as sharp as needle bush spines. "We released all the captured Talac. We defeated Ubica iron. In the end, we defeated a company of trained soldiers."

"Except Xain. If we'd just killed that crawler, our chances of arriving at our home would be much improved," Anan said.

Terja shrugged. "Xain lived. But so did we. Today we will see how we fare. But either way, they will remember who they battled."

He glanced at Terja's confident stance, staff and shield ready, knowing he was well versed with his weapons. Taking inventory of his own armaments, Anan was satisfied. From the finely spun bowstring to the lethal sharpness of the obsidian shards lining his battle club, Anan felt prepared for whatever today brought. A slight pain was the only remnant of his encounter with the deathspinners, the healing much faster than they had thought, but he was still concerned that it might create a fatal weakness. If their entire group became part of the Great Weaving today, at least they would have given the others time to travel deeper into Meke territory, and hopefully they could find their elusive cousins and petition them for help.

Terja settled beside him as they waited.

The sky above them roiled like the grasslands ahead of a high summer winds. With no glimpse of the Varas, time sat heavily on Anan. He questioned his decisions, but had to keep his fears to himself. A few moons ago, he had been simply the hunter who was Silbre's twining. There had been few decisions to make, none of which had any impact beyond the two of them.

Now? Now each decision could mean the end of the Kuri. The weight of his clan's survival rested on his shoulders. Should they have taken the half day to help the others travel farther? Could he have protected his twining better by running? They could have escaped if the two of them had left the others. But even beyond the bloodweaving,

Anan knew he could never abandon the people who had come to depend on him. Terja would never agree to it either.

He took a deep breath and used the whisper of matama from his connection with Terja. He knew it might weaken their First Twining-blessed link, but saw little choice. Anan wove a gossamer thin spell to check their back trail. *Oh by the First Twining, they are coming, and close.* He whistled out the mating call of the sunbird, the signal they had agreed upon, and sensed the others moving into position. They silently awaited the appearance of the Varas force.

OKA SHIFTED his feet silently across the bare red earth. The cold wind cut through him like a sharp iron blade. The fingercount of Varas accompanying them moved exactly as he would expect a group of red-mud Varas to move—like a herd of daggerhorn in rut. If the Talac couldn't hear them coming long before they arrived, they were not as competent an opponent as he thought.

He could easily sense Gurvan on the right flank and Daya to the left. Both men were awash in the tension of someone hunting a dangerous foe, as they should be. Oka pulled a pair of throwing knives free, gripping one in each hand, ready to release them in a heartbeat. The terrain around them had become rougher, the grass almost chest high, easier to hide a small force inside. The others of his forging saw the same possibility of a trap.

Oka stopped, his unease filling him as he cataloged the area surrounding them. The other Ubica dropped to one knee at the same instant, but Oka felt no change in their emotions. The Triad worked together, scanning their surroundings as a unit. All three felt the wrongness, but couldn't find its source.

Suddenly the golden Talac lunged from the high grass and grabbed a guard who had wandered to one side. With no more trace of their passing than a ripple in the ocean, the two disappeared. An instant later, another Varas gave out a strangled cry and grabbed at the arrow in her throat. As the guard dropped to her knees, a sling pellet cracked against the side of her skull.

Oka caught a glimpse of one of the attackers as they dove into a wrinkle in the landscape. He flung a blade toward them, but was uncertain if it found lodging in the Talac. Daya and Gurvan studied the grass surrounding them. Daya's hammer leapt, deflecting a stone aimed at Oka's head. Within the same heartbeat, Gurvan's sword flashed forward in a complex pattern, destroying an arrow an arm's length from them.

A Talac jumped from cover to engage one of the few Varas still standing. The brutish Varas bellowed at the sight of an enemy and charged, his sword swinging wildly. The Talac's lithe body twisted in a recognizable pattern, and in an instant blood poured from the guard's ruined throat. In the moment of stillness while the Varas crumbled, Oka realized this was one of the targets of their forging with the High Regent. This was the infamous hairless Talac.

Oka watched the man they would kill shortly for weaknesses they could exploit. Each mark had a weakness; the Ubica learned from a young age how to find them. He was removed from the action, trusting Gurvan and Daya to keep him safe as he evaluated their target. A second, furred, Talac appeared at the hairless one's side and a choked sound came from Oka.

"What?" Gurvan demanded.

"Both targets. They are here. In easy reach."

Gurvan deflected another stone with a thrust of his long iron blade. Stepping back into rest stance, he spoke without looking away from the action. "Use care, little Forge. These Talac are formidable."

"Distract the one with the bladed shaft. My stingers are hungry for the other. With any luck, our forging will be fulfilled and we can leave these Ancients' forsaken lands." He knew the other two exchanged a glance, but Oka focused on his mark. With a goal in mind, he could use the terrain to his own advantage as the Talac had initially.

He pulled the blowgun from his robe as he covered the ground between them. He was close when he slipped the dart in. Another guard cried out, but Oka felt satisfaction radiate from Daya as his hammer saved the soldier. Glad to know the others were moving as he'd asked, he refocused on his intended victim. He reached one of the deep-red rock spires and pressed his back against the unyielding surface as he listened to the battle around them.

A moment later it began to snow. The first driving flakes transformed into blowing sheets before Oka could breathe.

By the smiths, this makes it harder to find my target.

There was another gurgling scream that ended abruptly. Oka wasn't certain, but he thought they were down to the three Ubica, plus one or two Varas. He heard Gurvan's roar of attack, followed quickly by Daya's. He rushed forward, hoping to find his quarry. He knew he'd only have a moment before the diversion was lost.

He ran in a crouch toward the sounds of battle. Following his internal map, he knew exactly where the rest of the Triad were. Based on that, he moved toward his quarry. The snow thickened until he could only see for a few spans. Then he saw his target through the heavy snow.

Oka flicked his gloves to the ground as another gust buffeted against him. *Too much wind. The darts could be blown anywhere.* He tucked away the reed tube and then let a double-edged throwing dagger drop into each of his bare palms. He waited calmly, focused on his target. The big Talac paused and Oka released the two knives in rapid succession. He caught the glint of highly polished iron as they flipped through the air. Time halted for Oka.

Suddenly his world tilted out of control when a small Talac appeared between the spinning knives and Oka's target. Oka watched in horror as his weapons spun toward an innocent. The first knife struck and Oka recoiled from the impact. The second blade caused no less damage as it sank into the chest of the Talac he now knew was female. Her scream of agony filled his soul and came close to extinguishing his flame. His body crumpled to the ground where he stood, saving him from the arrow and sling pellets that passed through the space he had just occupied. The others of the Triad raced to him and pulled him from the battle.

ANAN STRAINED to find the Ubica Triad through the building blizzard. The Talac force seemed to be winning the day. He'd known how fierce his select group was, but he'd been surprised at how they had cut through the Varas. But something gnawed at the back of his mind as he scanned the rapidly thickening snowfall.

He ran toward a battle he heard close by. A Varas soldier fled but was hounded by Soneri and Joven. Anan snatched an arrow from his quiver and quickly released the arm-long shaft at the fleeing man. An instant later the satisfying sound of another Varas's death cry filled the air.

Then it hit him: the Ubica. He dropped to create a smaller target, and one of the Ubica's weapons flew at him. Anan's mind only registered the threat of death when a blur of motion shot between him and the attacker.

"Morea! No!"

The cry had barely left him when he caught the young woman as she pitched back, with two knives protruding from her chest. He lowered her to the ground, oblivious to the battle going on around him. Anan's weaver's sight dropped into place as he fought to save her. His emotions were overwhelming as he grasped for a solution. He plunged into the connection he shared with Terja in a desperate attempt to heal Morea.

A sob left him as he saw the dark shadow of the iron blades piercing her heart. He reached for more matama, with more urgency as Terja raced toward them. But the flood of matama had no effect this time. It was as if the iron had become the antithesis of the life-giving matama. He prepared to try again when a slender hand caressed his face.

"Stop. You can't save me this time. Did it not occur to you that a visionweaver would know the place and time of their own death?"

Anan held her close as she coughed. Blood collected at the corner of her mouth as she took another labored breath.

"Anan! Heal her! Take whatever matama I have," Terja said as he stood beside them.

Anan dove in again in desperation, but the darkness had spread. He knew no heroic spellweaving was going to cure her. There was something in the metal he didn't have the skill to reverse. He cast a web to ease her pain, but as the tears welled in his eyes, he knew Morea's end was near.

He sensed Terja spinning the spell for akhir, the final strike spell that would kill both Terja and the Ubica. Morea struggled in his arms, a hand held out toward Terja.

"No, stay with me. All. Stay" came the whispered command from the dying woman.

Anan focused on Terja as his heart was being torn in two. "Akhir would not help this time. You would kill the Ubica who did this, but you would die too. Morea doesn't want that."

A rattling sigh came from Morea and in a whisper she said, "No, Terja. No."

Terja reached for his sling, but Anan grabbed his arm. "No. Help me ease Morea from this weaving. She wants you with her." Soneri and Joven were beside them too, and he glanced around. "You also. She will not die alone. Have the others watch for attackers."

"After the knives were thrown, the Triad disappeared. The Varas were killed. It wasn't the entire guard, only a small group. But no Varas survived the attack."

Anan paused in indecision and then Morea whispered, "My weaving is darkening, Anan. Are you there?"

He grabbed the woman's hands and held them tight. "We're all here, Morea. We won. The Varas are gone."

Her eyes fluttered shut for a moment, then shot open to bore into Anan. "Not done. Careful. More coming."

Anan's hot tears flowed in rivulets through the velvet on his cheeks to splash on their clasped hands. Terja knelt opposite him and gently brushed the hair from her eyes. "Stay with us, Morea. We'll think of something."

Her chuckle became a coughing fit that left her gasping for air. "Funny, spellspinner. Always the optimist."

She gasped again as all four of them huddled around her. Her eyes were clear as Morea sighed—and then went silent.

The snow swirling around them turned ferocious. The white seemed thicker than the walls of a winter earth lodge.

A soft sob came to Anan and he turned to see Soneri scrubbing his eyes. Only a heartbeat later, Terja let out a shuddering gasp, followed by Joven.

"She kept me alive. When we were with the slavers," Joven said.

"Morea had an indomitable spirit. She wouldn't let me run her off when the Varas were sizing me up as a pelt. She refused to leave my side," Soneri said.

Anan rocked the lifeless body, frantically brushing away the accumulating snow. "Why? Why did she insist on coming? She knew. She told me she knew."

He felt the heat of Terja's touch and turned toward him. "She came because she knew she was supposed to save you. Soneri is right. She will be part of the central pattern in the Great Weaving. We need to do the unraveling now. I don't want to leave the body for a pack of longtooth to find."

"No!" screamed Anan. "I am taking her back. The whole Kuri clan should know the bravery of a lowly herdweaver. She will have an unraveling like no other."

He glared at the other three, daring them to question his decision.

After a moment Soneri stepped forward, and Anan stiffened. The big man held out his arms toward Anan's burden. "Let me carry her to the Kuri lands. I promise you I will forfeit my life before I let any take her."

Anan resisted for a moment, then nodded in agreement. Soneri took Morea in his arms like a newly born kit. He stood without a word, her cloak fanning out behind her as he turned toward the direction the other Kuri had taken that morning. A morning that now seemed lifetimes in the past.

TERJA STOOD with his arms crossed, the angry winds of Iceweaver a tempest around them. The tall grasses whipped him with the ferocity of the Varas lashes, while bits of ice battered him. To the side was the sight he tried to avoid seeing, Morea's shroud-wrapped body. Instead, he focused on Anan.

"We can't take the body to the winter village. You know this too. First Twining will guide her to the Great Weaving regardless of where we do rites," Terja said.

Anan paced the tent as Terja made the same arguments, again. His face was as immobile as the sandstone crags deep in the grasslands. He wanted her unraveling to happen once they reached the winter lodges. Anan became completely unreasonable as the evening, and the unraveling, drew closer.

Terja knew the reason. Their connection worked perfectly and left little room to miss Anan's emotions. He was overwhelmed with guilt. Terja knew soon he would have to force Anan into moving, but he wasn't looking forward to that moment.

He was considering his options when a faint scratching came to the tent flap. Terja untied the opening and held it while Soneri and Joven slipped inside. He lashed it back quickly, and Soneri began speaking.

"The storm is building. If we are going to do the unraveling, it must be soon. I think the break will not last long. Iceweaver seems particularly angry."

Anan scowled but Terja stalled his first words. "It must be done. All of us wish we could do as you say. But even Soneri agrees this is what Morea would have had us do. We all agree you should be the weaver."

He spun on Terja. "I'm the one who—"

Terja poked Anan in the center of his chest. "You did not kill her. Stop thinking that. But you can honor her sacrifice by performing her unraveling."

Anan sighed deeply and Terja felt the anguish through the connection, along with a thread of resignation.

"It doesn't seem right. To leave her away from our homeland," Anan said.

"She will be in the Kuri lands long before we are. She will be a part of the same Great Weaving if we do her unraveling here or at winter village," Terja said.

With a sigh of acceptance, he turned to Soneri and nodded. This would be the most painful unraveling since he and Terja sent most of the Kuri clan to the Great Weaving.

Terja laid one of the snowgrazer pelts over the fabric shroud and stepped back. Soneri slipped his arms under the covered body, carrying it to the doorway. He paused to allow Joven to open the door ties and then slipped through with Joven close behind. Terja glanced back to see Anan had steeled himself for the task. As he walked past, Terja gripped his shoulder and squeezed. Anan smiled grimly and patted his hand.

They walked toward a sheltered canyon Joven and Soneri had located. As they made their way through the encampment, the other Talac fell into line behind them. Those few too weak to walk were carried. The clan assembled around the natural dais while Soneri laid the body out before them.

Terja moved opposite him as Anan began the weaving that was the first one learned by any spellweaver. Terja let his spellsight slip into place and saw as Anan pulled the strands of existence from the lifeless body until the threads obscured the sight on the platform. Terja knew not to touch the colorless threads this time. He also knew the ritual was far less involved for a single death than for the bodies of most of a village, which had been his first unraveling. That time he and Anan had been recoiling from the death of their families. The first time their magics had worked together—and it had almost killed them both.

The sight before him shifted slightly and Terja could tell it was beginning to wind to a conclusion. The storm rose again, growling and tearing at their clothing.

The frigid wind blinded Terja for a moment, and when he could see again, an empty snowgrazer pelt fluttered between him and Anan. Their eyes met.

"That's never happened before. The unraveling always strips away everything," said Terja.

Anan stepped closer and pulled the pelt toward him. He studied it carefully as the winds built in intensity. Terja walked to his side and stood quietly for a moment.

"Should we leave it?" asked Terja.

"Look. It's clean. None of the—nothing is left. It's spotless."

"Anan, is it safe to take?" asked Terja. When a moment passed and he received no response, he grabbed Anan's shoulder and shook him.

"Anan!"

His twining seemed to break out of whatever held him transfixed. "Yes, it's safe. We need to get to shelter or they won't find our bodies until the spring thaw." He turned to the crowd that had formed; it appeared to be their entire group. "Strap the tents together. Share bedding. This storm will batter us for at least a day before the next one comes from the mountains."

Terja stepped behind him, sensing his twining's concern even as the storm's ferocity sharpened. He leaned close enough that the others would never be able to overhear. "This storm will be one of Iceweaver's most vicious in recent memory."

Anan nodded. "We will focus on surviving."

CHAPTER FIFTEEN

OKA PRESSED a sharp stone against his wrist until it broke the skin and a crimson stream started down his arm. He watched with apathy as his life force drained away, drop by drop by drop.

Gurvan yanked the rock from his fingers and threw it to the opposite side of the tent.

"Stop it, Oka. You are not responsible for the innocent's death. She jumped in the path of your weapons. You cannot be blamed for that."

Oka couldn't gather the will to lift his eyes. "I killed her. I felt the spiritblades feeding on her life forces. I must perform amia to remove the dishonor from my Triad."

"Your life is not forfeit. Your Triad does not require it of you; the Ancients make no such demand of you," Daya said.

The waves of depression overwhelmed Oka. He didn't understand why the other two failed to see that he had no other choice. He could hear the ring of the Ancients' hammer against anvil as they called him to the final forging.

"Give my blades back."

Daya shook his head. "No. I am responsible for your safety, and you would harm yourself."

Oka rolled himself onto the bedding and turned his back to the pair. "Leave me, then. If you are going to prevent me from saving my honor."

There was a period of tense silence before Daya said, "We need more wood for the fire, and there seems to be a lull in the storm."

Daya turned to Oka. "Can I trust you to not harm yourself while we are gone?"

Oka stared at the tent's dark wall, aching for a far darker blackness.

"Oka! Swear to me!"

Oka wiped his mouth on the sleeve of his robe and whispered a reply. "No...."

The worry and concern from the other two was palpable for Oka. But his despair thickened with each heartbeat. He knew his duty, regardless of the feelings of Daya and Gurvan. The ritual of amia would free his Triad from their mating and allow his reforging. The other two were speaking softly to each other. Before the words registered, they turned to him.

"Gurvan is going for firewood while I stay here to watch you. Our Forge will survive this crisis."

Oka sighed, thinking he had almost bought himself the time he needed. But he knew he would never be able to trace the scent of metal quickly enough now to end his life. He wriggled deeper into the bedding without a word.

"I warn you, I will put you in irons if that is what it takes to keep you safe from yourself. This Hammer will not compromise the well-being of his Forge."

Oka waited quietly, wondering what else Daya would say. After time began to stretch interminably, Oka felt the need to explain. "I feel her. They've done their passing ritual, and I still feel her. It's as if she stands beside me, judging."

Daya took a deep breath, knelt beside him, and clasped his shoulder. "We don't know why, but you will always feel each person you send to the final forging. If your Triad is a life bonding, the burden will be shared. That's why you haven't experienced the consequences before. That's also why each Triad is given a limited number of contracts. We can help each other to bear the burden. The forging with the High Regent would have retired our Triad. Now...."

"The girl wasn't in the count. Now we can't fulfill the contract. What will we do? We can't return to the Ubica council with an unfulfilled agreement."

"Gurvan is considering the choices. Typically a Triad would only forge one contract at a time. The Elders agreed to ours because of the circumstances."

"I've heard the punishment for a failed assignment makes the person yearn for death."

Daya cocked an eyebrow and pursed his lips. "Stories younglings tell each other to test their bravery are usually more fable than fact."

"Still, we are on perilous footing."

"We are on unknown footing. Gurvan will take care of it, and we will all return to the warm sunshine, blue waters, and white beaches of our homeland."

Oka glanced toward Daya to find a face locked in an iron façade. Without a word he turned away and began planning.

Xain watched Soja through hooded eyelids as the new captain paced the tent, coiling and uncoiling the whip between his hands. Xain's emotions alternated between fury, desperation, and fear. Their chance of recapturing the escaped Talac was much reduced from when they began. Kosemi's disastrous decision to try to cross the deathspinner colony had taken out a number of the Varas troops. Added to the ones lost to the Talac traps... only around half the troops remained.

The hope of delaying the Talac had resulted in the loss of all the soldiers who'd been sent, with the exception of the Ubica Triad, who were now standing before him and Soja.

"They are close. They couldn't have magically moved themselves somewhere else during the blizzard. We must move quickly," Xain said.

Soja studied him before turning to the Triad. "The storm has passed. We must prepare to march as quickly as possible in pursuit of the slaves. You will not fail the Varas again."

He spun and lashed his whip toward the largest Ubica. The iron fragment at its end flicked across his cheek and left a slowly bleeding cut. The other two tensed but no words came from the trio. "You will do what you were commissioned to do. You will kill the Talac's leaders. Once the ringleaders are fed to the longtooth, the others will easily be rounded up, and you can shackle them with the new Ubica irons you brought."

Gurvan slowly wiped the blood from his face and sucked it off his finger. He fixed a dispassionate stare at Soja. The expressions on the faces of the Ubica chilled Xain. Then Gurvan captured both of them in his gaze. "We will complete the forging created with your High Regent. But know this: we will not fight alongside you against the Talac. We are a Ubica Triad, not hired mercenaries."

"I see no difference. You were hired to help the Varas. Know that," Soja said.

Xain realized Soja was going to get no response to his statement, and seeing the determined expression, he realized this was an argument they weren't going to win. At least the Ubica would deal with the two leaders. Xain would have admitted it to no one, but his fear of the Talac leaders had grown since he'd managed to escape. Last time he'd used a spell he had learned while in the Varas pleasure houses. It had opened a fold in the Great Weaving, allowing Xain to escape. Of course, he'd killed the man after he'd gotten the information, to keep it from others. He had hoped he would never need to use it again. The Talac had told him many times the travelers through the Great Weaving often didn't return.

He became aware of the continued impasse between Soja and the Ubica, realizing he had been drifting in thought. Soja began uncoiling his whip again, but this time Oka took a step toward them with tensed muscles and a hard expression on his face. Soja flicked the braided leather serpent behind him. Xain hoped the Varas leader would not push the Ubica any further.

"What do you need to fulfill your agreement?" Soja asked.

"We have what tools we need. We will follow your troops into the Talac encampment." This time it was Oka speaking. Xain studied him but could read nothing from the man.

"Very well." Soja stepped to the tent flap and tugged it open to speak with the man standing just outside, who was obviously suffering from the cold.

"Sergeant. Pass the word. We will run down the Talac. The first set of troops attack at first light."

"Yes, sir!" The man snapped off a salute, turned, and moved at a sprint toward the row of tents.

A chill of foreboding washed over Xain as the Ubica left Soja's tent and Soja cast a hungry glare at him.

CHAPTER SIXTEEN

THIS TIME there was no doubt. Anan could see the first of the Varas soldiers spilling from the canyons a few fingerwidths of the sun behind them. They'd known the Varas were closing on them for several days. Anan and Terja had chosen this spot to meet them. Although, from what Joven and Soneri could determine in their scouting missions, there were still at least twice as many Varas as Talac, and many of the plainsmen were too injured or weak to fight. But they would battle to the last. He hoped these professional soldiers would retreat if the battle went against them. Anan knew if he was wrong, then their chances of survival were vastly reduced.

"They come."

Anan glanced toward Terja and couldn't keep in a soft chuckle. He was armed with the obsidian-edged shield gifted to him from First Twining, and the bladed staff discovered during their flight to save the Talac who had been taken from the Kuri homelands. The sling with which he was so lethal hung from his belt, along with a pouch of sling pellets. The humor came from the coat Joven had constructed for him. In the light of Terja's lack of velvet, Joven, along with a few others, had covered Terja with a robe made from the snowgrazer's pelt. It was constructed so skillfully that it would not impede his movement at all, but it would keep him far warmer than the velvet of the spellweavers. It also gave him the appearance of a wild animal. Anan hoped the attackers would pause too long and suffer the consequences.

"The groups are ready," Soneri said.

He glanced to find Soneri and Joven standing close. "They're here. Is everyone prepared?"

"Those that are mobile are armed with slings and staff. Ite did a good job of finding weapons in the barrens. Everyone has at least a sling. And...."

"What? We don't have time for secrets."

"No one will surrender. They each have a guardian bush thorn to end their lives if we lose. No one wants to be taken by the Varas again."

Anan sighed deeply. "This may be the last day the sun shines on the Kuri."

"If it is, we will be remembered," Joven said.

"It will be difficult to rebuild a clan with nothing left but memories. I wish at least the injured were continuing the journey."

"To be slaughtered like the herds were when they wiped out the herdweavers?" Joven said.

"I am not their leader. The Kuri are an independent people. If they choose to fight until none are left standing, I can't do anything to stop them."

Terja stepped beside him, shoved his arm into the shield's straps, and shot Anan a determined glare. "Your concern has an easy solution. The Varas must never get past us."

Anan cocked an eyebrow at Terja and then looked at the Varas advancing through the tall grass. It was certain their numbers were greater than the Talac, even if everyone were well. But the soldiers were covering the distance quickly and the time for planning or miracles was gone. He pulled his bow from his shoulder and waited for them to move into range.

Every member of the Varas century carried either a spear or an iron short sword, but several also held crossbows. While they didn't approach the range of either Anan's longbow or the distance possible from those skilled with the sling, they would wreak havoc when they moved close enough.

He and Terja faced the oncoming Varas alone. This time they didn't have the benefit of darkness, and were still outnumbered.

"I'm taking out the lead. They are trying to work up the courage to charge. It should delay them," Terja said.

"The others know to fire when they are certain of their mark. I see no reason the best with the sling should pass up a shot."

Terja pulled out his weapon and dropped one of his pellets into the pouch. He flipped the loaded sling around before releasing it. The dark stone arched through the sharp air and found its mark. The guard's head snapped sideways and he crumpled. A grim satisfaction filled Anan as he watched the closest Varas run to the downed man, who never regained his feet.

"Excellent shot. He won't be fighting us today."

Before there was time for a response, the other Talac launched a volley of stones across the field. The missiles sped toward the Varas for a heartbeat before landing like a swarm of cloudfliers diving for grubs. Many missed, but a surprising number found their mark.

The soldiers rushed forward, but a call from far behind their lines brought them to a stop. Anan could barely hear the commands shouted over the battle cries of the Talac fighters. He had half expected to hear Xain's voice, but the one shouting instructions was clearly a Varas. His rage flared a heartbeat later when he identified Xain standing beside the commander. Anan's anger flamed higher when he saw three darkly clad men moving into the battlefield. The Ubica.

"There are the assassins. How do we draw them to us? I don't want to lose anyone to them because they are hunting us."

"Cut through the Varas like herdweavers on a harvest day. That will get their attention."

"Did you see who leads them?"

Terja nodded. "Another Varas, but Xain is at his side. But I'm less concerned about him than the Triad."

"If it's with my last breath, I will kill the traitor." Anan shared his anger with Terja through their connection. He refocused on the Varas and found they had divided into three groups, and large shields appeared from somewhere. It would be much harder to score on them now with slings. But he knew they had no choice. They must either defeat the Varas, or the Kuri would no longer be one of the Council of Five.

"They're coming," Terja yelled out a warning.

The soldiers screamed with fury and broke into a run toward each of the Talac groups. The hiss of thrown missiles filled the space as Terja delivered one throw after another. Anan wasn't certain what damage had been inflicted, but they had succeeded in getting the soldiers' attention. Now it was Anan's turn to thin the attackers. He drew his ironwood bow and let the first arrow fly. It split the wooden shield being held by a soldier and buried itself to the fletching in his chest. There was a moment of disbelief on his face before he pitched to the ground.

He quickly released several more arrows, each one ending the life of a charging Varas.

"It's us and them now."

Anan felt Terja's love flow through him as he stepped beside him with shield tightly tied in place and his bladed staff ready. The lead Varas came too close and Terja moved in harmony with the man's frantic motions. An instant later the soldier fell back, his throat sliced from ear to ear.

Two soldiers raced at Anan, spears held low. Anan stepped toward the closest and drove the obsidian shards lining his sword into the man. The blade buried itself in the Varas's chest. As the body fell, Anan grabbed the spear, spun, and embedded it in the other soldier's chest. Feeling a presence behind him, Anan spun, the sword clearing a path. It came to a sudden halt, wedged against the largest iron sword he'd ever seen, wielded by a huge Varas.

The man ripped the blade free with a growl, his foul stench filling the air. "I'll enjoy your pelt, Talac. I've used your kind before, in the pits."

Anan growled at the thought of the Talac who ended their lives in the worst Varas sex houses. He swung the obsidian-embedded sword and met the iron blade in midair. With each blow he lost some of the sharp, but fragile, blades creating the sword's edge. *I have to find another way to overcome this attacker.*

The Varas stepped forward in an overhand blow with enough power behind it to slice Anan in half. On instinct, Anan jumped just as the Varas shifted the directions of his sword swipe, and missed the blade by a fingerwidth. Had Anan been one heartbeat slower, he would have been gutted. But a searing pain came from his leg injuries, warning him that he had few moves of that type left in his arsenal.

The soldier left the back of his neck unguarded as he spun from the force of his own attack. Anan's injuries screamed out as he turned and sank the warriorglass sword in deeply, almost cutting through the man's neck. Thick muscle gripped at the blade, resisting its release. An instant later, Anan wrenched it free, and the still twitching body of the Varas hit the ground.

What he saw made his blood run cold. One Ubica battled Terja, while the other wielded a war hammer in an exchange of blows with Joven and Soneri.

He spun to where he'd dropped his bow and quiver, cursing to find only one arrow remained. Then he saw the third Ubica, standing a few spans away, intently studying Anan. He recognized the man. He was Morea's killer. Even if it cost him his life, he would take this man into the Great Weaving with him.

He drew the arrow, taking a moment to aim, and released the shaft. The Ubica never moved as the missile sped toward his chest. A glow came to the Ubica's eyes when at the last instant he stepped aside and snatched the arrow from midair.

Anan felt defeated. He'd missed. He had not kept his promise to avenge Morea. Then he realized the man still hadn't moved, other than a faint swaying. As the battle raged, around Anan a new tableau played out. One that was strange and unbelievable. The Ubica's eyes glowed as if a fire burned inside. He gripped the arrow with a manic expression on his face and plunged it into the middle of his own gut.

Anan was immobilized with shock. The man had relegated himself to a long painful death as his body poisoned itself. He reeled from what he just witnessed. The instant the arrow entered the Ubica's body, the others dropped their attacks and dashed to their fallen Triad member. The sword bearer lifted the wounded Ubica into his arms, and with no pause set off. The third man cleared their path through the skirmish…. Neither seemed to care about either Varas or Talac fighters, so long as they did not impede their sprint off the battlefield.

The Ubica's retreat seemed to demoralize the Varas troops. The captain had directed his soldiers from behind the battle and he held their line for a short period of time, but without the Ubica his troops gave way, step by step. When Soneri and Joven rushed the few holding their position, they folded. Anan couldn't imagine what was happening, but was relieved when the Varas soldiers broke formation and fled.

"What happened? Why did they leave? I don't know how much longer we could have held out," Terja said as he stepped beside Anan.

"He caught my arrow. He was safe. I didn't even have another. Then he stabbed himself with it. Why? I don't understand," Anan muttered.

Terja glanced at him with a confused expression. "What are you talking about? I was fighting the swordsman, and I was hard-pressed to stay alive. Then he ran."

"Ours did the same. He held his own with the two of us, then he just sprinted away," said Soneri.

Anan tried to explain. "The thin one. The one who killed Morea. I saw him, and shot. He caught my arrow, then stabbed himself in the stomach with it. The others raced to him."

"I've heard of a tradition of saving your honor by killing yourself with the Ubica. But I know no more," Soneri said.

Anan nodded slowly, absorbing Soneri's words. But after a moment of consideration, he still wasn't certain what happened. The entire situation left him confused. From the expressions on the faces of the others, they had no more sense of what had happened than he did.

The wind whipped around them, blanking out anything more than a few brief steps away. The cold burned through Anan, and the feeling of foreboding grew with each tendril of cold that cut through him. This he knew intimately, as did anyone who had grown up in Talac lands. This was their savior, and greatest enemy. He turned to the people who had congregated around him.

"Iceweaver is coming. We need everyone in shelter and to care for our dead."

OKA LAY quietly in the tent, the unbelievable pain washing over him in wave after wave. The reek of bowel that filled the tent was a testament to his success. He had sought death, and found it. He had no choice but to lie quietly with Daya watching him more closely than a prairie glider watches the unaware springtail. He'd tried to finish the amia, but the Triad stopped him each time. Now his body had weakened to the point where he couldn't resist them any longer. But though they weren't letting him complete the formal amia, he knew he wasn't much longer for this forging. The blood seeping into his robe slowly leached the life from him and he could sense the Triad bond fading. The cold penetrated every part of his being, even through the layers of bedding he was covered with.

"He's fading. What're we going to do?" Daya asked.

"I don't know. It's fatal and he would already be with the Ancients if he'd had another moment."

"You know I should have been allowed amia to save the honor of the Triad," Oka said.

Gurvan spun on him and bellowed, "You are part of our Triad! We treasure you. We will have you live or both of us will die in the attempt."

Startled, Oka glanced first at one and then the other. "I've killed an innocent. The Ancients decreed I must die for the good of my Triad."

Daya shook as he turned on Oka. "You are not listening. We refuse your petition. We will find a way to heal you."

Oka's eyes fluttered shut as a faint whisper came from him. "It's too late."

OKA WOKE and gasped as a new level of pain lanced through him. Once he could think past the agony, he realized they were outside. He was rolled in a blanket, with Daya and Gurvan carrying him down a narrow canyon. When another stumble from them left him roiling in pain, he gasped out, "What are you doing? Why are we out in this weather?"

There was no response other than increasingly heavy breathing as they wound their way deeper into the maze. They finally slowed and laid him carefully on a slightly raised flat stone. He watched, unable to do much else as his strength became less with each beat of his heart. Daya and Gurvan moved close to him and began a ritual that Oka recognized even in his pain-filled daze. "By the Master Smith, what are you doing?" Oka asked.

"Calling the Ancients."

Oka tried to sit up in shock at Daya's words. He collapsed as a result of his attempt, gasping for breath. He slipped from consciousness, and when he drifted back it was to the heat and scent of a forge. He could taste the coal dust drifting up from the floor beside his nostrils. For a moment, he felt like a youngling in his father's smithy. But this one seemed to have no boundaries.

"Is this the forge of the Ancients? Have I died?"

Before he could think any further, the largest smith he'd ever seen stepped through the smoke and haze. Heat-worn leather covered him from waist to foot and his bare upper torso and arms rippled with muscle. Daya and Gurvan both dropped to their knees before his gaze came to rest on Oka. The studied examination made Oka want to crawl onto his stomach in reverence too. The man's eyes glowed with the heat of the deepest coals, where iron is either tempered or burned away. He lay quietly as the man knelt beside him and held a hand over his wound.

After a moment or two he began speaking, and with each word Oka heard the ring of hammer on anvil. "You have little time left, youngling. But I sense you would prefer that. Your Triad is trying to save you, but you refuse the gift. Sadly, if you had let them try, I do not believe they would have succeeded."

There was a pause with more tension than the testing blow of a long sword.

"And I will not."

Oka heard what sounded like a choked sob, or perhaps a gasp. Regardless, he was too tired to care. Even yet, the next words spoken shocked him.

"But your enemies can."

Oka snapped his eyes open to look into the depths of fire staring back at him. Even in his disbelief, he could only manage a whisper. "I killed an innocent, a daughter of the Talac, and you would have me ask them for a healing? Amia would be unneeded."

"Perhaps, perhaps not. Think beyond the moment. Is there something they want more than your death?"

Oka glanced at the others, and he could feel the mixture of awe and reverence filling them. "The gods of the Talac are not demanding retribution. If you are spared, then perhaps what your Triad tells you is true. The death was not your fault. Also, tonight are the obsidian moons, when coal is harvested for the most sacred rituals. From the utter darkness comes the hottest fires. This time is also seen as holy by the Talac. Their weaving is particularly strong in the darkness of the twins."

The smith studied the blood-encrusted wound in Oka's stomach. "You will not live to talk with the Talac as you are now. The Ancients will let me extend your time."

The smith reached down, one hand on either side of the arrow shaft. Suddenly it was as if two red-hot pieces of iron were shoved inside the wound. Oka screamed as darkness enveloped him.

TERJA SAT in the bitter cold, looking toward the night sky and the points of light that filled it. The stories of the obsidian moons had frightened him since he was a tiny kit. They hadn't lost anyone today, but the only uninjured left were he and Anan, along with Soneri, Joven, and Ite. The others would fight tomorrow—Terja was certain it would be tomorrow—but they would be cut down by the Varas troops and the Ubica.

"They will survive. The Kuri will return to their homelands. Our people can live through more than they realize," Soneri said.

His deep voice resonated through Terja but he lacked the will to turn. "There are many more of them than us. Helpless Talac will be killed."

Terja could almost feel Soneri's head shake. But he continued. "Our odds are better than the two of you against the slavers. We saved almost everyone."

Terja nodded toward the darkening sky. "The dark moons have aligned. They foretell a major change in the lives of the Talac. It's also thought to give spellweavers exceptional healing abilities. But our Elders were not born yet when the last obsidian moons occurred. What if the gods have left us? They took Morea from us."

"Losing Morea has been horrible. I miss her deeply. If it weren't for her, I wouldn't have survived the slavers. But we are not kit's toys for the gods. We make our own choices and the weaving goes on," Soneri said.

They stood and watched as the moons slid slowly over each other until only a single pale disc stood in the sky. Then the moons began to be eaten by the circle of darkness that formed the most feared part of the black moons. Terja's pulse pounded in his ears; the light dimmed. As the moons were devoured, Terja's anxiety grew. The light was a thin crescent blade when Anan seemed to materialize at his side. Terja found comfort in Anan's firm squeeze.

"It won't last long. No great change is prophesied."

"Anan, I know you are probably right, but I can't help but worry. I was raised that way."

The slice of light vanished and an involuntary gasp escaped Terja. It was as dark as the depths of a cave. The pinpoints of light he had admired earlier did little to illuminate his surroundings.

"Talac. The Ubica Triad stands close. We come for a peace forging."

Terja swung his staff and shield into place, but then stopped. Other than faint scrapings he couldn't identify, there was no way to tell which sounds were Anan and Soneri, and which the Ubica. A full Triad. But they said they were weaving a peace.

Anan began to speak. Terja oftentimes forgot the power Anan could weave into his words, if he so chose. He was twisting wisps of matama into his voice.

"Why are you here, Ubica? You are our enemies, and have sold your place in the Great Weaving for iron from the Varas. Why should we trust the word of assassins?"

The silence became deafening as Terja and the other Talac waited for a reply. Terja began to wonder if they had disappeared into the darkness when a different voice came to them.

"Our Forge is dying. He has little time. Without him...." The speaker's voice caught. "Without him our Triad is no more."

A hard edge filled Anan's voice. "The knife thrower? Are you thinking to request our skills of spellweaving to save him?"

"Yes, Talac. Oka is our Forge, and as such is an expert on throwing weapons. We plead with you to save him."

Anan's tone turned to ice. "He killed a precious friend of mine. I hope his death is lingering and painful."

Harsh laughter filled the air around them, chilling Terja. "I told you I should die. I killed the innocent and you stopped me from finishing amia. You even tried to have the Ancients heal me. It is time for my death. My actions will break the forging between us. Let me die. The Elders will assign another Forge."

The original Ubica spoke again. Only this time it was obviously aimed at their dying companion. "You foolish man! We were the ones who invited you to share the forging between us. We love you. There will be no replacement Forge and no breaking of our forging. This has nothing to do with fulfilling our contract with the Varas. This is about saving your stubborn self."

Terja caught a thread from the conversation. "What does he mean, he killed an innocent? What's he talking about?"

"The Ancients decreed no innocents could be killed by a Triad under punishment of amia. Oka killed the girl. But she wasn't his target. Now he feels his life is forfeit."

Terja glanced at Anan, feeling the rage barely below the surface from his twining. But his mind began to spin together another thread, one that might help them survive.

"What would you give us in exchange for a healing?"

He knew his words were fanning the flames already roaring inside Anan. But he felt this was the right weave. The silence lasted only an instant.

"We would void the contract. The Talac would not need worry about a Ubica Triad for a generation."

"And who are you to make such a statement?"

"I am Gurvan, son of a senior Elder of the Ubica. I would swear it on all the smiths in my family's lineage."

"That's their most sacred oath," Soneri said.

Terja wasn't certain why, but he was comforted by Soneri's words. He turned to Anan. "We have to try and heal him. Think how many Talac lives we might save over the course of a generation."

Anan lowered his voice to a bare whisper. "There is no deathspinner fiber left. I don't know what I can do for him."

Terja tugged the thick snowgrazer pelt around him, brushing the hairs away from his skin where they seemed to want to adhere as he considered their predicament. Finally he shrugged. While they had been talking, the moons had moved, and the time before they reappeared was short. Without the dark weaving of the obsidian moons, even he and Anan might be unable to save the Ubica.

"If we save him, how many Talac will live? Morea would not thank us for misusing her sacrifice."

Shock filled Anan's face as the full request sank into his thoughts. "You want me to heal him?"

"I would have the Kuri back as a clan. Without the Ubica hunting us, we have a chance."

Darkness settled on Anan, and Terja wasn't certain how his twining was going to react. His eyes hardened as he stared at the dark silhouettes of the Ubica. "Bring him closer."

THE ASSASSINS acted quickly, moving their mate to just in front of Anan. His expression never shifted as he knelt beside the dying man. His anger and hatred of the man before him made it impossible to focus on the weaving. His hands trembled as he worked to control his emotions. He couldn't move past hearing Morea's last breath as he held her. *How can I dishonor her memory by healing the Ubica?* He tried several times with no success before a firm hand squeezed his shoulder.

"You can do this, and you know time is running short. The moons will soon reappear. What would Morea tell you if she could?" Before Anan could answer, he heard the thin tinkling of dewclaw rattles of the kind Morea loved to wear. Without answering Terja, he knew the answer. This time when he tried to relax, the spellsight slipped into place without a moment's hesitation.

He followed the strands running through the man's body in front of him and was amazed that he still lived. He had done an impressive amount of damage to himself with one strike from an arrow.

His bowel was punctured in at least a fingercount of places and the results had spread the poison through the rest of his body. In addition, his lungs were damaged too. The dark strands of wound poison wove their way through his body. The deadly fabric was woven through most of the Ubica's system. Anan spent a moment more surveying the extent of the damage before withdrawing his awareness with a shake of his head.

"I don't know how he lives. Wound poison is woven through his entire body. Even if I had a kilt filled with matama, I don't know if I could save him, and we have no matama."

Terja said, "Is there something I can spin closed?"

"No, the threads of poison fill his body. As I said, he should not be alive."

"The Ancients granted him enough time to get to you."

Anan turned to see the comment had come from one of the Ubica. "The Ancients?"

"Yes, the Triad of Ancients who created the world for the Ubica. They sent the Ancient Forge at our call. They said to come to you. Oh, they also said to give you this, that it was the forging you needed."

Anan took the small fur the Ubica offered him. He turned it in his hand, amazed at its softness and the quality of its creation. It took him a moment to realize it was from a snowgrazer. He peered at the man who had given it to him. "Why do you have a snowgrazer pelt? They are animals of the far north, many days from the Ubica lands."

"We found it after the Ancient Forge left. Both Daya and I felt it should be brought to you. We know nothing further about it."

"Why would we need this? It's amazing craftsmanship, but what we need is deathspinner fiber."

Anan stroked the pelt, enjoying its silky texture as his mind searched for a pattern. He lifted his fingers to find them coated with long hairs that seemed to be fighting to flow toward Terja. The tapestry snapped into place. He tossed the pelt to Terja.

"Spin the matama using the fiber from the snowgrazer."

"What? It can't be done. Only—"

"Terja, please. Try. If we fail, we have lost nothing. If we save him, then you're right. The Kuri have a chance at survival that I hadn't envisioned before."

Terja hesitated for a moment, but then he began spinning. It took a few heartbeats as if he wasn't certain what type of fiber he used. But the thread he spun was wonderfully strong. The smile crept across Anan's face as he saw the white fiber of the snowgrazer turn delightful shades of blue, and more importantly, the green this healing needed. Once there were a few more lengths of thread, Anan began his weaving.

Taking the delicate threads, he ran the strands of fiber back and forth in a fine web that drifted across the prone Ubica. They worked quickly together, with Terja feeding him a seemingly unending supply of matama-embedded threads. In a weaving where he had no choice other than to use it as it came, Anan still thought he could use the multitude of colors.

His hands faltered as he noticed the pure tones becoming grayed. He glanced at Terja. "What's happening to the matama?"

"I used up all the Talac matama. I had to use from the Ubica. I think the obsidian moons are also changing the matama. I can feel them fulfilling my need."

"Our tones will be tinted with the iron from our forges," Gurvan said.

Anan glanced toward the Ubica who was speaking. "What do you know of this? Is your matama dangerous to us?"

"The Ancients forged the Ubica from iron freshly taken from the earth. We are a mixture of strong iron and the elements. The ore of our being will not cause you harm."

Anan glanced at Terja, who replied, "I believe him. If he is wrong, it is their mating who will die."

"We are not wrong."

Anan studied the muscular Ubica again before returning to his weaving. The muted tones of the grayed matama darkened the corner of the webbing, but otherwise Anan could sense no problem. The man barely remained alive. Anan could sense him only through his spellsight.

With a mental flick, he released the gossamer weaving. The matama disappeared into his dusky skin, with the weave wrapping itself around the dark areas inside him. The snowgrazer fiber didn't behave like the silk from the deathspinners, and Anan had to be constantly vigilant to keep the threads true and square. This healing wouldn't survive the slightest flaw in his weaving.

That was Anan's last extraneous thought as he focused on the healing he wove. He forgot who lay below him as he entered the man's system. The matama wrapped itself around the dark threads that filled his body and slowly constricted until the matama and the wound poison blinked out of existence. Time stood still as he struggled with the new fibers and the ore-dusted matama, forcing them to conform to the healing he'd woven. The weaving cleared the toxin, but the healing was not progressing fast enough for Anan. As he began to struggle to control the power, a flood of matama flowed into him from Terja.

He sent a wash of thanks to his twining, then redoubled his efforts. The Ubica's color returned to normal as Anan worked on the most serious of the wounds in his abdomen. Now he closed the damaged tissue. The pockets of infection were quickly extinguished and the wounds woven shut. He could sense the healthy tissue restoring itself. As he neared the surface, he paused for a moment and considered creating a trap like Xain had made inside Joven when he had "healed" the young Talac. When the trap sprung, Joven had almost managed to kill Anan. He would have succeeded if it were not for Terja, and the trap had still managed to severely injure Anan.

But the thought of doing the same to the Ubica passed quickly. They had an agreement, and he had no intentions of compromising his integrity. With a twist, he sealed the last seeping injury and left the healing. He knelt at the man's side as the last vapors of the healing drifted above the skin like a fall morning's fog over the grasslands. He waited, but after a moment he could see that the Ubica still barely lived. He turned to Terja.

"We need more matama. I can't eliminate the last bits of poison. He should be awake, but instead his breathing and heart are no better."

"We have no more. Even with the Ubica matama, we had little before we began. I have no place to accumulate matama."

"We have more. A tiny bit," said Soneri.

Anan turned to him. "Where? How do you know of more matama?"

Soneri smiled slightly. "You and Terja were more focused on other things. It's matama from the deathspinner poison from your leg."

Terja looked stunned. Then his expression changed to one of intensity. He dug through his pouch and pulled out the puff of fiber with its multicolored edge. Without a word Terja spun it and passed the thread to Anan.

Anan studied it for a moment before turning to the intent Ubica. "I don't know what this might do. It could kill him."

They studied each other and then turned to Anan. "We cannot save him. Do what you can."

Anan wove a strange web that seemed natural, with the color combinations from the new matama. He released the spell and it disappeared almost immediately.

A heartbeat later the final islands of darkness in the poisoned man disappeared. Rocking on his heels, Anan studied the now resting man before him. Only a moment passed before his eyes fluttered open.

The young Ubica met his gaze and Anan barely kept himself from lunging away. His eyes burned with an amber flame, and a faint glow from his skin created a light around him. Anan felt as if he could hear the crackle of coal in the forge. Then he watched as a crystalline tear formed in each eye to slowly cut its way across the man's cheek as they watched each other. The Ubica's tongue slipped out and moistened his lips.

"Why?"

Anan glanced at the other Ubica. "What is he asking?"

"He doesn't understand why you saved him."

He hardened as he turned back to the Ubica, who had not moved from his spot on the cold ground. "It was not out of some mercy for you. You killed my friend, and for that I can never forgive you. But your twining said she was not your target, and you regretted her death. Beyond that, they gave us their word that the Talac will not be a target of the Ubica for a generation. My people have lost almost everything. Safety

169

from attack sounds like a thick woven blanket during a cold Iceweaver storm. Saving my people—that is the reason you still live."

The man's eyes flamed even brighter, and Anan fought the need to look away. In a moment the flames quenched in his eyes, and the glow left his skin. The Ubica began to speak.

"I am known as Oka. These are my Triad mates Gurvan and Daya. I will improve on their pledge. Our descendants will protect the Kuri clan of the Talac for so long as the Holy Triad fills the skies, Hammer and Anvil at night and Forge during the day."

Anan's jaw dropped at what had just been pledged. In the stories of the Kuri, there had never been a time when they were not attacked and enslaved by the Varas. That this could be stopped was—impossible.

"This is not something you have the ability to give us. These are our homelands, and we have faced the Varas over and over again. How would you stop them?"

"There are ways. The Ubica have a network of Triads through the lands north of the great waters. Our Triads are prolific too." His mouth quirked. "The Ubica like a challenge. Keeping a forging for the rest of time will be a suitable one."

Anan's mouth opened and closed several times before it shut and stayed that way. He turned to Terja, who nodded in return. He could feel relief travel between them. But before he could reply, Gurvan began to speak.

"We support our mate in his change of our agreement, but we also must tell you. We cannot help you defeat the Varas who close with you now. We cannot break that contract by helping you escape. We will leave, denying them our help, but that is the most we can do."

Anan was shocked when he heard Terja's soft chuckle. Their gazes met, and he could sense the warmth of victory through their connection. Terja turned to the Ubica. "Having the three most lethal fighters removed from the battle against us would be a boon. But they won't let you leave, will they? Xain knows your contract, doesn't he? He will call what he feels is due."

This time, smug laughter came from the Ubica identified as Daya. "We have no intention of going to the Varas encampment. Gurvan and I have packs with what we need to begin the trip back to our homeland.

We have no intention of giving the Varas an opportunity to claim debt. Our Triad was warned by the Elders to prepare a retreat path as we moved into this cold wasteland you seem to love. We can get to our first cache by nightfall." He looked at Oka. When their eyes met, Anan was shocked to sense the love passing between the two. Gurvan joined the pair and their mating bond was obvious. He'd never expected this experience from a Ubica Triad. But the love and devotion between the trio was unmistakable. He realized Gurvan was still speaking.

"But now that you have healed our Forge, we can move quickly. We wish to be away from these gods-forsaken barrens before the winter rains come to our home."

Anan's tongue flicked to his lips, tasting a bit of iron dust from the Ubica matama he had woven. The metallic taint reminded him of the taste of blood, and memories flooded him. After a moment he turned a baleful eye to Oka.

"I saved you. You've made a pledge to my descendants and me so long as the twining moons are in the sky. But if I see you again, I cannot guarantee my reaction."

Oka uncoiled from the ground with more grace than a longtooth in full mating dance. He stepped closer to Anan, and then, before he could react, the Ubica had grabbed his hand tightly and rammed a throwing spike through both their hands. Somehow Anan knew this was not an attack, but what it was, he wasn't certain. The pain was excruciating, but he refused to release his grip. A moment later, the Ubica reached down, yanked out the spike, and ran his tongue over it. Their gazes met and the weapon disappeared into his topknot.

"We are now bonded. I cannot harm you."

Anan gripped his hand tightly as the blood slowly dripped from the wound. He was shocked at the act, but strangely comforted too. A few heartbeats later he looked at his hand and found the injury was healed and the pain had stopped. His mouth dropped open and he looked at the Ubica.

He was met with a smile. Silently Oka turned and disappeared into the darkness. The other two nodded first to Anan and then to Terja before following.

CHAPTER SEVENTEEN

ANAN STRAINED to see through the thickening snow that had been falling since the deep gray of predawn. They had moved to the top of the highest butte to watch, but since he could see nothing past the ends of his fingers, it did little good. He knew the Varas soldiers were close, but he became frustrated when he couldn't find them. His bow was ready, the arrow nocked. Each action had to count toward victory. The Talac would fight until their last breath. He didn't believe the Varas guard had the same level of dedication.

"Can you sense them?"

He shook his head and answered Terja softly. "Nothing. But they have to be close. The snow seems odd too. It changes direction and speed with each breath. Perhaps it's blocking the threads I wove to find them. But this is too perfect for their attack." He tilted his head toward Terja. "Are you ready?"

"I have my sling if I get a chance to use it. But I think Iceweaver is decreeing a battle where we see the faces of our foes."

A gust of wind howled past, and Anan was challenged to see his hand before his face. A few heartbeats later the wind eased, and he could see Terja, but no more. The restricted sight left Anan with even more concern about their enemies. If the Varas timed it correctly, they could overtake the Talac before they could respond. The five of them had to stop the Varas. Anan expected the best they could do was sacrifice themselves to buy the others time.

Anan stripped more matama from the threads of snowgrazer fiber braided around his wrist and sent a searching pulse through the web he had erected to detect the Varas. Then he felt another surge of energies flowing into his guardian web, this time from Terja. With his help, the web surged farther than Anan could have pushed it alone. A moment later every nerve in his body told him the news he'd been dreading. The

172

Varas had arrived. The world seemed to slow around him as a multitude of decisions were made in a beat of his heart.

He turned to Terja with a grim expression. "They are closing quickly and we are outnumbered. Alert the others. Even in this storm they will find us." Anan pulled Terja in for a quick kiss. "I hope our twining survives."

"As do I."

He was surprised when Terja grabbed him again and pulled him into a passionate kiss that left Anan gasping. Terja clasped Anan's face between his hands and their gazes locked.

"I love you, Anan. Even if we are both destined for the Great Weaving today, our love will go on."

Anan's throat tightened as the words penetrated his being. *He said he loved me.* He turned to Terja with a shake of his head. "You have the worst timing."

Terja flashed him a smile before turning to disappear into the storm.

Anan's emotions tore through him far too quickly to categorize. But then a rush of warning flooded his body as the Varas boiled onto the flat ground between canyons to overwhelm the outnumbered Talac. He braced himself to hear and feel the first impact of body against body, but his focus was on finding Xain. Anan knew the traitor must be killed, but he wasn't certain how much power the man held. Xain was a spellweaver. He should have none of his stolen matama remaining. But Anan couldn't be certain. *Perhaps Xain drains our spell panels even now.* But all that remained was in snowgrazer fiber, not deathspinner. It did not behave the same. Perhaps he couldn't steal from snowgrazer-blended matama. The last time they had clashed, the man had escaped when Anan had thought it impossible. He silently whispered a prayer of good hunting before bringing all his energy to search for the man he wanted dead more than any other.

When he did, it happened with amazing brevity. One instant the snow was blowing thick, gathering on Anan's exposed velvet, and in the next it cleared and Xain stood before him. In one smooth motion, Anan drew the arrow to his cheek and then released the feather-tufted shaft.

As it hissed past his ear, Anan's worst nightmare happened. There was a far too familiar twisting of the air between them. A choking cry escaped Anan's lips as Xain disappeared as he had in their initial confrontation. The arrow cut through empty space. *He's found a way to steal matama from the snowgrazer fiber.*

But Anan had no time for regrets as two of the High Regent's guards bore down on him. One wielded an iron-tipped spear and the other a short sword. From the expressions on their faces, they expected to overcome him with little problem. Anan grabbed his warriorglass dagger in one hand and the obsidian-edged sword in the other and released himself to his battle weaving.

The spear bearer lunged, thrusting with his weapon.

Anan stepped in and pivoted around the deadly strike. He swung back in a vicious arc with the dagger, managing a shallow cut across the Varas's face. Out of pure instinct, Anan spun and blocked the other guard's sword strike.

The two soldiers synchronized their movements and attacked Anan at the same instant. He leapt toward the sword wielder with a lethal upward swing that ripped him open from groin to neck. The iron sword slipped from the man's hand as he fell with a gurgling cry. Anan yanked his sword free and dropped to one side as the tip of the spear left a bleeding score across his own chest. But to Anan's salvation, the other man overextended himself in his attack, and Anan took advantage of the opening he left.

Anan blocked out the sounds of fighting around him and focused only on the single foe. He pivoted, swung his sword in a backward arc, and felt it bite. The teeth of obsidian sank deep into the Varas's neck and shoulder. A scream of pain echoed through the snow-covered terrain.

He jerked the blade free. The attacker pitched forward as Anan stood on the defense. The soldier fell to the ground, jerked once, and slumped into the snow.

Anan surveyed the battles around him. Soneri, Ite, and Joven held their own against the Varas. Terja was down to a single assailant, but the man was a match for his bladed staff.

He sprinted toward Terja when the air around him rippled in that achingly familiar way, causing Anan's chest to knot. He crouched low, trying to spot where Xain would appear. A searing pain in his thigh answered his question. He fell to one knee and turned to the man.

"Your time is over, weaver." Xain glared at Anan.

As Xain aimed the crossbow, Anan rolled to one side, his dagger ready, and flung it at the man. There was a blast of fury and the familiar ripple, as Xain again used the fold to disappear.

He lay gasping for air, waiting to be struck down. But the pain lessened as he waited for another attack from Xain.

Able to focus on his injury, he looked down to see a throwing spike buried halfway into his thigh. His fingers drifted to the strands left on the snowgrazer cordage around his wrist. *Do I have enough? Are others in more desperate need?*

His question became irrelevant when he heard a gasping yell he recognized as Terja. He sealed the blood vessels that had been severed by the spike and then yanked it from his leg. The pain left him blinded for an instant as he fought to stay conscious. But a moment later, battle fury numbed him and he staggered toward the indistinct shape he recognized as Terja.

Time seemed to have stopped for him as he struggled to reach his twining. The spellspinner was tiring as the Varas sergeant hammered against Terja's shield. Terja was struggling to keep him at bay with his bladed staff. Anan knew he didn't dare shout encouragement, but he could, and did, send it through their twining connection. He sensed a feeling of relief and became more determined to reach his mate.

He followed the sensations as the snow thickened again. With the winds whirling around him, he spotted Terja. He used the last of the matama to block the pain. He would pay later when it echoed back at him. But he had to live long enough to pay that debt, and right now he needed full use of his limbs. The cool numbing of his injuries allowed Anan to focus on helping.

Anan gripped his sword with both hands and raced at Terja's attacker. His first blow was deflected, but Terja stepped forward, creating an offensive pattern with his blade his father taught him years before. His skill was shown again as the obsidian tip buried itself deep in the Varas's shoulder. But when Terja yanked backward, the dark blade broke in half.

With a wild scream of pain and a berserker's fervor, the sergeant lunged at Terja, who backpedaled, fighting to escape. Anan lunged, ready to help his twining. His body moved of its own volition, countless days of practice letting him function automatically. He had almost reached them when Terja pitched back, losing the grip on his bladed staff. Terja crawled to retrieve the damaged weapon, trying for something against the Varas. Anan didn't see how he could escape.

In desperation he stopped, drew back his sword with a double-handed grip, and threw it at the Varas with as much strength as he could muster. Anan hoped it would delay the man for a moment.

The black glass-lined weapon sliced through the thickening snow as Anan raced forward. The weapon struck with a wet thud and a bellowed scream.

Terja retrieved his staff and with a deft motion sliced the broken blade across the Varas's throat. The man's hands flew to his ruined neck as the last of his life pumped between his fingers. A moment later he fell to the ground.

He turned to see who else needed help and was shocked to see the Varas retreating into the heavy snow. Their captain seemed to be calling them away from the battlefield. Terja moved beside him as the last short figures disappeared into the gathering storm. He started to relax.

"Don't move. Not a breath. Nothing. Or one of you will die from the Ubica poison on this arrow. No amount of your healing will save you."

Anan's muscles knotted at the voice he recognized all too easily. Xain.

"You can only kill one of us. The other will take your life easily enough."

A menacing chuckle filled the space between them. "I will disappear, and this time you'll never know where I will appear again." Xain tossed two pairs of manacles toward them. "Put them on. I had these specially made for you two. It cost me a fortune from those thieving Ubica."

He pointed toward the black shapes with his chin. "Pick them up now or one of you will be dying in the other's arms."

With his eyes locked on Xain, Anan picked up one of the cold metal rings. His fears were instantly confirmed. The sinister darkness absorbed any weaving he sent at it. He had no chance of unweaving these pieces of iron.

Xain motioned with the crossbow, almost growling at Anan this time. "Talac! You are trying my patience. Do as I say, or you will be another rotting carcass in this gods-forsaken place."

Anan moved imperceptibly to shield Terja from the arrow aimed at them. He knew he had a fingercount of heartbeats left in this life.

Neither of them would allow themselves to be taken alive, back to the Varas homelands. Better to be sent to the Great Weaving. Terja tried to fight him as he wove his last battle tapestry through their connection. He could almost feel the sobs, and he could not have said whom they originated from. Perhaps both of them.

He turned to Xain prepared for his end.

"Foolish Talac."

The sound of metal against wood filled Anan's ears as Xain started to pull the trigger.

Xain jerked upward, launching the quarrel into the darkening sky.

A dark shape grabbed Xain from behind, slapped a hand over the traitor's mouth, and then sliced into his throat, coating the ground with crimson. It held the struggling man until he stopped thrashing. The body dropped to the ground.

Anan and Terja stood together to face this new threat.

The snow and wind danced in an ever thickening weaving, but the dark shape moved closer with each heartbeat. Then Anan realized that the form standing before them was the Ubica he'd saved. Oka moved within touching distance, casually cleaning the blade of his knife. He hid it in the folds of his clothing so quickly Anan had no idea where the blade had been stored. A smile crept across his face as he looked at Anan and Terja.

"I told you my oath was good. I and mine will guard the Kuri clan until the last forge goes cold."

Anan frowned. "But you said you couldn't break your contract with the High Regent. You also said your Triad was leaving for the Ubica homelands."

The other three joined them as Oka's smile broadened even further. "Ah, that is not an issue. Xain was under contract by the High Regent. He was never to return to the Varas courts. So I fulfilled the final layers of our contract. We returned because I convinced my Triad this would complete our tempering."

Anan considered the Ubica's words and realized the implications. "Xain was one of your targets."

"He was," Oka said. "The High Regent was adamant he never set foot along the great river again."

"You've bought us time. It will take the Varas a few days to regroup and continue the chase," Anan said.

Anan nodded slowly as the others joined them. They were all still moving without help, but some were at the last of their threads. He turned to Oka, carefully schooling his conflicting emotions.

"What is your name? Your real name," Anan asked.

The Ubica's smile grew even wider. "We have no compulsions against sharing our names. We do not believe they hold special power over us. As you know, I am Oka." He motioned to the other Ubica who had appeared. "My Triad mates are Gurvan and Daya." Oka smiled in a way that unnerved Anan. "Daya has news you will appreciate."

One of the other Ubica nodded. "The Varas have all retreated. It would seem the guardians of the plains were more than they wanted today."

Oka paused for a moment, pulled the hood of his robe tighter, and met the gazes of the men in front of him. The wind whistled around them and the Ubica began to talk again. "If you want to know something the Ubica would rather you didn't, ask us. Each Triad has three people, one for each of the Ancients: a Forge, Hammer, and Anvil. If you want to destroy an entire mated Triad, kill the Forge."

Anan studied him for a moment, then asked. "Who is the Forge for your Triad?"

"I am."

"So if we were to kill you…."

"Gurvan and Daya would die. Our Triad is forged by mating. I had a Triad before and lost both Hammer and Anvil. But we were not mated, so I survived their passing as Gurvan and Daya lived past their untempered bond with their Forge. One additional detail, a Forge who commits amia releases his Triad from the mating bond so they could find a new Forge."

"Where would they find someone like that?"

"Only in our homeland. Each Forge is trained from birth to control the fire within. They are the only ones who can kill in that way."

Terja shook a little as he watched the dark-skinned man. "So you could kill us all by looking at us?"

"It is not that easy. It takes time to build a killing fire, which is almost impossible to do in a battle. If I were to start now, you would likely slay me first. If I were to release the fire, I would be exhausted for days afterwards. It's a weapon only used in desperation."

Oka first met Anan's gaze and then Terja's. "You now know the fatal flaw in the Ubica Triads. As I said, the Kuri will never be a target again. We will see to that. But the Ancients say this storm is a working of your Iceweaver. We received her message. The Ubica are not welcome. We will be traveling back to our lands with all haste." He shivered slightly. "We do not see how you can live in these ice-covered plains."

Anan said, "Our winter lodges are secure and warm—and many days away. If Iceweaver is angry, none of us may survive the journey."

Oka gave them a final nod and then disappeared into the storm. The other two paused for a moment, nodded to the gathered Talac, and followed their Forge. Anan thought he could detect a faint glow from Oka, but wasn't certain.

He stared at the point where the assassins had disappeared and then turned to the other four. "Iceweaver is not happy. Let's catch up with the other Kuri and hope we can find a sheltered area for our tents."

CHAPTER EIGHTEEN

TERJA BUNDLED himself against the howling winds. After their battle earlier in the day, the combatants had not lingered on the windswept battlefield, but had raced after the remainder of the Talac. When they overtook their people, they found them scrambling to combine shelters so they could huddle together to keep from freezing. With only a few fingercounts of Kuri remaining, they needed to combine their resources as efficiently as possible, but Terja was concerned that it would not be enough. Anan had already treated some of the clan for snowfire on their fingers. Terja didn't see how it could get much worse.

"We're being attacked!" called one of the sentries.

Varas? They followed us this quickly? There is no chance we can survive.

"Terja. Soneri. Joven. Ite. Follow me!" Anan yelled.

The five of them plunged through thigh deep snow surrounding the tents. A call sounded that filled the air and Anan signaled a stop. "Did you hear that? That was nothing to do with the Varas."

Soneri nodded. "It was not from the Varas. But I fear it will be even more devastating…. It was a snowgrazer call."

Terja cringed at the thought of the vicious animals attacking their weakened group. But he lifted his staff, with its broken head, and stood beside Anan. He'd barely halted when the other three stepped beside them. At a rustling sound to their rear, Terja glanced back to find all the Talac who could stand with whatever they could find to serve as a weapon. If this were a snowgrazer herd with their scent, they would likely all be killed. They were known to track down and kill hunters who had taken an individual from their herd.

But Terja couldn't help but admire the Talac's determination. These people had made a remarkable recovery from the cowed slaves they had been a moon ago.

After another, distinctly male, snort from the bowels of swirling snow, Terja prepared himself. He and Anan stared into the snow-blinded landscape, trying to gain a moment of advantage, when the huge animals charged forward.

"Do not fire," a voice called. "We are Talac too."

Terja's hands went numb as his jaw dropped open. Anan looked equally shocked. From the shifting feet and muted voices behind him, everyone was dumbfounded.

He trusted nothing at this point in this twisted journey. Then the voice cut through the winds again.

"We are Meke. The Twined Ones came to me in a vision, and Iceweaver has led us to you. You are the Kuri captured by the Varas, correct?"

"How do we know you are Talac? How do you know the Kuri?" Anan asked.

A chuckle drifted through the air around them and gave Terja a feeling of comfort. *This woman must be a clan leader. She fills me with a strength that seems familiar.*

But her voice never wavered. "Who else but a snow-blinded Meke would stand in a storm and argue with their southern kin? We all should be seeking shelter before Iceweaver sends us to our final sleep."

"She's right, Anan. We need to find shelter or we'll be another victim of Iceweaver's indifference." Something occurred to him and he turned to the woman. "We heard snowgrazers. Did you see them? We hunted in the great herd. They may be pursuing us."

Another laugh curled around Terja, and he saw the shapes coming closer. His chest tightened and his heart pounded as his apprehension grew. He struggled with his fears, which became almost unbearable as a double fingercount of monstrous snowgrazers formed a semicircle in front of them—a Talac riding each one.

Terja tried to talk but could only manage a squeak. The woman on the largest bull let out the now-familiar chuckle. The rider swung her pelt-covered legs to one side and then dropped from her mount. She tapped the bull's knee and it gracefully knelt beside her. When she pulled back her hood, Terja was shocked to see another spellspinner.

She watched him for a moment before turning to the other mounted Meke. "Form the snow tents. I don't know if I can spin enough matama for them, but it's our only chance to save the Kuri." She sounded two ear-piercing whistles and motioned. "Form up the heavy snow patterns. Get the ko into their places. Everyone should be easily worked into the patterns."

The woman began pulling matama and spinning it into a thick cord. As loop after glowing loop gathered around her wrist, Terja became fascinated. There was a similarity between their spinning styles. Terja quickly learned her pattern and duplicated it. His loops of cordage were close to hers as they spun the last threads of matama from the air around them.

"Do you have a powerful weaver? I have one with us, but she is little more than a kit and has only just come into her powers."

"My twining is skilled," Terja said.

As if he were summoned, Anan appeared at his side. He stared at the Meke for a moment before speaking. "What do you need from me?"

"The snow drapes are spread between the ko in a crystalline pattern. Use the matama-filled cordage and connect them to each other with the poles between each ko as the anchor points. It will form a great tent that will shunt the snow and wind away, and between our body heat and the warmth from the ko, we should survive the storm."

A frown creased Anan's face as he strained to do the weaving described. He struggled at first with the strange fibers of Meke spinning.

Then he smiled with relief, and suddenly the fabric shifted and with a snap, a line running to the first ko tightened and the shelter began to take shape. As Anan's hands flew, sheet after sheet snapped into place as he sent the matama through the fabric. Soon it was larger than the biggest winter lodge of the Kuri. The last of the matama crept into the seams and a contented sound came from one of the animals.

"Hurry, get everyone inside. This storm is getting worse," Terja said.

Anan barked off a few orders and the Kuri made their way through the deep snow with the worst of the injured helped by others. The Meke worked with them to arrange the people around the low-walled tent. Supplies and other gear were piled against the outer walls.

Terja followed the last Kuri inside and was shocked to find the enclosure was already almost balmy. He moved to the center, where space had been left for him and Anan. As Terja shuttled forward, he noticed two things. First, even though it was warm, there were no fires.

Second, the ko themselves were being used to anchor poles the Meke had brought, and Terja thought they were also likely responsible for the majority of the heat he was enjoying.

"You can lay against them. They like the attention."

Terja looked up to see the woman had taken off her thick, hooded coat and laid it over the animal's shoulder. She lowered herself until the two of them were nestled against each other.

"You might as well get comfortable. This shelter would seem short even to a Varas. But Iceweaver is releasing a lot of anger with this storm and the low tent will resist the worst of her fury. This could last for several days."

Terja watched the huge animal for a moment, then settled to the ground several steps away. It was not as warm, but Terja wasn't quite ready to trust an animal that looked a lot like the ones who killed one of their group. Given their situation, he was happy the animals had arrived, but he wasn't ready to use one as bedding.

The Meke watched them for a moment and then wriggled against the longhaired animal under her. "I am Isiliva, a spellspinner of the Meke clan, and a ko rider."

Something passed through Terja at her words, but it left quickly as he focused on another part of her information. "Where did the ko come from? Why do none of the other Talac know about them?"

Isiliva studied him for a long time. She tilted her head toward the two. "We have kept the ko for generations, but we have our mountains. The other Talac do not journey to the high pastures where the ko are kept. And the ko do not like the lowland's heat. But they are perfect for winter travel. We normally come from the mountains to trade with the Pero. But the feather weavers are no more."

"No, the Varas slavers that attacked the Kuri also wiped out the Pero. We have a few Pero survivors, but they will likely be adopted into the Kuri. How did you find us? Did you know the Varas were trailing us?" Terja asked.

"This is close to our normal path, but finding you was woven by the gods. We did not know you had enemies following. But it makes us no difference. We will always help the other clans. Especially to avenge the Pero."

Terja glanced up as Anan lowered himself beside them. "The tent is warm, Isiliva. But we haven't eaten in more than a day. Can we start fires, or will the ko be afraid?"

"One or two cooking fires away from the ko should be fine." She paused for a moment and scanned the area around them. She spotted a pair of packs that must have come from one of the animals. Isiliva pulled it to her and dug inside for a moment before bringing out a stack of woven bowls with the top one filled with rocks. She handed Anan the equipment with a nod.

"Here are bowls and cooking stones we've been using. They aren't quite as tight as those from the Kuri. But they suffice."

Anan took them and moved to the largest open spot where he piled tinder, struck firestone to iron, and grew the first tendrils of flame. Once Anan rolled the rocks into it, he turned to the Meke woman. She studied Anan but met Terja's gaze when he looked at her.

"Thank you. Your sharing saved Anan time that he didn't want to waste."

"I thought it might. Once the stew is cooking, we have travel food that would taste better prepared."

Terja nodded and moved slightly closer to the big animal Isiliva leaned against. Its deep brown eyes turned toward Terja as it let out a low call. He was hesitant to move closer. This animal's horns looked even more deadly than its ancestor the snowgrazer, and he had seen what that brute could do.

"You can touch him. He likes it actually. He is very gentle."

"Gentle? I've seen what a snowgrazer can do to a grown man. These animals are even larger and it looks like you sharpened their horns."

She stared at her mount as if she'd never seen it before. Several moments passed before she turned to Terja. "I've raised him from a tiny calf. His mother was killed by a pair of nasty creatures we have in the high mountains. I forget how he looks to others."

"He is intimidating. You can trust my word."

A yelp and a muttered curse drew their attention to Anan, who was nursing a finger and wearing an expression that was a combination of anger and embarrassment. Isiliva tossed Terja a storage envelope.

"Sounds like the water is hot enough. Here's some dried daggerhorn and root edibles. They are better cooked together. But at this point I think he'd take instructions better from you than me."

Terja walked to the small fire and watched as Anan used two sticks to drop another stone from the fire into the liquid-filled basket. It bubbled and roiled for a few heartbeats before sinking beneath the surface. He glanced to Terja, who held out the filled storage bag. Anan studied it for a moment, and then his eyes flicked to the calm woman.

"Give her my thanks. Hot food is going to improve everyone's outlook."

"I agree." Terja paused until Anan looked at him again.

"Something else?"

Terja smirked. "Did you want some help cooking?"

Anan gave him a confused expression. "No. Why?"

"It sounded like you might need help a moment ago."

Anan appeared muddled for an instant but then tilted his brow and scowled at Terja. "Sometimes I miss the painfully shy spellspinner I found in a hole. Go. Talk to the fascinating Meke. Maybe you two have something in common."

Terja was still smiling when he returned to the woman. This time he did sit within reach of her mount. It studied him calmly for quite some time and then dropped its head to the ground with a soft snort. Terja reached out and touched the tip of its nose. He was startled when its long tongue curled out and washed the underside of Terja's wrist. Strangely enough, he found the gesture more endearing than startling. He held still for a second pass of the animal's tongue before looking up to see Isiliva staring at him.

"What? Was I not supposed to let it lick me?"

"No. No, that's fine. It's just that he's never done that with anyone other than me before."

Terja sat, trying to work out how to respond, while Anan brought them each a bowl of stew. A moment later he returned with a third bowl and sat beside Terja. The ko lifted its head, stared at Anan, and then snorted, hitting Anan in the chest with a thick clot of mucus.

"Ah! I didn't need that! Isn't it enough that you are forming the center pillar for my home tonight?"

Isiliva smiled, waving her finger at Terja. "That was more what I expected of my fine mount."

Terja chuckled as Anan cleaned the slick substance from his clothing. As Anan began to eat again, a question occurred to Terja.

"How did you know about the Kuri woven bowls? You said the Meke don't venture far from their mountains," he asked Isiliva.

"That's true. Most Meke do not. But I was twined with a Kuri for a few years, so I know about their weaving."

"My mother was Meke. But she died while I was still a kit. I don't have memories of her. Only a few Kuri knew her, but they didn't like to talk about her. They said the memories were too painful."

Isiliva turned her gaze to him. "Kit, what is your name?"

"Terja."

"And your father was?"

"Gade. He was the leader of the spellspinners in the...."

Isiliva grabbed Terja and pulled him close as if she were just seeing him for the first time. Tears streamed down her pale face as she studied him. "You're alive!"

Confusion and apprehension filled him. The Meke woman was on the edge of hysteria, but Terja was not ready to accept the logical conclusion to what was being presented him. "My mother died," he said coldly. "A long time ago. My father told me this. The other spellspinners said the same. My mother is dead, or she would not have left me. My mother—" He turned to Anan, his gut in the biggest snarl he'd ever felt. "She is dead. My mother would not desert me to live with my father. She wouldn't."

"Terja, who told you that she was dead?" she asked.

"My father. The others. Everyone in the village."

"Think carefully. Did they tell you directly, or were they answering without answering?" Anan asked.

"Yes. They...." Terja considered the question. "No. Only him. No one else said the words. Only him."

He turned to the woman claiming to be his mother as anger and disappointment filled him. "Why did you leave me? Was it because I was too small? You had to know I would not be the son most mothers want. Was I not enough? I was never even told your true name."

"Oh, my poor kit. You were perfect. You were my entire world. You were the most beautiful child ever born."

Anan squeezed his shoulder. "So he hasn't changed much."

Isiliva shook her head, wiping the freshet of tears from her eyes. "Oh no. The man before me is the fruition of the potential I saw in my little kit." She cupped Terja's face in her hands and their eyes met. "He told me you were killed in an accident with a daggerhorn while I was away visiting my family. He must have hidden you with his friends."

She smiled sadly at Terja. "Some of his friends never approved of his wild Meke wife. I did not act in a way they found befitting a spellspinner."

She released Terja, grabbed Anan, and then pulled all three of them together. "I see the twining between the two of you. It seems your father's bigotries didn't ruin your life."

"It. We. There were—" He looked at Anan with a silent plea.

Anan nodded and squeezed his shoulder again. "It was difficult, for many reasons. Not the least of them being the decimation of most of the Kuri. But we have survived and will fulfill our bloodweaving."

Terja found himself wanting to believe. *Could this be my mother? This wild Meke who rides a huge war beast? The mother I thought was dead and mourned many times. There is no reason to doubt her... but I cannot trust what I am being told.*

"If you still doubt, we could do a pair spinning."

Terja snapped his gaze to the woman. "That is for a twining, not a mother and son."

"It can be for either." Her voice gained a comforting tone. "You may have come into your spinning early, but there are still a few things your mother might know that you do not."

Terja turned to Anan. "You're the weaver. What do you think?"

"I know the pair spinning is for more than twining, but any more...." He shrugged.

"All right. I have to know the truth. What do I do?"

"Follow me. We'll be using matama from the people, but also some from the ko."

Isiliva pulled fibers to her and Terja immediately knew he was in the presence of a master spinner. The threads she created were beyond anything he'd seen before. At first, he could see no places where his meager skills were needed, but then gaps in the creation called to him. He picked up threads from his and Anan's kilts and created with his mother. The threads drifted around them, intertwining in ways Terja knew only happened with family. Isiliva's skills in creating the matama-laced fiber was unlike any Terja had seen before, but they also had a familiarity he found comforting. When he spun the matama from the Ubica, he felt a tug from his mother and they slipped out of the work.

"What were the darkened matama? I have not seen them before," Isiliva asked.

"They are Ubica."

She leaned forward to ask more questions, but Terja waved her to silence. "I can tell you what we've been through later. I need time. I've just discovered the woman who I was told was dead is alive and well."

Terja started to hug Isiliva but then took a few stumbling steps backward before spinning and walking away.

CHAPTER NINETEEN

TERJA STOOD, leaning against his mother's ko. He and the bull had gotten to know each other well throughout the three-day storm, as had he and his mother. The fears he'd had before about both were largely gone. The animal was as tame as any kuri in the clan's herds. And Isiliva... well, he and his mother were working on some type of relationship. Considering they were relative strangers, he thought they were doing well.

They had spent days having in-depth conversations. He felt now that his father was to blame for their separation, although he didn't understand the man's motives. Isiliva was more certain of the rationale, but she had years of mistrust to build upon. Terja wasn't quite ready to heap all blame on his father. But he was forced into agreement; the weight of blame had shifted toward him.

"Are you ready to start back to the mountains?" Isiliva asked.

Terja exhaled softly, trying to diffuse some of the tension about a topic they disagreed on. This was the singular decision that they could not agree on: what the group should do next. He readied himself for the discussion again as he turned to Isiliva. "We are continuing to the Kuri winter village. That has been our destination always, and it will continue to be so. Too many people died to make it possible for the rest of us to continue."

She turned to him with that same look of determination that she'd worn for the past several days. "How are you going forward? Your drags will be hopelessly buried in snow, and you are still most of a moon from the winter village. And that is if Iceweaver decides to be kind."

"The drags are being made into sleds. Also, some of the Meke are showing us how to make snow sandals that will allow us to travel across the deep snow. We will finish the trip."

"Have you asked the Twined Ones for guidance again?"

Terja drew his mouth into a thin line. *Why had Anan thought sharing that bit of information was a good idea? I would like to use some deathspinner glue to stick my twining's lips together.*

"We do not need to call on the Twined Ones. Our path is clear. We are going to the winter village. Some of the kuri might have survived. They are clever animals and would follow the same migration pattern they have for generations. Without them, the Kuri clan is no more."

Isiliva's face flushed red. "You can stay with the Meke. We will help you as soon as it is safe to travel across the barrens. The lands between here and the winter lodges are filled with hungry packs of longtooth and who knows what else. Bandits sometimes make a winter home in the recesses of the barrens. You are not a large group."

Terja's resolve hardened. "We are going home. This group has been through too much. The promise of our homelands is all that has kept them moving at times. We can make the new equipment we need in a few days and then we will travel southwest. The grasslands will welcome us."

"You'll never be ready in a fingercount of days, certainly not in a smaller number. Making the snow sandals alone will take more."

Anan stepped beside Terja and met Isiliva's glare. "We have matama stored in the snowgrazer fur. We've been able to comb some fiber from the ko too. Joven and I can make things go faster than it would have otherwise. We can be ready to leave in a few days."

Isiliva was visibly angered. "You have to come with me. I can't chance losing my son again!"

"Isiliva, we've known each other only a short time. Anan and I are twined and we will go together. We have discussed the options. We will try to take what remains of the Kuri back home."

She looked first at one and then the other before walking away without another word. Terja watched her disappear into the blinding snow before turning back to Anan. "You look like you have done something I will not be happy about. What is it? And don't lie to me."

Anan hesitated before he sighed and nodded in agreement. "I wanted confirmation."

Terja's gut twisted. "You called the Twined Ones? Without me?"

"It's not finished. It needs you to open it. But it is ready."

Anger mixed with fear as he looked at his twining. Finally he sighed and motioned to Anan. "Take me. We will talk about this later. Don't think this is over."

Anan turned and walked down a side canyon that the wind had scoured clear. They had traveled for a double fingercount of spans when Anan disappeared around a corner. Terja followed him and saw that he had set up one of the old tents in the tiny blind canyon he'd discovered.

They ducked inside, and Anan handed him the knife from his waist. Terja cut across his palm and let the drops fall into the pattern Anan had already created. Anan released it an instant later and the now-familiar effect began. Except this time the snow began to pelt against the sides of their shelter until they were buried inside the dome of an ice cave.

Once sealed inside, twin snow whirlwinds formed with them, only there was no wind moving that Terja could feel. The Twined Ones had been waiting for an invitation. The swirling winds grew to fill half the enclosure when, with a snap, the funnels disappeared and First Weaver and First Spinner stood before them.

They were dressed in fiber woven from the ko, but not like the Meke garments. Their appearance was more what one would expect from Kuri. The kilts, leggings, and outer clothing were similar, but thicker. First Weaver's velvet was thicker than before. But First Spinner was bundled until he looked like he was covered in thickly woven tapestries. He looked content in his layers of warmth, though. First Spinner smiled at Terja, and he felt some of his fear lessen.

"Next time you need intervention, could we do it during the warm moons? Terja and I are not as prepared for cold as you velvet wearers." First Spinner winked shyly at a shocked Terja.

First Weaver laughed and nodded conspiratorially with Anan. "They want our velvet in the cold moons, but they say we are hot during the fire moons."

Anan chuckled and met Terja's raised brow with a wink. "You know he is right," Anan said.

"Ah, but these two are not here to drink fermented kuri milk and talk of the challenges of being twined. What questions would you have for us, kits?" First Spinner asked.

Terja nodded and explained. "We are in the middle of the barrens. The Varas are beaten back, at least for now. The Meke have arrived with their wonderful ko who can travel during this season. Our goal was to reach the winter home of the Kuri, but we do not know what the trip might hold. We desperately want to return and see if any of our herds remain, but if we lose anyone else….” Terja fought back his tears. “I can't send any more friends to the Great Weaving.”

The silence surrounded them. Eventually First Weaver began. “You already know that we can foretell the future with no real degree of accuracy. But in reward for saving generations of Talac from Ubica Triads, the Blessed Ones have given us leave to share some information.” He nodded toward First Spinner who took up the narrative.

“The Varas still live. Neither the battle with you, nor the storm, wiped them out. They are the High Regent's personal guard, so if they were to return without the Talac—it would not go well for them. Also, there are creatures far worse than longtooth that leave their icy mountain retreats to hunt on the plains through the cold moons. Iceweaver has no more pity on you than the hunting animals. If you choose to continue, there are many obstacles.”

Terja felt defeated. The hurdles listed by First Spinner were as bad as what they had already faced. The only good thing was their bargain with Oka, and that had been pure luck.

“No, youngling. It was not luck. You chose the greater good rather than revenge for Morea's death. That is a weaving many would refuse.” Terja started at the idea of the avatars reading his thoughts. But First Weaver picked up the tale again.

“The trip to the Meke homeland has many of the same perils. Their lands are closer to Iceweaver's realm and her fury is not trivial. Your mother wants you to accompany her, but she knows either trip will be dangerous. The journey to the Meke lands she knows well. She would put herself in peril for your sake.”

Terja groaned and pressed his hands against his forehead. “This is not helping. All I know now is either choice could work, or could wipe out the entire clan. And now I know the Varas will pursue us until we are either captured, or they are dead.”

The Twined Ones shared a significant look before turning to the pair. “We do have one additional piece of information. We hesitate to share it with you, because it will likely make your decision for you.”

“What? What could make our choice so easy?”

"The kuri herds still live. And some of the herdweavers."

"The herdweavers live? How?"

"They were the youngest. They were hidden by the older kits before they fought the Varas. Most of these kits are barely old enough to be tending the animals. They are trying to find the winter lodges too. But their memories are far less accurate. Without help, they will never live to find the winter grazing lands."

"The herds, and more importantly kits from the clan, must be saved. It's a miracle they are still alive."

First Spinner smiled slightly. "We thought that might be your decision, regardless of what we shared. The young are protected by the Blessed Ones when possible. These kits are dear to us, make no mistake. But we would have respected your decision, regardless."

Terja felt as if he were about to lose his last meal. "We must go. It's urgent now we find the kits. Regardless of the danger, we must save them. They are more important than even the bloodweaving."

"The last strands of the bloodweaving are woven with these kits, and the last of the Kuri. Focus on saving your people and your oath will be fulfilled." First Weaver glanced at his twining. "And yes, you are right. You have little time and we have nothing else to give."

With that the pair became more and more translucent until they returned to the swirls of wind they had been. The ice was cracking from the fabric when a voice spoke in both of their minds. *We are still available to you. If you need us, you know how to reach us. We might at least see more than you.*

A moment later, the coating of ice shattered and the tent fabric started to ripple again. The pair sat in shock for several moments before Anan turned to his twining.

Terja felt as if his body was tied in knots. He was trying to digest the news from First Twining, but it would take time. He turned to Anan, who had a look of shock on his face.

"The kits still live. Some of the herds with them. We must hurry. There is no time to spare now. I'll see to the workmen and motivate them to finish their tasks more quickly."

"I'll say my good-byes to my mother. Then we can start packing as much food as we can gather. The Meke brought more than they needed, thinking we would be coming with them."

In a joint moment of relief, they embraced each other tightly. Anan grabbed Terja by the shoulders. "More live. We can save them."

Terja returned his infectious smile. "Yes. We can save them."

Epilogue

TERJA STOOD at the edge of the encampment as the people around him prepared to leave. The sun reflected off the sparkling white snow the blizzard had left behind. The barrens were engulfed in a blanket of snow at least a hand length in depth. But the Talac's focus was on their new mission—rescue. Word spread quickly that herdweavers and kuri were still alive. And that it was up to them to find the kits and safely guide them to the winter lodges.

The news had been the push needed to force the exhausted Kuri into action. Even with Anan's spellweaving, Terja wasn't certain they could finish the needed changes in their gear in time, but they had finished quicker than anyone's most optimistic projections. Now, only a few days after their call to First Ones, they were preparing to leave.

"Have you found her?"

Terja turned to find Anan moving to his side. "No. I can't imagine where she went. I would have liked to tell her good-bye and that I plan to see her again."

"There are very few of us. She must be hiding from you."

"Not hiding so much as trying to work out the new rules," said a woman's voice behind them. "I had made a petition to Iceweaver."

Both men turned to find Isiliva standing behind them. Terja wasn't certain what to think or ask. Finally the words began to tumble from Terja: "I wanted to tell you I have no choice. I wanted to have time to talk to you. But we're leaving now. Will you come see us at our fire season encampment? I would like to see more of you, speak with you more."

"No."

Terja's heart sank at the refusal. He'd hoped she would understand.

"No. There will be no reason to visit. I'm coming with you to the Kuri pastures. I think you could use some help to find the missing herdweavers."

Terja's mouth opened and closed several times, but he had no words. Anan took over the conversation to help an obviously upset Terja.

"Are all the Meke traveling with us? What about the ones left behind?"

"Only three of us are coming with you. The others are returning to the mountains. They need to know that the remains of a Varas century are in our lands. But three of us are coming with our ko."

Terja studied the three of them. Isiliva had chosen one male and one female rider. Although he wouldn't have been able to identify them, Terja was thankful they would have more riders than one. He felt the need to say something to them all. "We welcome you. The Kuri will protect the Meke with our last breath. Thank you again, my fellow Talac."

The two smirked slightly and the male began to speak. "We've always wanted to see beyond the mountains. This should be an enjoyable trip that will take very little time. Between us and our ko, there should be nothing we can't overcome."

Terja felt an odd combination of amusement and horror at their naiveté. He started to say several things, to outline the dangers they had already faced, to point out the difficulties that might lie ahead. But in the end all he could muster was a nod. He looked back at his mother to see if there was some bit of humor he was missing.

She lifted both eyebrows and shrugged. "They have—interesting—ideas."

"Hey! Get away from me! You thread-eating bird!"

Terja turned to find Anan flailing his hands at a small bird that seemed determined to perch on his shoulder. The spectacle continued for several moments longer before Terja got an idea.

"Anan. Stop. Let the bird alight."

Anan shot him a look, but then slowly lowered his hands. As soon as he did, the bird landed on his shoulder. Anan cringed and shifted uncomfortably for several moments, and then stopped.

"What's it doing?"

"Nibbling at my ear. But very softly." He scowled at Terja. "If this diggerbird bites me, you will pay dearly, my cherished twining."

The spectacle continued for several moments until Anan chuckled at the attention. "It tickles."

With that, the small predatory bird launched itself and circled the head of Isiliva's ko before zipping to the southwest. The small group stood transfixed for several moments, and the bird reappeared. It backwinged, chattering furiously at them before darting again to the direction of home.

"Well it looks like it wants us out of its territory," Anan said. He turned to Terja. "How did you know it wouldn't bite? Usually they're aggressive."

Terja considered carefully before answering. "It wasn't trying to run us off. It wants us to begin our trip."

"Why do you think that?"

"Morea's totem was the diggerbird."

JON KEYS's earliest memories revolve around books. Either read to him or making up stories based on the illustrations, these were places his active mind occupied. As he got older, the selection expanded beyond Mother Goose and Dr. Seuss to the world of westerns, science fiction, and fantasy. His world filled with dragon riders, mind-speaking horses, and comic book heroes in hot uniforms.

A voracious reader for half a century, Jon recently began creating his own fiction. The first writing was his attempt at showing rural characters in a more sympathetic light. Now he has moved into some of the writing he lost himself in for so many years—fantasy. Jon has worked as a ranch hand, teacher, computer tech, roughneck, designer, retail clerk, welder, artist, and, yes, pool boy; with interests ranging from kayaking and hunting to drawing and cooking, he uses this range of life experiences to create written works that draw the reader in and wrap them in a good story.

E-mail: jon.keys@ymail.com
Blog: jonkeys.com
Facebook: www.facebook.com/jon.keys.773
Twitter: @Jon4Keys

OBSIDIAN SUN

JON KEYS

Obsidian Series: Book One

Differences must be put aside when vengeance becomes all-consuming.

Anan, a spellweaver of the Talac people, returns from a hunting trip to find his village decimated, his mate dead, and everyone else captured by Varas slavers. The sole survivor is Terja, a young man without the velvet that covers most Talac, marking him as a spellspinner. Since Talac magic requires both a weaver and a spinner, Anan and Terja must move beyond their ingrained mistrust. All that remains is revenge and a desperate plan to rescue their tribesmen before they are sold to Varas pleasure houses. A goal Anan and Terja are willing to die for.

With the blessing of the Talac gods, they discover new and surprising ways to complement each other's power. But as they race through terrain full of enemies and dangerous creatures to reach their people before they pass into Varas lands, they must take drastic steps to face the overwhelming odds against them. Understanding their connection might be their only hope.

www.dreamspinnerpress.com

HOME GROWN

Jon Keys

Peter Stevens believes nothing tastes better than a vine-ripened tomato tended by a farmer's hands. The craving for heirloom tomatoes leads him to his local farmers' market and his favorite vendor, Ethan Hart. As Peter becomes a regular customer, the two find they have more in common than a love of good food. Just as Ethan begins to relax, Peter's ex, Jay, appears and is all the things Ethan is not. A perfect storm of mistakes and poor choices, as well as Ethan's haunted past, has him ready to admit defeat. With the guidance of friends and a goat far too smart for her own good, Ethan realizes he needs to have a tender hand and patience to grow a home for Peter.

www.dreamspinnerpress.com

Also from Dreamspinner Press

EVELYN ELLIOTT

FEATHER FALL

SPELL SLAVE: BOOK 2

www.dreamspinnerpress.com

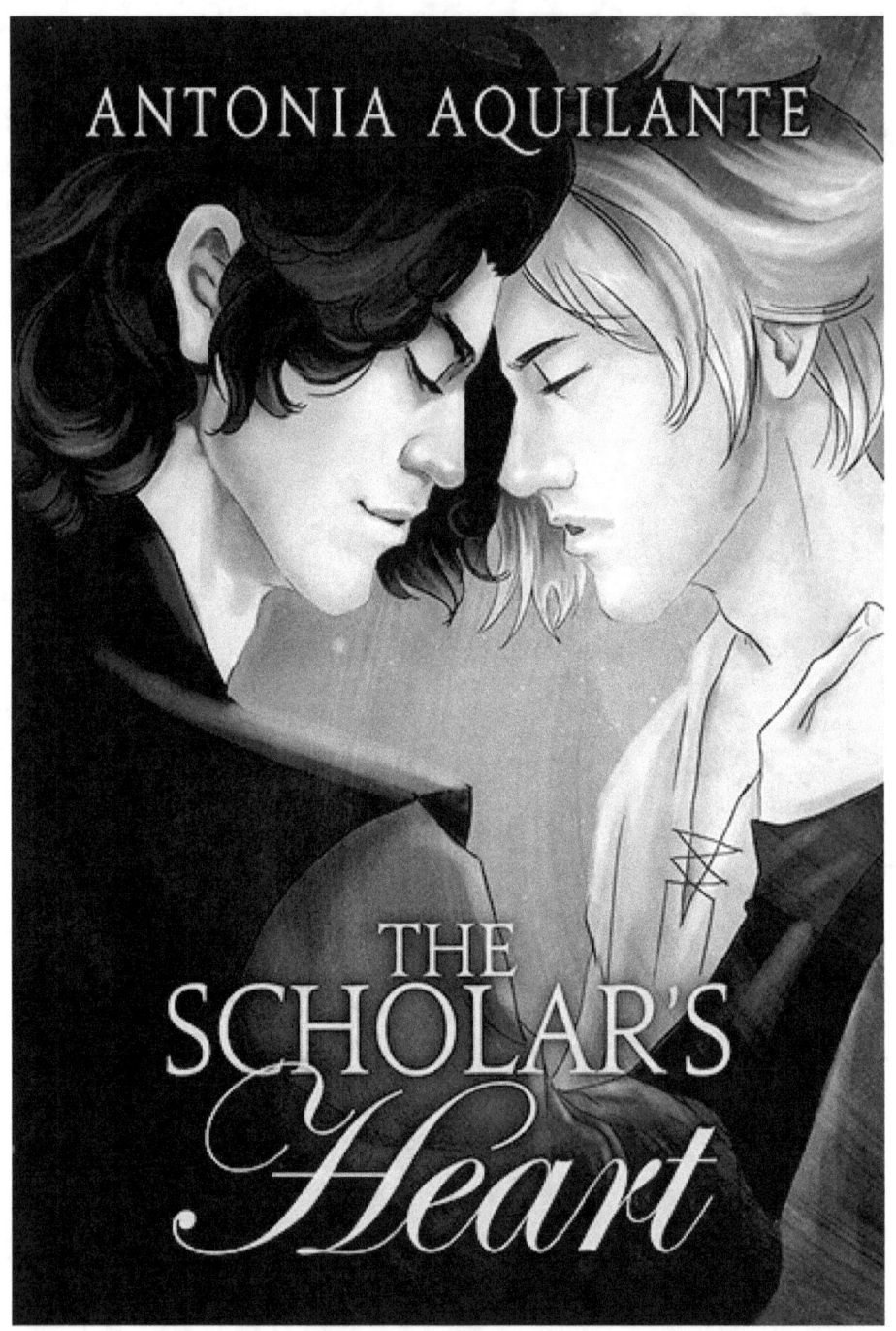